TO BE
HONEST

TO BE HONEST

a high-brow novel of questionable lows

by

R. Tim Morris

EMPIRE STAMP

Empire Stamp trade paperback edition: April 2019
ISBN 978-1-7750598-3-7 [eBook]
ISBN 978-1-7750598-8-2 [Paperback]
ISBN 978-1-7750598-2-0 [Hardcover]

"If you tell the truth, you don't have to remember anything."

—Mark Twain

Chester K. Eddy, Everyone

I eat my boogers.

There. I said it. I pick my nose and eat my boogers. Basically all the time. The way I figure it, if nasal mucus is mostly just water and dust and pollen and other germs we inhale from the air, then it's good, right? They say kids need to get dirty, they need to be exposed to germs, to build up their immune systems, so this is essentially the same thing. Plus, I've gone my whole life without any major illnesses or injuries, so it's got to mean something. If it ain't broke. What's the big deal, really? I'm pretty sure everyone does it.

I'm doing it right now.

"Hey, man! Get your finger outta your nose!"

But welcome to society. It gets worse here every day.

"What do you think this is? A preschool?" So, that's the director — Luuk Meijer — yelling at me in his weirdo, European accent. The guy is a shitshow of uselessness, but for some reason, he keeps getting work in this city. Playwrights practically line up to have him read their scripts. I'm not completely sure why, since everything he's touched lately has turned into a dog's asshole after too much wet Alpo.

Oh, wonderful. Now he's clomping right on over here in his vegan Doc Martens. I overheard him make a point to mention the fact his shoes were vegan to the playwright sitting next to him during my audition. Meijer didn't actually *tell* me she was the playwright, he only introduced her by name; as though Maya Custner is so instantly recognizable a name, right? *Whoa, THE Maya Custner? Be still my out-of-work and nearly-dead heart.*

But I remembered her name from the script sample in the audition package. I'd never heard of Maya Custner, so she's no doubt new to the New York theater scene. Best guess? She's straight out of somewhere uncharted yet darling, like Erie Community College, finding "fame" for crafting popular radio plays which were no doubt about misunderstood liberal bigotry, or the first Jewish woman to work on the Ford assembly line, or something of that ilk. I only recalled the name because the first time I read it on the audition script, I thought it said Maya *Cuntster*. And you don't forget a name like that.

She's kinda sexy, though. It's the glasses. God, I dig a quality pair of glasses.

Meijer's on the tips of his vegan toes — *What does "vegan shoe" mean anyway? Do you eat them? I have no idea when it comes to these sorts of things* — and I can still see only his sad, square, pancake face digging his chin into the stage.

"And that's my kazoo, man. You don't pick your fucking nose and then touch my fucking kazoo."

I don't step back at all, even though he spits a little on my frayed Chuck Taylors. *Please, dude.* "So, when *should* I pick my nose?"

"You don't. You DO NOT pick your nose. You're a god-damned adult."

I beg to differ. I've been constantly led to believe adults have their lives together. They're happy because they're doing the things they *want* to do and they have the things they *want* to have. They aren't thirty-two and still auditioning for seventh-billing of an off-off-Broadway theater role on a Sunday. *A Sunday?* This one's a musical and my character doesn't even sing. How do you get away with being the owner of a music store in a musical and not have a song? I wasn't even expecting my *own* song here; at the very least just a melody in someone else's number. But nope. I don't think they ever told me the name of this play either. Probably not even anything to do with kazoos.

Of course, Luuk Meijer doesn't want to hear my sad, Charlie Brown story. And he'd much rather continue his bogus lecture than just do his job. "That kazoo is a prop, man. Other auditioners need to touch it too, and some people might not want to find your boogers all over it."

"Can I just finish here, or are you going to keep interrupting me?"

He looks at me, a fire in his eyes. No, it's more like a seething suppression of a base-instinctual need to kill me right here on the spot. An animalistic desire to rip the flesh from my bones and take what remains of me to his sticky cave in Central Park. There's a lot more serial killers in this city than the authorities and census reports would have you believe. But he glares back at Maya Custner, like her being a witness to the whole event would only complicate matters. Yes, you can read a lot into the most minute of actions if you pay enough attention. Usually I don't. But I know I'm on the ball this time.

Inevitably, Meijer returns to his seat, but because he's still keeping an eye on me, he plants himself awkwardly back in his obnoxiously high director's chair, and falls down on his ass. And then the chair proceeds to collapse onto his face.

I can't help from laughing. Come on, it's funny! At some point, something's bound to *not* be a social faux pas, right?

And yet it still comes as a surprise to me when, not even a minute later, I find myself being escorted from the theater. Who knew this run-down theater employed mafioso thugs? The scruffy but steely-armed stagehand even chucks my bag into the alley (right into an open dumpster of feces and human remains blanketed by the morning's snow) instead of having the courtesy and grace to hand it to me like a gentleman. The stink-wall of urine hits me immediately, and — *Here I go again* — I crowbar some crusted mucus from my left nostril.

Some helter-skelter rustling shakes me from my momentary cloud of small victories, and an indisputably-homeless homeless woman pops her head out from her handmade fort of cardboard boxes, snowbanks, and Hefty bags. My eight-year-old self would be pretty jealous of the setup. Actually, I'm still a little bit jealous of it.

"Hey, kid! Get ya finger outta ya nose!" she yells at me sanctimoniously, like she wasn't just back there pissing into an old Yop bottle.

I was about to flick the snot back at the door from whence I came, or just eat the thing up if I couldn't gracefully snap it off my finger, but instead I wipe it onto her Pampers box, collect my tossed and freshly-dampened canvas satchel — *I hope that's just snow soaking through the bottom* — and walk away. I figure any further foreign germs are not going to make a dent in the situation she's got going on here.

As I step out onto Ninth Avenue, I hear my name being shouted from back in the alley.

"Chester K. Eddy!"

At first, I think it's maybe the homeless woman, which literally makes NO sense at all, because how could she possibly know my name? Did she think I was cute? Does she want my number? Does she *have* a number? 21st Century homeless culture in New York probably includes cell phones, wouldn't you think? It's not the same game it was twenty-five years ago. She's arguably more attractive than the *last* homeless woman I slept with, I'll give her that much. Granted, it was kind of shady back there. And before anyone asks, there was enthusiastic consent, so none of that Harvey Weinstein shit, please. Thank you very much.

But then I see Maya Custner standing there, a sort of wobbly look about her. Like she's already reconsidering. She asks, "Can I talk to you?"

"Talk to *me*?"

"Just a few questions."

"I know where I was last night, y'see. But two nights ago is a bit blurry. Does that help?"

She cocks her head like I'm speaking Greek with a Chinese accent.

"It's a detective joke. You know: *I want to ask you some questions? Do you have an alibi for the night that lounge singer was found in her motel bathtub, strangled with her own cinnamon chewing gum? YOU'LL NEVER PIN IT ON ME, COPPER!*"

"Um. I was just going to suggest you take a different role in the show. If you're interested, that is."

"You mean *that* show?" I motion toward the theater with my chin, holding my satchel over my shoulder like I'm trying to channel James Dean but probably looking more douchey, like Justin Bieber in a Calvin Klein ad instead.

"If Luuk Meijer hasn't scared you off, of course."

"Meijer doesn't scare me. It's the stagehand goon with the prison neck tats that made me shit my pants."

"So, you poop your pants *and* you pick your nose?"

"Trust me, I'm quite the catch." *Cue patented eye sparkle: Wink!*

"The truth is, I think you're better suited for another part. I wrote it with someone like you in mind. Someone who doesn't put up with other people's crap the way you do."

"I do?" Obviously, I'm not quite used to such emphatic flattery. "Or, I *don't* do, is probably more grammatically accurate."

"The way you talked to Luuk in there? It's not often I see that kind of bold bravery. That's what I mean."

"I wouldn't call that bravery. I was just being honest."

"Well, I thought you were great. And I'd like to see you given another chance, Chester."

"I'm sorry?"

"Another chance at this show."

"No, the first thing. You said you thought I was *hot*, I believe?"

"I did not."

"You did too. But I can admit to having a piss-poor short-term memory."

"Maybe making a career out of memorizing dialogue is not the best decision then?"

"For the record, I'm terrible at pretty much everything. People call me Charlie Brown because, despite my lack of real-world adequacies, I keep trying. 'Cause, you know, *God bless my weary but workman-esque, proletarian soul.*"

"Who calls you Charlie Brown?"

"Just me, really. But I know people are thinking it."

Dramatic pause. She scrunches her little mouth to the side, deciding what to say next. "What am I thinking right now?"

"That there's not really another role you want me to audition for? That you really just wanted to come out here to hit on me?" Sure, maybe that *wasn't* her actual intent, but it's out there now, tabled for discussion. "Am I close?"

"I'd say you should add 'mind reading' to the list of things you're not very good at."

"Listen, that list is getting close to unmanageable. So there really *is* another role?"

"There is."

"And you think Meijer would let me just waltz back in there and re-audition? After I laughed at him like he was a drunk circus clown?"

There's a bitter breeze blowing through the alley now, and the cold produces a tear from Maya's eye. She doesn't wipe it away though; it runs down to the tip of her nose instead. Maya's nose is oddly-but-wonderfully shaped, like a perfectly flawless avocado: still weird and bumpy, but with a curve to die for. Her fine choice in frames is also doing it wonders. What can I say? I appreciate a good pair of glasses. *Where are you when I really need you, 1995 Lisa Loeb?*

I watch the tear dry up until she says, "Probably. But the whole audition process is BS, isn't it though?"

"It definitely can be. Though it all seems to come down to this game of cat and mouse; of the casting director and the actor feeling each other up."

"Out. They feel each other *out*, not up. Feeling up is where the trouble begins; where the whole #MeToo/#MeThree movements created this current culture shift."

"Boy, it's gotten out of hand, hasn't it? I mean, who saw *that* coming, right?"

Maya pulls her glasses off dramatically, making a point. And really, the pulling off of glasses would have been sufficient enough, but then she still feels the need to say, "You mean, aside from literally every woman working in the industry over the past four decades?"

"You know, people use the word 'literally' too liberally." She continues to stare at me, unflinching. "Could you put the glasses back on, please? I feel like this conversation was going much better with the glasses on."

She complies, her temper seemingly extinguished by my dousing of blunt candidness. "So, why do you do it?" she asks. "Why do you keep putting up with the bullshit?"

Question: Why do I do it?

Answer: Because I'm inherently stubborn, embarrassingly clueless, and totally lacking any actual, real-world skills.

"Because it's my passion," I say instead.

She looks at me with a gaze that says, "*Wow, I totally respect that,*" and, "*You are an amazing, beautiful, glimmering star of hope for humanity,*" with a little bit of, "*I want to place my hands on you right now, but I don't yet know if it's for sexual or spiritual reasons. Hold on, let me dwell on this— Yup, this shit is definitely sexual.*"

But she doesn't actually say anything. Probably too lost for words.

"I've been doing this for so long now," I say. "I know how to take rejection. It used to be hard, no doubt about it. But I know it's all just a part of the business."

So brave, this Chester K. Eddy. A beacon of artistic inspiration.

She asks, "And how do you handle yourself when you *do* land a role?"

"I'll let you know when that happens."

She smiles the sort of smile that tells me she knows I'm only joking.

I smile back like I'm pretending I really am.

"Listen, Maya. I appreciate the whole 'damsel in distress' vibe you've got going here. But I'm just not sure I'd be up for taking a different role."

"Damsel in distress?"

"Yeah. Like you're tied to a railroad track while some sinister jerk in a dusty bowler hat gesticulates above you, twirling his mustache. I know you need to just get this production going here, and Luuk Meijer — *The Easy Bake of Dutch Ovens* as we call him in the biz — isn't helping with his whole Sieg Heil attitude. Wait, is he Dutch or German? Is Dutch-German a thing?"

"No idea. What was your point?"

"My point is: You're desperate. And I'm right here."

You're Desperate and I'm Right Here should be the name of my own musical. Autobiography, maybe. Mental note made.

She blows out some pent-up air and says, "When I was in college, struggling and writing women's-issues radio plays for extra credit," — *BAM, I totally called it* — "I always assumed getting to New York would mean I'd made it. That all my work wasn't for nothing. That it was worth it. That *I* was worth it." She leans against the theater's old red brick wall. Fun fact: Sidney Poitier once leaned against this very same spot. I remember seeing the photo in a Playboy article from the 70's. "But Luuk Meijer has been everything that's wrong with the business. He's arrogant. He's oblivious to what the play is really about. And he couldn't care less if it ever gets off the ground because he's got fifty more scripts just waiting for him to ruin."

"What *is* this show about?"

"It's an homage to life, to love, and to the performing arts." *Sorry. Barf in my mouth.*

"You should cut the ties. Go do your *own* thing. You've got the chops, kid."

"You think so?"

"Sure. Plus, everyone in this town knows Meijer's a train wreck. The longer you're associated with him, the worse it'll be."

"So why did you audition for it?"

"Because I knew *you* wrote it." *Shhh. Is that angels swooning that I hear?*

"Really?"

"Really." *Not really. Do swooning angels even make a noise?*

There's a weirdly comfortable-yet-uncomfortable silence here, like she's unsure what she should be saying and I'm just waiting for her to say it. I love these moments, but then I usually get ahead of myself and ruin them by saying something childish. *Don't go that route, Chester. Don't take that road. Rise above! Don't say anything childish. Don't say—* "You know, at first I thought your name was *Cuntster*."

Well, that's out there now. I might as well pick my nose while I'm at it.

As I do, and for yet one more time in this conversation, Maya simply stands there, jaw agape, not knowing what to make of what I've said just now, or probably anything we've covered in the last ten minutes. "It probably happens all the time," I say for no real reason other than I must have missed the sound of my balls shrinking. "But people are just too conditioned to not say anything about it," I add, because why not at this point?

She continues to say nothing, and the sky rewards her patience with the parting of clouds and a burst of sunlight upon her face. She turns away, and brushes her shoulder-length hair with her fingertips like she's been practicing for this moment. And I'm rewarded with a little extra toss of those dark locks, and a view of the temples of her glasses, winding their way over the helix of her ear.

Yes, glasses temples and ear helices CAN TOO be hot.

Let me stop right here for a moment. I'd like to point out, in case there's any doubt later, I am NOT a sexual predator. Okay? Good. I may look a bit like the depraved lovechild of Matt Lauer and Louis C.K., but that's not me. And trust me, there's been plenty of moments when I've stopped in front of a mirror and thought, *Holy shit. I am a god-damned sexual predator, aren't I? No normal person would be thinking the kinds of thoughts I'm thinking. I am the second coming of Mike Tyson, but without the money and face tattoos. I could get a face tattoo, though. Nothing's stopping me, really.*

Am I actually dealing with some sort of low-grade insanity? Self-diagnosed, obviously. I mean, it's not like I can afford a real evaluation from a legit doctor, but I have had a baker's dozen of ex-girlfriends tell me I'm insane. I think that counts, if one is right in assuming the proper ex-girlfriend-to-doctor ratio is around 13:1. It counts, right? I'm pretty sure it counts.

So, what I'm doing here — *the way I am ALL the time* — does not make me wrong. Would a perfectly sane person pick his nose and eat his boogers so much?

Maybe don't answer that.

"Do you have some sort of mucus build-up problem?" Maya says, snapping me back to reality.

"I'm sorry?"

"Your nose. You've always got a finger knuckle-deep in there. You're going to make it bleed if you keep that up, you know."

"Never mind that. Can I ask you something, Miss Cun—I mean, *Cunn-istin-er-son?*"

"It's *Custner.*"

"Can I just call you Maya Cuntster? It would make things so much easier."

"Is *that* what you want to ask me?"

"No, that was a side question. I was going to ask: why are you still standing here? After I embarrassed your boss, took a dump on women's rights, tried hitting on you, made fun of your name, and picked my nose like I'm foraging for rare black truffles. Why are you still here?"

"You were hitting on me?"

"In a Charlie Brown kind of way, I suppose."

"I don't remember Charlie Brown ever hitting on anyone."

"You should read the later *Peanuts*. It gets pretty erotic. Or the fanfic."

"Charlie Brown fan fiction? Never mind. To answer your question, the reason I'm still here is because I'm drunk, okay? And I need the fresh air."

"You're drunk right now?" *Why do my eyes light up when hearing information like this? No, it's not the sexual predator thing.*

"I can't do these auditions without a few drinks beforehand. And I cannot hold my liquor. At. All."

I'd just like to stop again, and say once more for the record, just to be clear: *I am NOT a sexual predator.*

***

So anyway, because booze and mental disorders are a notoriously bad combo for making sensible decisions, we end up in the sack. After enthusiastic consent was given, of course. *Consent for the win!* Turns out she *was* pretty drunk. Luckily, my brother's place — *I'll explain later* — was merely a single train from the closest station, so she didn't even have enough time to pass out before we got to the apartment and started bumping uglies.

I thought it was all right, maybe even sort of memorable, but when I wake up the next morning, Maya Custner is nowhere to be found. The only detail here now that wasn't in this bedroom the night before is a note scribbled on my canvas satchel in black Sharpie that reads:

Congratulations Charlie Brown,
You really are terrible at everything.

I'm going to assume this means I'm not landing the part.

Blame It on the Twain

TBH, I've eaten a scab or two. Or, more likely, a few. I figure it's kind of like eating a bug — *Maybe a beetle? A weevil? Wait, is a weevil a real thing? Sounds made up* — though I suppose without the protein that bugs are said to have. But maybe scabs *do* have protein? Maybe they are protein monsters and nobody knows about it? I could really be on to something big here. Scab bars. You heard it here first, people: scab bars.

I wasn't always like this. Believe me. I once had career aspirations and an actual girlfriend. People would often tell me: "*I can see you doing this,*" and "*I can see you doing that.*" The *This* and the *That* were usually something stupid like hansom cab driver and dog walker — *Even if I've always expressed a fairly obscene dislike toward four-legged creatures of all kinds; don't even get me started on Central Park squirrels* — but at least they were concrete, realistic *somethings.*

I'll tell you, I'm a naturally creative person. I've had business concepts too. How about this one: You know when you've got that visitor coming by who won't eat anything you already have in the pantry, and blatantly makes a point to very specifically mention what it is they *do* eat, so then you go out and load up on non-dairy cheese and non-meat steaks and fishless filets that barely even get consumed and once your annoying friend is gone you're left with a giant bag of tofurkey and a 4L carton of fucking flax milk? Introducing *The Visiting Vegan*™! Vegan products for annoyingly picky friends, in smaller servings so you don't have to choke it down like you're in a Fear Factor elephant shit eating challenge once they've left to lord their lifestyle over someone else. Could even incorporate scab bars in there somewhere.

And that's just one idea. I've got a bunch more.

The fact remains though: I, Chester K. Eddy, used to be someone who could say with a modicum of confidence that I had a decent degree of success in life. Not everyone can say that.

But, like everyone, I also had my secrets. MEcrets, I call them. All those little things about ourselves we pretend to hide from everyone else:

My favorite slushie flavor is cream soda, but I tell everyone it's cola 'cause cream soda sounds emasculating.

I think Hot Tub Time Machine is actually a pretty solid movie.

Would anyone notice if I adjusted my balls right now?

But guess what? Everyone else has got their MEcrets too, likely just as embarrassing as our own. And they all add up. We run ourselves ragged trying to keep our own lies and secrets straight.

And then one day, through the unintended but watchful guidance of Mark Twain, I figured it all out: What's the point of hiding any of it?

It was three days ago actually, a sunny but freezing November morning, when I was watching two drunks in Washington Square Park; the two of them were both rocking some thrift-store quality Mark Twain cosplay and taking turns reciting a few of his more famous quotes. Let's see if I can show off here, and recall some of them from my cobwebby high school memory banks:

There's: "Something something stranger than fiction." I believe Twain based this on that Will Ferrell movie.

Also: "Death is like this and death is like that." Dude had a LOT to say about death. Seems unhealthy to me.

And, of course we can't forget: "Golf sucks." That was the gist of it, at least. What? Am I sitting around reading Mark Twain quote books every night? Are you? I'm not sure if those boneheads in the park were out-of-work actors — *I didn't recognize them, at least, so I know they'd never beaten me out for roles* — or if it was a contest for prizes, or if they were just trying to impress a couple of hot NYU chicks who were sipping mocha frappuccinos around the crowded fountain. Someone even drunker — *Boy, there's a lot of daylight drunks in Washington Square* — yelled out: "It's finger-lickin' good, ya homos!" Though he must have thought they were Colonel Sanders impressionists. At least I hope so.

Anyway, to get to my great moment of clarity, I clearly recall the shorter Twain saying the following words: "The truth is fucking awesome 'cause you don't have to remember shit." Now, I can't verify the accuracy of the quote, but it sounds like a line a Freemason with a brushstache and a stark white suit might say. Taller Twain had no rebuttal for that. Also, he didn't even *have* a mustache. Man, that guy was barely trying. Still, each of them landed one of the two hot chicks, so they were definitely onto something there.

Bear in mind, I was also pretty drunk that morning, so for all I know, those actually *were* Colonel Sanders impersonators. Damn, now all I want is some juicy fried chicken.

But that one quote about telling the truth totally resonated with me. Why not just quit it with all the little lies? Why bog down my already sub-par mental acuity by keeping track of them all? Why hide MEcrets? So:

I pick my nose.

I eat my own boogers. I roll them up and toss 'em in my mouth like any cartoon character ever eats their popcorn.

Instead of farting in public and blaming small children and the elderly, I just say, "Yep. That was me. Sorry everyone in the broken elevator."

I kill bugs because I can. Maliciously, too.

I still smoke cigarettes, not because I've been addicted since I was twelve, but because I actually fucking like them. Sue me.

The last time I flossed was when the dental hygienist did it for me, and I don't remember when that was, but I do remember the blood geyser that blew out of my mouth. Got to miss school that day, too.

I have an assorted, and mind-blowingly large collection of dingleberries I'm open to show to anyone who asks nicely.

And there's more too. LOTS more. But more than anything, there's absolutely no more of the *"Who ME? I don't do THAT. That's GROSS!"* I'm done with it. And it's totally freeing.

Sure, I no longer have realistic career goals or a girlfriend, but I'm happier. That has got to count for something.

I'm happier.

Yes, I'm happier.

Pretty sure I'm happier.

I'm trying here, at least.

The Great Mendota & The Not-So-Great Monona

TBH, I don't give a shit about calories. The good ones, the bad ones (I don't understand why there's a difference; *is* there a difference?), or why anyone counts any of them. Seems like a pretty stupid thing to be counting, and an impossible thing to accurately measure anyway. Like the limits of the galaxy. Or the number of hairs on my ass. Or just how much porn is actually online.

So, my brother's real name is Chase Eddy, but everybody knows him as Ace. For as long as I can remember, I've called him "Acehole" when I'm pissed at him, but it's becoming increasingly hard to get pissed at the guy since he basically supports my maladjusted Charlie Brown ass. He calls me "Chesty," and although I'm still merely in the very early stages of full-on man-boobs, I continue to let him get away with it.

Question: Why?

The Obvious, Simple Answer: Because he's better than me, that's why.

We grew up in Madison, Wisconsin, each of us the product of a happy family and healthy lifestyle. In my eyes, the only thing that truly separated the two of us was he got the bedroom in the basement and I didn't.

Bear with me. This is going to take some explanation.

I'm seven years older than my brother, and should have had a leg up on him in everything, but Ace Eddy just don't roll that way. He was great at everything: he would climb taller trees than me, he could hit any target imaginable with a broken Dollar Store squirt gun, and, even though the Racecar playing piece is far superior to the Thimble, he still beat me at Monopoly. Every time with the fucking Thimble. I quickly learned to never agree to partake in any of his challenges, but his competitive nature could never stop him from attempting to make a worthy opponent out of me.

ACE: "Hey Chesty, you up for some Billiards?"
ME: "Who says 'billiards?'"
ACE: "Darts?"
ME: "Go fuck yourself, Acehole."
ACE: "Backgammon?"
ME: "Are we living in an English pub, or something?"

He's probably the most athletic and enthusiastic person I've ever known; but I avoid sports like the bubonic plague and have about as much ambition as a...uh—*You know, I can't even be bothered to come up with a good metaphor here.* He was great at everything, but ice hockey was really his sport. In fact, when he was only ten, Ace Eddy was garnering attention from hockey scouts, and at fifteen he was granted "Exceptional Player Status" in the hockey world by some suit whose job it was to proclaim ridiculous things like that.

But that basement bedroom! Even after all of this, he still got the fucking bedroom in the basement, which meant he could easily sneak girls into his room in high school, whereas I was stuck with the room upstairs, trapped at the end of the hallway so I had to Mission Impossible my way across those perpetually-creaky floorboards past our parents' room, and *Goddammit, Stuart and Lorraine Eddy, why on God's great earth did you never close your bedroom door?* They just left it wide open so I had to sneak the girls past, concealing them behind a Fraggle Rock bedsheet just to make it to my room.

Confession time: There were never any girls.

Confession, part the second: There definitely *was* a Fraggle Rock bedsheet. I wouldn't make up shit like that.

Sorry. I get carried away sometimes with the childhood bedroom thing.

Seriously though, ours was the only house on the block without a tree out front for horny teens to invite even hornier teens up into their STD dens. Not even a lattice or a fucking drain pipe. It was abysmal.

Damn, I thought I could let it go.

But all I'm saying is that when I was in high school and my brother Chase was a booger-picking — *God bless his innocent and MEcret-free soul* — eight-year-old, I practically begged my parents to clean out their weird museum of Stairmasters, VHS tapes, and Grandma's lamps (which sat upon *other* Grandma's doilies) from the basement so I could move my Daryl Hannah poster and my pimply boner down there. I may have even tried to bribe them more than once with weekly payments of pilfered Arby's coupons. But would they have any it? Fuck no, they wouldn't. *"Seriously, Stuart and Lorraine? THREE Stairmasters? We already have two whole flights of stairs in this house!"*

Again, sorry.

But the one time I did convince a girl — *With consent!* — to head on over to Chester's Mack Shack™ I had to lie and tell Vicky Henderson the pool house out back was actually my bedroom. *"Bed? What bed? Beds are bad for the sperm count. Everyone knows that, Vicky. Now let's get this over with fast because it's fucking freezing out here. And yes, those pool floaties and algae nets ARE the only source of insulation in here, thank you for asking. What do YOU use? Oh shit, so that's where the raccoon's been living all winter."*

What was I talking about here? Oh yeah, Ace Eddy.

Okay.

When Chase turned thirteen, without even asking for it, Mom and Dad just up and gave him the bedroom in the basement. They cleaned their shit out of there and just handed him the keys to the high school equivalent of the Bang Bus. I was twenty, still living upstairs and still being quite bitter about the whole thing. But hey, I was now attending Madison Wisconsin's most prestigious school for acting — *Yes, the "most prestigious" can too also be the "most shitty"* — while working part-time at that shop that only sold party balloons. Also, I was rocking a pretty sweet mustache at the time, which no thirteen-year-old, not even my brother, could possibly compete with.

So, obviously, life was chugging along pretty great for me, and I assumed the joke was finally on my brother.

The joke was *never* on my brother.

I even look at pictures of us from back then and realize my mustache looked more like a ferret tried to Jheri curl his pubes. You win again, Ace Eddy.

I was still working part-time at The Balloon Attic (sounds like "Ba-Lunatic" is you're slurring your speech enough) when Ace finished high school. He didn't even go to college. He just played hockey.

And get this: at eighteen, Ace Eddy was drafted first overall by the New York Islanders in the NHL Draft. Eight-*fucking*-teen! He started playing the very next season, and after a record-breaking rookie year, Ace signed a nausea-inducing, pimply boner-deflating, major multimillion-dollar contract. Life was pretty sweet for the Eddys for a while there, and I even moved to New York City with him, right into his swanked-out Park Avenue pad while I looked for stable acting work. Okay, I wasn't really "looking," per se.

Yes, things were good. Until three years ago, that is, when some Slovakian tank on skates broke Ace's neck with a body check into the steel frame of the goalie net. Mlynár Blubálž even cracked his stick over my brother's head for good measure, just to make sure he was down. I was at that game too, trying to impress a girl with the free tickets Ace had given us, but she ended up just giving a hand-job to the dude on her left while still eating *my* candy floss. How rude.

There's that old saying: "I went to a fight and a hockey game broke out." Well, *Ho Lee Shit* did Hell ever break loose at the game that night. I can't even watch hockey anymore, that crimson sheen of blood on the ice scarred me so much. And I'm usually not such a pussy for a little violence. Also, when the Zamboni began resurfacing the ice, shaving the top layer off into a flaky, frozen pile of red, I nearly gagged. Dracula's Snow Cone, I called it later. Yes, a good joke will always help speed up the healing process.

So, all of a sudden: *POOF! Done. Smell you later, hockey career.* And even though Ace was put on long-term injury reserve, he continues to get paid, not only due to the terms of his contract with the league, but also from the major lawsuit that all of Slovakia is probably having to pay out.

Still, being forced to retire at twenty with millions of dollars in the bank? Sounds like a pretty sweet deal to me. And the money keeps coming; the dude signed a fifteen-year contract.

It's been three years now, and I don't see Ace complaining about shit. Also, even with the neck brace he's still required to wear sometimes, Ace Eddy continues to get the quality ladies. Meanwhile, I keep seeking out the damaged goods because I tell myself girls with lazy eyes, daddy issues, and Tweety Bird tattoos are my only option.

If Madison Wisconsin itself could be used to explain the dynamic between Ace and Chester Eddy, then he is the Mendota and I am the Monona. Don't worry. Most people don't care to understand it either.

***

I'm in the kitchen right now, the morning after my romp with Maya Custner, trying to wash her black Sharpie'd insult off my satchel. I have to relocate the sticky pile of week-old cereal bowls from the sink so I have enough room to scrub the damn thing with some dish soap and a wire brush. Finally, I just submerge the entire bag into the bubbly water.

Walking away, I stop momentarily to consider whether I had any smokes or condoms still in there.

Ace is in the theater room (a renovated dining room — *Who in this city is still dining, anyway?*), playing a video game. Hockey. Go figure. I can't help it, but just seeing that shit on the eight-foot projection screen takes me back to the night he nearly lost his head.

"How can you keep doing that to yourself?" I ask him, leaning against the door frame.

Ace says, "You've got to move on, Chesty. I have." He barely moves his head to acknowledge me. But he can't really move his head too well anymore anyway with that contraption on his neck. "If you keep letting it bother you, how do you ever get over *anything*?"

"I don't know if I do, really. But with my new Honesty Movement? I know I'm going to start seeing some changes here."

"Oh yeah. Your new religion. What's it been, like a month?"

"Three days. And it's not a religion. I'm calling it a *movement*." I slump into the leather recliner next to the couch.

He pauses his game, just as he's winding up for a big slapshot. "Wouldn't you need more people for it to technically be a movement? I wouldn't trust you to move *anything* on your own."

"Says the dude in the neck brace who's playing video games at nine in the morning and not wearing pants." He *never* wears pants anymore. Claims *no-pants* is good for his rehab. Some days I'm lucky if he actually puts underwear on, at least. Whatever. "I'm no hygienist, Ace. But I'm pretty certain Donald-Ducking it around the house has got to be breaking some health violations in this place."

"Is it nine o'clock already? Also, it's MY place, so I get the last say on what counts as a violation." He unpauses the game, and the puck rockets into the back of the net. Ace Eddy scores again. My brother only ever plays an older version of the game, the one where he's still a rookie and his stats are rated like he made the game himself.

Out of curiosity, I ask him, "Do you ever think about how good you could have been in the NHL? Like, do you think you would have been better than Gretzky?"

"No one will ever touch Gretzky." Player changes are made, and the teams line up for the next faceoff. Ace Eddy's still out there though.

"How about—uh, actually, I can't name another hockey player."

"Come on! I took you to that party at Sidney Crosby's house! You literally sat on Sid's face while he was passed out on the couch."

"Doesn't ring a bell."

As soon as the referee drops the puck, a player on the opposing team — *I can't verify whether or not he's Slovakian* — throws a punch, knocking Virtual Ace Eddy on his ass.

My brother shouts out, "Mother fucker!" And he chucks the controller across the room, missing my head by inches. Instead, it hits his hockey jersey on the wall, his #89 New York Islanders rookie jersey, cracking the glass frame it's displayed behind.

"See? I knew you hadn't moved on," I say to him. "Bad shit's hard to get over, isn't it?"

"That dirty Slovak nearly killed me, Chester! KILLED me!"

"Yeah, but look at *all of this*," I say, emphasizing this crazy room and the view of Central Park out the window. The sunrise from the East reflects off the steel and glass of Midtown, like the city is made of diamonds. Yeah, I know I can sometimes — *Sometimes?* — be a sarcastic prick, but this is an amazing city to be in, from no matter where you're standing. "Now you get all of this, and you don't even have to do shit anymore to earn it."

"Maybe you're forgetting that *you're* the lazy one in this family, and not me."

"Well, laziness is all very subjective—"

"I was getting up at five in the morning when I was eight years old to go to hockey practice before school. And then the Scouting Combine, the training camps, the bag skates—"

"'Cause, I mean, I've actually left the apartment in the last week. I wouldn't say that's lazy. That takes *some* degree of effort."

"At first, I agreed with you. I thought this would be great. I mean, *after* I realized I wasn't dead and would probably still walk again. I think they gave me a sixty-five percent chance at the time, which sounded pretty incredible. But now reality's hit. My C2 through C5 vertebrae are fused together. They had to make sure I still had enough bone left from my hip surgery, so they could take some more out and put it in my neck—AND I SWEAR TO GOD, don't you DARE give me a hip-check joke right now."

Damn. He's good. Clearly, Ace either knows me all too well or I'm way more obvious than I thought I was.

"The doctor gives me injections every month, which really only helps with the arm pain. My physical therapist is here six times a week. I take twenty-two pills a day. Beer only makes the pain worse. This is my life."

"If it's any consolation, beer always makes *me* feel worse too. But maybe try a nice, dark, German ale? That might do the trick."

"And, to top it off, I have no idea when the hell you're moving out of here."

"*Moving out?* I thought this was a lifetime commitment we made."

"Shut up, Chester."

I get up from the recliner — *Also, I almost thought right here that, "Christ, it's really difficult to get out of this chair. It's so fucking comfortable! Like I'm sitting in a warm bowl of oatmeal or something." But I didn't because, hey, #89 Ace Eddy is sitting over there with a broken neck and it's probably pretty fucking hard for HIM to get anywhere, so what the hell am I complaining about? What gives me the right? But I didn't think that, so = Growth! Yay! Points for me! Wait, I guess I did still think it though, didn't I? Whatever —* I pick up the tossed video game controller, and hand it back to my brother.

And I say, "Consider this Nintendo controller my olive branch, fair Ace. Though, now that I think of it, the controller would have to have been *mine* first in order to symbolize an offer of peace. As it is, I think I'm probably just giving you back the olive branch that you chucked at my head. Not sure if the message still counts in the same way. What do *you* think?"

"It's a PS4, not a Nintendo."

"Nintendo, Nintitto, am I right? But seriously. Don't you realize that this change I've made, my Honesty Movement—"

"You mean your *dirty secrets* movement?"

"Whatever you want to call it. It's doing wonders for *you* too. Look, three days ago I had no idea you felt so shitty. Now I do. You should be thanking me, really."

"Get out, Chester," he says to me, like someone serious in a movie. He nails it, actually. If this was his whole audition, I'd totally give him the part.

"What—?" I ask, even though I heard him and I comprehend what he's telling me, but I figure I can buy more time by asking him to repeat it.

"Get. Out."

Sounds even worse the second time. Definitely should not have asked him to repeat it.

"Chester, you said you'd only be here until you found work."

"I've been looking!"

"For *three* years? I keep bending over backwards for you—"

"Which is completely inaccurate, 'cause, y'know, you *can't* bend over backwards anymore."

"—And all you do is continue to take advantage of me."

"Who buys all the groceries?" I ask, hoping for a lifeline.

"You do." *Thank you very much. Point for me.* "But we don't have any groceries."

"Well, no. 'Cause I ate them all."

"And you use *my* credit card." Goddammit, Ace Eddy scores again.

"The bank refuses to send me one. It's not my fault I'm hogtied by Visa."

"Whose fault is it then?"

"Uh, Morgan Freeman's?"

"What?"

"He does the voiceovers for the commercials. He's in on it too. You have no idea how high this goes!"

"You're an idiot, Chester. And it's about time you start figuring out how to function on your own."

***

So, by the graces of the great Mendota and the not-so-great Monona, I've Charlie-Browned myself out onto some dirty Park Avenue sidewalk, barricaded by slushy piles of blackened snow. Only a *SisQó Tour 2000* hoodie to my name, and my vandalized satchel still dripping dish soap bubbles from sitting in the kitchen sink. Turns out I *did* have some smokes and condoms in there. Half of an uneaten Big Mac for some reason too, which I still ate, despite its mushy, waterlogged-ness.

I take back what I said earlier about this city being so great, no matter where you are. This town straight up sucks from where I'm standing.

The Dank, Steaming Unknown (Enjoying the View from Down Here)

TBH, I've had dirty thoughts about the Golden Girls. Filthy, actually. Does this have anything to do with the glasses fetish, though? Not sure. I don't even know how many of those old codgers even wore glasses. But when it comes to 80's sitcoms with *ahem* older lady ensembles, my thing was really with those Designing Women. Dixie Carter and Annie Potts? Come on. There's some Southern heat right there.

So, what's a fella to do when he suddenly — *and unjustifiably, I might add* — finds himself homeless in New York and has nothing but six soggy smokes, a bruised ego, and one hanging audition? A hanging audition, by the way, is how I refer to a part I've auditioned for but haven't yet heard back from. Common sense tells me the Maya Custner play is not-so-hanging, but common sense and myself have been at odds for a while now.

Well, the first thing I decide to do in my quest for personal-betterment, is clearing some snow off the sidewalk in order to dry out my cigarettes on a subway vent. I don't think I could look *more* homeless, so, you know, my personal-betterment is totally running at a 100% success rate so far.

Next step? Fuck Ace Eddy. That's right. He thinks his life will be better off without his own brother in it? We'll just wait and see who breaks down and comes crawling back first. We'll see who sticks whose neck out first, in a manner of speaking. This is no different than him being in the basement bedroom when we were growing up; only now he's just nineteen floors up. And me? I'm—well, I'm back in the fucking pool house watching Vicky Henderson walking away from me, aren't I? Not to mention the fact I don't even have an apartment key anymore, since I chucked it at Ace's television on my way out.

That may have been a somewhat irrational decision on my part.

My fist slams the subway vent, and two of the six smokes fall into the dank, steaming unknown. I could admit that, yes, it's fairly comical, but I'm not going to. Instead, I'll keep my focus on the future. Because that's what winners do. *Chin up, Chester! You're a winner!*

Okay, so: Dry off Dishwater-Soaked Cigarettes, Check! Give Little Bro the Middle Finger, Check! What's next?

I got it: Time for a drink! I bet I can double-checkmark this one.

I know a great little place within stumbling distance from the apartment, just a couple of blocks East of Park Avenue. Philly's only stays open until midnight — *though I'm usually kicked out by nine o'clock anyway* — but the best part about the place is that it opens at ten in the morning. A full day of drinking has never been a hindrance for someone about to embark on a quest to better his life, right?

Let's not answer that one just yet.

The original owner of Philly's Bar was named Baxter, but he died in the 80's, and nobody (not even Darren, the current owner) had any idea why the guy ever decided to name the place Philly's. Of the folks who creep around here, no one had ever met old Baxter. He wasn't from Philadelphia, nor did he appear to have a thing for cheese steaks or cream cheese. As it is, Philly's is just a confusing name for a bar, especially if it's located in Midtown Manhattan and there's New York Jets paraphernalia everywhere in the place. Not to mention, someone's carved, "The Liberty Bell's a sad, lonely bitch" into the bar's old, wooden sign with a knife. Honestly, it wasn't me. I've never been to Philadelphia, but I've heard it's a cesspool. And also, the guy who broke Ace Eddy's neck played for the Flyers, so The City of Brotherly Love is certainly not doing itself any favors in my opinion.

Darren's working when I come in, but there's not a single other soul in here. The old beast of a television is on, turned to that weird channel which seems to only ever show reruns of *The View*, though thankfully, at a low volume.

Darren is hooked on *The View*, which — *Okay, I'll man-up and admit it —* is partially my fault. I'd asked him to turn it on one morning. Completely dead to the world with a hangover that could only have been made worse by the intensifying shrill of Barbara Walters' voice, but I asked for it nonetheless. Darren wondered why in the name of all that's holy I would ever request *The View*. And I told him:

ME: "They've got all these ladies lined up on chairs, legs crossed, right? And when they inevitably need to re-cross said legs because of varicose vein and obesity numbness, sometimes, if you're cagey enough, you can see up their skirts."

DARREN: "But you're talking about Joy Behar and Rosie O'Donnell here. Yuck, man."

ME: "Even so, there's like four or five of 'em. PLUS guests! Believe me, it's the best odds on television. Also, Rosie wears pants most of the time anyway, so you're not going to see anything too offensive."

DARREN: "Fair enough."

He couldn't really argue with that logic, and he's had *The View* on every morning since. But even though a strip of black electrical tape has been pulled over the cracked screen for months now, covering up the hosts' midsections, he still watches. I assume that, like most things, patterns are simply formed and it's hard to change our ways. Even if it means a grown man watching old episodes of *The View* alone while he cleans beer steins and dried puke.

I sit up at the bar and order an Old Fashioned. Darren comments, "You're in early."

"Got a big day, Dee. Decided to kick things off right. You know, a half-dozen to full-dozen bourbons? Maybe a handful of those free nuts of yours. *Hey, whoa!* Careful now. That's not innuendo. Don't be getting any funny ideas!"

"Sure, sure," he says, ignoring my standard fare repertoire — *Something tells me he's heard some of these lines before* — and pouring a generous volume of bourbon onto ice. He slides the glass over to me, right into my hand like he was an Olympic curler.

"This is going on my tab, eh?" I double check. *For no reason at all, Darren. No reason at all.*

"Course it is. How's Eddy doing?"

Darren always asks how my brother's doing. And I guarantee he'll ask within three or four sentences spoken. Also, I think he only calls Ace "Eddy" because that's what it said on the back of his hockey sweater. The fact it makes me feel like I'm no one at all? I try not to let it bother me too much. I still try for some of the spotlight though: "I've been better."

"I meant your brother." Boy, that spotlight fades fast, doesn't it?

"Who, Chase?" I reach over the bar to find the phone charger Darren lets me use, and I plug my dead phone in.

"Ace."

"Right. He's good. In a bit of a mood today, but you know him: he's never one to complain about much." Except for his brother being a freeloading loser with no hopes, dreams, or prospects worth living for. Except for that.

Darren just nods in my general direction and goes about his business of cleaning glasses and general prep for the day, but I sense his eyes on me as soon as my finger goes into my nostril. "What's this, then?" he asks, cringing a little at what he's witnessing. "Dude, get your finger outta there!"

"It's this cold weather, Dee. Dries my nose out so much. Doesn't it ever bother you?"

"Not the cold, nope. But I *am* bothered by *that*." He smacks my arm away from my face. "Can I get you a tissue at least?"

"Nah," I say, choosing to wipe the snot on my hoodie sleeve rather than swallow it. "I started a movement, you see. Honesty. No secrets. Inspired by Mark Twain, or a reasonable facsimile thereof. Nothing but pure, unfiltered, open book honesty now. But without being super annoying, like Whoopi Goldberg."

"What is it with you and those View ladies?" He turns the television off with a well-placed hand on a hidden remote control.

I just shrug. "Beats me. But hey, even though I've only been doing this thing for three days now, I think it's really working for me already."

"It's *not* working for you. It's disgusting."

"Come on, Dee. It's gonna catch on. Trust me."

Darren grabs another glass, but like any barkeep worth his weight in salt-and-pepper chicken wings, he knows when something's amiss with his clientele. "What's on your mind, Chester?"

I gulp down most of my first Old Fashioned. "T and A, mostly."

"I mean, what's bothering you?"

"I think it's the fact the T's seem to be getting smaller and the A's seem to be getting bigger, and nobody seems to want to complain about it anymore."

"What's to complain about? Guys like us, we should be happy with *any*."

Guys like us? Where does he get off lumping me in with him? Darren's a thirty-something ticking time-bomb of inappropriateness with no sincerity, self-respect, girlfriend, or visible musculature of any kind whatsoever. Also, he's clearly smart, but doesn't seem to realize how annoying he—

Oh.

My.

God.

Shitting.

Gods.

That's not Darren; that's a fucking mirror I'm looking at, isn't it? The only difference between Darren and me is *he* has a job and I very clearly do not.

Still. How does one actually admit one's unhappiness and dysfunction to someone else? With pure, unfiltered, open book honesty? Let's not go that far quite yet. Not just yet. I tell him, "Listen, Dee. I'm womanless and incredibly horny. I'm unemployed and virtually unemployable. What am I supposed to *do*, man?"

He pours another bourbon into my glass, right over the ice that has yet to melt. "Well, I'm not servicing you under the bar, I'll tell you that much."

"Thanks for the offer though."

"But seriously. I know you're ambitious. Nothing ever shakes you for long."

"Thanks, Dee. Do you mean that, though? You're not just shitting on my ego right now, are you?"

"Partly."

"You partly *are*, or you partly *aren't*? Wait, those are really just the same things, aren't they? Are we experiencing a paradox right now?"

"I think what it really is, Chester, is that you just can't seem to take a hint. But that's admirable too, in a way."

"Oh." Is this how it feels when somebody tries opening your eyes to the truth?

"You don't know how to quit because you don't really know how you started anything in the first place."

Is this a revelation that's happening right now? A revelation kicking me right in the honesty-balls? No, I think something could only be a revelation if I was *believing* any of it. Darren doesn't *really* know me; he just pours me drinks on a daily basis and listens to my drunken, droning, verbal diarrhea.

"You're an actor. Aren't there any parts out there right now?"

"Sure there are. This is New York." I flash a pair of Jazz Hands to help verify our location.

"So then, you're not landing any auditions?"

"No. I am."

"Well what's the deal then? You on a director's blacklist list or something?"

I swallow half the drink in a single gulp. "I just always seem to find a way to blow them. The auditions, I mean. Not the directors."

Darren places the bottle of bourbon back under the bar; out of sight, out of mind. "It's always low-brow or no-brow with you, isn't it?"

"Is that a problem? I'm sensing you perceive it to be a problem."

"Of course it's a problem, Chester. And it's not just that—"

Don't tell me he's got a fucking list.

"—It's your unrelenting pessimism, and your lack of reverence and integrity."

He's actually got a fucking list. And it's one of those annoying lists with big, five-dollar words in it. I knock back the other half of my drink and push the empty glass back toward him in a display of audacious contempt — *There's your five-dollar word for you!* — but my finger slips and the glass fails to move at all.

"I have integrity," is the best response I can give at the moment. I could let it lie (especially since I don't really wish to get into a second argument already this morning, and I certainly don't want to get kicked out of a second home of mine) but one does not call upon Chester K. Eddy when one needs a situation diffused. I am not the expert on letting things lie. "I'm *built* on integrity. Like a Ford truck. Is that their motto? Who's got more integrity than me?"

"Oh, I don't know. How about Abraham Lincoln? Or the Dalai Lama. Or fucking Superman."

"Oh, come on. Those are totally unfair comparisons. Two of those guys aren't even real."

"Gandhi? Oprah?"

"No mononymosity! Someone with *more* than one name."

"You're just being difficult now."

"Okay. Let me rephrase that: who would you think has *less* integrity than me, but actually has more?"

"Huh? I don't even understand the question anymore."

"My point exactly." *Hey, look. I win! But what's this? Am I still talking?* "Let's set the bar real low then." *Oh shit, I'm still talking.* "I bet you can't name a single serial killer with more integrity than me." *Wow. I really just went there, didn't I?*

Darren leans back, arms crossed. "A serial killer will at least own up to his shit, man."

"So, a serial killer has more integrity than me? Is that what you're saying? Jeffrey Fucking Dahmer is basically a better person than I am?"

"He'd probably pay up his tab, at least."

"That's not fair! He was gainfully employed!"

"Gainfully? Are you saying Dahmer was more employable than you?"

More ambitious, maybe. I'll give him that much. "I recall reading he worked at a chocolate factory and a sandwich shop."

"Jeez," Darren says, shaking his head like emerging from a drunken stupor. "That is probably the last guy I would want handling my food."

"No kidding, right?"

Where were we going with this?

We both stand our ground now, neither of us sure about what the hell we're talking about anyway. Or what to talk about next. Coolly, I reach over the bar to find the remote control so I can turn the television back on. Lena Dunham is on *The View* now, talking about angry things and wearing an inappropriately short mini skirt while doing it.

Finally, Darren offers: "Listen. I'll talk to my brother if you want. He's a construction contractor in the city. He could probably find you something."

Construction? That sounds an awful lot like work to me. "Do you have a sister?"

His appetite for helping me is seemingly evaporating by the second. "I do. But she's married. Sorry."

"Is she happy in her marriage? Do you have a picture?"

"Are you for real, Chester?"

I am, unfortunately, very for real indeed.

"I'm just trying to do you a favor here," he continues. "I'm attempting to treat you like a grown-up."

But as I sit dithering, unsure whether or not the next thing I say will only be digging myself a deeper hole in this conversation, like a police megaphone announcement before a house party raid, my charging phone rings from behind the bar, saving me from further trouble.

Well, "ringing" is a polite way of describing what it's actually doing. A while back, I set my ringtone to *Random-Lyrics-from-Me-So-Horny*. Because that's funny, right? Wait, don't answer that. In my defense however, I do keep my phone set to vibrate, but ever since I dropped it into the toilet, it does still ring sometimes, and only ever during the *People-Are-Standing-Around-Judging-Me* times. It's not like I'm desperate for attention. I keep telling myself that if I can't fix my buggy phone, I'll at least change the offensive 2 Live Crew ringtone. But it's just one of those things you keep saying you'll do, though not right now because you don't have time, but definitely the next time you've got thirty seconds to spare, right? Definitely. But then you still never do. It's one of those kinds of situations.

Dee looks down at the lit-up screen, scrunches his eyes and furrows his brow, like he's unsure what it is he's looking at. "Are you expecting a call from a...*Pornstar Jugz Sixty-Nine*?"

"As a matter of fact, I was." I yank the phone away from the charger, trying to keep as straight a face as possible. Maybe Darren will assume it's a very grown-up business call. "I'll be taking this call outside however, thank you very much. Y'know, *work stuff*."

But as I exit Philly's, Darren calls after me: "If that's Jeffrey Dahmer, maybe you can ask him to lend you a few bucks to pay your fucking tab!"

I don't think he bought my attempted "grown-up" stratagem.

Heh, Ha, Right

Christ, it's suddenly freezing out here. I thought daytime boozing was supposed to warm the body. "Hi, Melissa," my words clatter off my teeth and into the phone.

"*Who* is yelling *what* at you now, Chestnuts?" she asks.

"You expect me to keep track of things like that?"

"I suppose not, especially when it seems to happen on such a regular basis. This person does know that Jeffrey Dahmer's dead, right?"

"I'm pretty sure everyone—"

"Bludgeoned to death with an iron pipe."

"Melissa. Honestly, you mean the world to me, but is this really how we're going to start a conversation?"

"Buzzkill?"

"Little bit, yeah. Plus, my phone has got like a decimal point of power left so let's keep it short."

"You know I don't like things when they're *too* short. That's why I like you. *Nyuk, nyuk.*"

"Heh. Ha. Right."

This is Melissa: former co-worker, current compadre (#1 on the Champion Chum List for sixty-two weeks and counting), and sort-of-sex-friend. Well, more than sort-of.

And the best I can respond with is: *Heh. Ha. Right.*

What the hell is wrong is me? My Honesty Movement requires me to disclose that, although we've been best buds with benefits for more than a year now, the truth is I can't help having those *you-know-what* feelings for

Melissa. The ones that start turning the *sexy-good-times* feelings into more of the *can-we-just-watch-a-funny-movie-in-our-Snuggie-Blankets®-tonight, maybe-with-some-mint-chip-ice-cream?* kind of feelings. I know. It sickens me too. But my *Heh, Ha, Right* response is indicative of the fact the world only works in messed-up ways. Why can I not just be myself when the *real* feelings start creeping their way into conversations? Why, at the very thought of liking someone this way, do I turn into some bumbling, no-fun, sweater-vested dad from a bad 80's sitcom? What the hell kind of an answer is: *Heh, Ha, Right?*

But she ignores the two left feet lodged in my mouth and asks, "Are we still on for tonight?"

"Actually, Mel. My place isn't going to work for the next little bit."

"Define, *The Next Little Bit.*"

"The foreseeable future?"

"I've never seen the future very clearly, Chestnuts."

This is another obvious part of the problem. Melissa's right: she doesn't look into the future at all. Which, in a way, makes it difficult for me to think about it also. The future's so obscured by our relationship's big, fucking, spooge-covered question mark, that we just keep it all so very status quo. But those Snuggie Blankets® are sure starting to sound like a good idea.

I say, "My brother sort of kicked me out of the apartment."

"What are you—"

"I can't get into it right now, Mel. I'm serious, my phone is the technological equivalent of Australia. There's no reason it should still be functioning."

No response.

"Hello?"

Nothing.

"Melissa?"

Kaput.

There's an oncoming winter gust of cold air that blows around the corner, and it mixes with the warm blast from a subway vent below me. I can't tell if I like the feeling very much. Still, the city has a nice quietness about it at the moment; like I'm the only one out here.

Am I the only one out here?

Before I head back inside Philly's to recharge my phone, I use this God-sent, dead battery of a moment to confuse my place in the world even further. Meekly, watchfully, making sure to catch my hound dog reflection in the bar window, I say into the lifeless phone still pressed to my ear: "I love you, Mel."

Yep. This is exactly where this story is going. Turn back now if you can't handle awkwardly-emotional, downward-spiraling men in their thirties.

pornstarjugz69@aol.com To See You, BOSS

TBH, if I find any amount of cash anywhere at all, I'm totally keeping it. No questions asked. I'm not even going to elaborate on this or give an example. I'm just broke and rapacious and lacking some real basic morals.

After two or three more drinks (or, after my phone was up to seven of its ten battery bars — *Who measures time with drinks anymore?*), I call Melissa back.

Voicemail. Shit. *"Hey, it's Mel. I'm probably in rehearsal for a show right now, 'cuz, you know, my ubertalent is so utterly demanding. Leave a message and I'll call you back just as soon as I wake from my fever dream. I'm not delusional. Oh, look up there. A unicorn!"*

I've told Mel a thousand times that a unicorn is strictly the name of a horse with a horn on its forehead — nothing more, nothing less — but she refuses to grasp the singularity of the whole concept.

MEL: "Listen, Chestnuts. All mythical, magical horses fall into the unicorn family. Winged horses, sparkly horses, zebras, Seabiscuit. All of them."

See? How do I not love her so much?

I don't leave a message, instead choosing to have another drink — *Or two? Again, drinks are not an accurate measuring stick for time* — before being kicked out of Philly's Bar around four o'clock.

Four o'clock! Yikes, where has the day gone? How long was I talking to that gold-digging Jezebel — *The one with the super fake tits, but I still kinda wanted to touch them because I've never actually felt a fake tit before. Is it more jiggly? Less jiggly? Same amount of jiggly?* — at the bar anyway? Obviously not long enough for her to realize I am not the kind of gold mine that's worth excavating. There definitely ain't naw gold in them thar hills.

Then I recall Melissa asking me about tonight, combined with the fond memory of being kicked out of my brother's apartment and the snow that's now coming down hard. I duck under a sidewalk canopy, brush the flakes from my SisQó hoodie, and I wonder, *Where am I going to sleep tonight?*

I try Melissa's number once more: Nothing. Not even voicemail this time.

***

A couple of years back, I'd done quite a bit of temporary work in the city. Terrible stuff, but a fairly regular — *if not on the near lowest-of-scales* — paycheck, and it was never the kind of work that demanded overtime or had any requirement to take it home with me. This was mostly random, generic office jobs, but I Heigh-Ho-Heigh-Ho'd my way into every one of them, thinking of the work as nothing more than research opportunities for the acting landscape that was my real life. Nine-to-five improv classes is what I treated these temp jobs as; these positions which seemed to only bring depression, misery, and big numbers in early suicide rates to the unfortunate few who called it their actual career. I was the Daniel Day Lewis of the virtually unknown, and peculiarly unhirable stage actors of New York City.

But these offices continued to mystify and bemuse me; their innocuous street entrances (revolving doors, dented buzzer plates, generic concrete planters exploding with faux-exotic rubber plants) which all led to their virtually near-identical interiors, the same employees in the same cubicles with the same miniature stacks of post-it notes, and the same lingering smell from when Erin — *there was ALWAYS an Erin* — burned her sad leftovers in the microwave. They lived like this, these never-defiant, yet permanently-seething denizens of a world we know nothing about, aside from the fact we still somehow need it to survive.

I loved being a part of it; I lived for the logging of hours-worked subtracted by the half-hour lunch but not the two fifteen-minute breaks. And I blatantly acknowledged my obliviousness to the fact that I could literally be replaced by a fresh-off-the-boat immigrant, a borrowed zoo monkey, or a disgraced Food Network star tomorrow.

When was I placed in a data entry position at the Deutsche Bank, I met Melissa on my first day on the job. Her position was the same as mine, though she'd already been there for three weeks. The wily veteran of data entry! Melissa was tasked with the responsibility of training me on that first day, but the only thing I can recall is how we primarily ended up sucking face in the janitor's closet. It was that grabby, expectorating, no-limits kind of a make-out session, the kind that can only be improvised on the spot. No amount of pre-planning can get those same sorts of results.

It didn't happen every day — *"Routine kills routinely," old married folks like to say* — in fact, it really didn't happen all that often, and when we presumed others were on to us, we began crafting codewords, hand signals, and even rudimentary pirate maps to indicate where in the office we would rendezvous next. I took the time to really authenticize my pirate maps; crinkling the paper, burning the edges — *I only set off the sprinklers once!* — and adding super unnecessarily-detailed hand-drawn compasses in the corners. Since I was a kid — *and for no real reason at all, other than ignorance and a poor memory* — I could never remember what side was East and which was West. Until Melissa came over during one of my pirate map crafting sessions and whispered into my ear all sultry-like: "Never Eat Soggy Wieners, Dumbass."

We had to be extra careful too, since we were both pretty certain our boss was a robot. Yes, an actual, whirring-cog type of robot. She took her coffee black (re: oil), never forgot anyone's name (re: data processors), and mysteriously closed her door once a day for an extraordinarily precise amount of time (re: sleep mode). And like any good robot, she required an acronym to define her pre-programmed role for which she was specifically designed for in human society. Melissa and I agreed upon BOSS: Brainless Office Shit Supervisor. The best part was that BOSS had no compunction with our calling her "BOSS" instead of "Ms. Whatever Her Actual Name Was," so this was a win for everyone.

BOSS always had her head on a swivel with the two of us. Kind of to the point where I would think, *"Why the hell does she even keep us around? We're obviously doing more harm than good."* But when you steal BOSS's cereal bowl from the staff kitchen and then lay low for a few days, you start to fade into the background a bit. Just a tiny bit. *Was Chester K. Eddy really just peeing under his desk into my once-presumed lost vintage Bionic Woman melamine cereal bowl, or was he just a figment of my imagination?*

The job at Deutsche Bank was basically digital filing of customer statements; the kind of personal information jackhole underlings like Melissa and myself should definitely not be left in charge with. Of course, it was against the air-quote/air-unquote rules, but sometimes you've got to fuck the rules. And we were the Kama Sutra masters of rule fucking.

On our lunch breaks, Melissa and I would call customers with unfounded good news (*"Mr. Wainwright, the Deutsche Bank has come across some extra money and, congratulations! has randomly selected your account to be ameliorated."*), erroneously tragic news (*"Ms. Taylor, we're sorry but your home has been arbitrarily repossessed. All paperwork will be mailed to you posthaste. Please file accordingly."*), or just devious and outright terrifying news (*"Mr. Toy, the Deutsche Bank has reason to believe there's someone in your home right now. We will be facilitating your safe evacuation. Please stay on the line and await further assistance. No, just stay on the line. Of course we're totally authorized to be doing this. Thank you for choosing Deutsche Bank! Your service is valued."*).

A few months into the job, we came across the mother of all personal data. Some clown's business account was registered under the email address of pornstarjugz69@aol.com. Without a doubt one of the classiest ways to make any business look professional, made even classier by the changing of the *S* to a *Z*.

To put it bluntly, this was undoubtedly one of the greatest discoveries of our modern times. No exaggeration.

At first, we weren't sure what to do with this information, but eventually decided that we had to meet. Melissa and I had to know who uses pornstarjugz69@aol.com professionally and takes themselves seriously. We were obsessed; we were in love with this person, like any good creepy stalker should be. It was like *Sleepless in Seattle* but without Meg Ryan showing up and ruining it all. We called Brook — *Brook was a dude, by the way; color no one surprised* — and asked if he could come in at his utmost convenience to discuss amortization, 401K plans, compound interest, and the bear, bull, and bandicoot markets. No real pressure. Nothing too urgent. Just doing our job, you know. Just trying to help, like, ain't we the sweetest?

So anyway, we arranged for Brook to come in and meet with someone about something or other; we had it all set up for a Friday. But then I go and get myself fired on the Thursday. Something about downloading porn at work? Turns out, these kinds of things are still very much monitored.

This was the game, for curious minds: Melissa and I each had two minutes on my computer to find THE most offensive image on the internet. She won every time — *and easily, too* — mostly due to my lack of focus and inability to look at porn from a "strictly business" point of view. I don't know if you know this, but the internet's a pretty fucking deep place once you start digging.

I denied it to no end, even though I'd happily admit to it nowadays. Maybe honesty would have saved my job? Probably not, but it's up to me to believe in ideas like this now.

In the end, I got fired. Mel didn't. I equivocated Melissa's involvement, and that it was all on me. You know, just looking for something fresh to jerk off to.

> *BOSS:* "So, you like getting off to pictures of angry dudes having sex in bunny rabbit cosplay who paint their junk to look like carrots and radishes?"
> *ME:* "Um...................yes?"
> *BOSS:* "How is that even a thing, Chester?"
> *ME:* "Would you believe I was Googling '*Testy Icicles?*'"

So how does Melissa repay me for saving her ass? Whenever I'd see her, she would rub in the fact she got to meet this Brook guy and I didn't; telling me tall tales of who he really was. Like, "*He had a subtle and discriminately tasteful neck goiter,"* or, *"Oh my god, Chester. He was wearing an old lady blouse. Like with a broach and that Bank of England smell and everything,"* or, *"Turns out it was just Brooke Shields. I had to buy an accent pillow off her just so she'd go away."* Never the same answer. Her creativity was uncompromising.

And I repaid her by changing her name in my phone to "Pornstar Jugz Sixty-Nine".

***

Finally, my phone rings. Unfortunate too, since I feel like the guy walking by had assumed I was homeless and was just about to toss some change my way. Until he heard 2 Live Crew blasting *"I have an appetite for sex, 'cause me so horny"* from my phone, that is.

"Hiya, Chestnuts." Ah. Exactly what I imagine they'll say to me at the gates of Heaven when I show up for my first day on the job.

"About time, Mel. You've been busy today."

"Or *getting* busy, right?"

"Heh. Ha. Right." Oh, fuck. And there I go again.

"Seriously though. My phone died on me too. We're just so perfect together, aren't we?"

What I want to say is, *"Yes! Yes, of course we are!"* But I know she's just being facetiously impudent with me, and isn't actually expecting a response. I pick at the inside of my lip instead.

"So anyway," Melissa continues. "I don't really want to hear about whatever it was you did to your brother this time—"

"So, you're just assuming it was *my* fault, are you?"

"Law of averages, Chestnuts. But what's our plan then? Where are we headed tonight?"

Still, even through all of my internalized awkwardness, we continue to hook up on a bi-weekly basis. There's no further commitment, right? Because look at us: We're healthy! We're young(ish)! We're kinda, sorta happy! We're free to nail anyone we please! And we are totally, *totally*, Toe-Tall-Eee content with simply being friends. We are, aren't we?

Melissa even calls us The Bum Chums (which, of course, is derogatory slang for two men in a gay, strictly-sex relationship) because, as she phrases it: "*I like to think of us as just a couple of best bud dudes who like to get it on.*"

Jesus, does my Bum Chum bum ever need a healthy, heterosexual relationship enema.

I fiddle with the wallet in my pocket and figure as long as Ace Eddy has my name listed on his joint account, I might as well use it to my advantage. "Meet me at The Kitano? Seven o'clock?"

"It's Seven-Thirty now, Dumbass. Race you there?"

"Race you there," I say with an electric crackling in my bones. She hangs up before I even say goodbye.

Double Entendres

TBH, whenever I see a limousine I make sure to flip them the bird. I think I assume whoever's in the back is either better than me (the most-likeliest of scenarios) or just being a dick (kind of like me, but going about it in an entirely different manner). I've heard it said that because of the cost of New York cab fare, it's typically cheaper to just rent a limo for an hour to get where you want to get, and be a self-important asshole while you're getting there. Of course, there always exists the possibility of a third option; that the back of the limousine is actually empty and there's no one there to receive my message. But I don't like that option. That car is getting the bird regardless.

I make it to The Kitano Hotel, just a dozen or so blocks down Park Avenue. Its brown brick veneer stands out amongst the buildings surrounding it, like a giant chocolate milk carton. Wherever Melissa was calling from, she's already beaten me here. It probably didn't help that I slipped on five different patches of black ice on my way. My body is going to be sore tomorrow, in more pain than it usually is after a night with Melissa.

She's in a white blazer, dark t-shirt, and jeans. Wearing boots stained from the sidewalk salt. Her dark, silky hair is tied back into a long ponytail, but "pony" is kind of insulting it. I mean, come on, nobody respects ponies! Her hair is much more like a powerful horse's tail than a pony's. I had a Black Stallion novel when I was a kid, and I was weirdly transfixed by the tail on the cover; there was something incredible about it, and I imagined what that luscious, shiny tail of his (*hers? does it fucking matter?*) would feel like. Brushing it with the palm of my hand, the tail coursing through my fingers, across my lips, whipping my face, tickling my bathing suit area. Yes, I had pretty fucked-up thoughts as a kid, too. That, combined with my answer of "Beastiologist" when my third-grade teacher asked me what I wanted to be when I grew up, is probably what was raising some questionable concerns for me in school. But seriously though, how does a dude write like twenty novels about a fucking horse? Was there a character arc for The Black Stallion? Did it have a love interest? Did it even have a name? Calling a horse character The Black Stallion is like naming Captain Kirk *The Horny Spaceman*. Were there actual people in the books? I don't remember. Anything other than that tail is a blur of childhood confusion.

Anyway, I sometimes like to think Melissa's hair is the tail of The Black Stallion. Is that so weird? Okay, that's still pretty weird, now that I'm actually thinking about it.

Whatever. Go ahead and judge.

The snow's started up again, and yet Melissa has somehow brought both the American and Japanese flags above the hotel entrance to a complete standstill. And me too, as I stand here frozen like I've accidentally wandered into a private Christmas party at a dildo factory. Yes, I often wonder what kind of holiday parties employees at a dildo factory will throw. I'll bet it's mind-blowing.

Whatever. Continue to judge.

Melissa doesn't put up with any more of my dumbassery than she needs to, and simply asks, "Why sushi tonight?"

"I figured since you were acting so fishy today, I might as well stick to a theme."

"Hey, *your* phone died too, Romeo."

"Yes, but I was the *first* one to say my phone died. You gave the exact same excuse later."

"So, I'm not allowed to have the same thing happen to me on the same day as you?"

I dismiss her immediately. "Too much of a coincidence."

"I should have lied then? Simply for the art of creative deception?"

"Wouldn't have had me wondering so much."

"What if I told you I was involved in a hostage situation on the subway?"

"Instantly more believable."

"And I didn't answer the phone because I was making out with the sexiest terrorist of the bunch?"

"I'd believe that too. No questions asked. Well, *one* question: could this be a lesbian terrorist? Do they have those? It would make this hypothetical scenario much more palatable."

"Let me see if I understand. So, getting hot and heavy with a lesbian subway terrorist is more likely to happen than both of our phone batteries dying on the same day?"

"Melissa, there must be fifty different hostage situations in New York on any given day."

"You're an idiot."

"And you are the idiot's abettor. My dim-witted coadjutant, if you will. So, who makes who the bigger idiot?"

"I don't even ride the subway."

"Fair point," I concede. "Let's eat. I've got a hankering for hamachi."

***

The restaurant isn't busy tonight, almost like we've booked the place for ourselves. Our chubby, listless waiter treats us like the place is packed, however, and like he's the only one working the dinner shift. Still, the milieu is wonderful, and the two of us are comfortable pretty much anywhere.

We've been stuffing our maws with sashimi, hotate, and Wagyu beef shabu-shabu for an hour now, mostly discussing my audition yesterday (ME: *"I'd be surprised if I didn't get the part."*), trendy craft ideas for empty Pringles cans (*HER: "Okay, can you think of just one idea that doesn't involve putting your penis in it?"*), as well as further tidbits concerning the ignominious pornstarjugz69@aol.com (*ME: "You say he had a HOOK for a hand?" HER: "A literal, fucking cartoon hook."*).

She knows we don't have to worry about the bill, since I'm always packing Ace Eddy's credit card. I've got a suite booked here at The Kitano Hotel, too.

And — *here's the big AND* — I've decided that tonight, right after we do the dirty deed, I'm going to tell Mel I love her. I have to. My new Honesty Movement commands it! Let's face it, if I'm all of a sudden finding myself running around the city telling total strangers and legitimately respectable members of society that I'm eating my boogers, scratching my bunghole, and actually giggling at bus stop posters for movies about talking babies (*Babies vs Crows: "It's Poo Poo Caw Caw Time!"*), then I've got to also be true with Melissa.

I do, don't I?

It seems like I should be.

Of course, I don't think I can tell her about the bunghole stuff, 'cause she's always liked me how I was. Why ruin that with any excess dirty MEcret stuff? *Just the love part, Chester. Just the love.*

But then, that's not really being completely honest, is it?

Shut up, Chester. Shut up.

As I'm thinking about all of this, all the while, I'm just hoping Mel doesn't notice anything's up with me. How could she? I'm seriously like one of those Buckingham Palace guards over here. Like I'm Liam Neeson playing a Buckingham Palace guard. Or Robert De Niro playing Liam Neeson as a Buckingham Palace—

"Why are you being so weird tonight?" she asks. *Shit.*

"I, ah—I'm just pissed off at my brother. And wondering exactly what I'm going to do next."

She dismisses my worries with a wave of her hand. "You've never really been a *What-Do-I-Do-Next* sort of guy, Chester. You'll be fine."

"I will?"

"Of course you will. I know you better than anyone, don't I?"

Our waiter pours some more saké for us, and mumbles something about our being a nice-looking couple. "Are you married?" he asks, with chin wattles jiggling.

"Not married," Melissa answers. "OR dating for that matter," she adds, with some insulting degree of emphasis.

"A shame. Saké good for the libido," he says, and he elbows me not so subtly. "Going to be a good night, yeah?" *Yeah! Tojo here is on my side!*

"Don't worry about Chestnuts and me," Melissa says. "This isn't our first night on the saké."

As politely as one can, I ask him, "How do you say, *Hot Beef Injection* in Japanese?"

He looks at me with a face: I can only assume he knows the proper translation, but he sure as hell isn't about to tell me. I miss the times when

New York waiters actually *worked* for tips.

***

The room I've booked was the only one still available: twelfth-floor, single-bed, with a view of Park Avenue. Not as nice as my brother's place, but at least this bed has seen its 700-thread-count Egyptian cotton sheets washed at least once within the last calendar year.

The best part? There's also a phone charging station at the desk in the room, so I'll be back up to 100% before you can say, "Sex and friendship don't mix, Chester."

Shut up. Yes, they God damn do.

We're on the bed, still fully clothed, my arm wrapped around her. I don't care that it's fallen asleep, gone numb from the weight of her laying on top of me. Melissa has never been a fan of the postcoital snuggling, preferring the *Wham Bam, Thank You, Chester Eddy* technique instead, where she'll immediately jump into the shower to wash me off her, leaving me alone with nothing to hold on to but that lingering moment of wonderful clarity and my flaccid monster still leaking on my stomach.

But she'll typically give me this *pre-coital* moment instead, where I can listen to her go on about her Chester-less Deutsche Bank exploits, any still-hanging auditions she's got out there, and her boyfriend Jack; whether he's in the good books or bad books with her on any given week is not of much consequence at all, really. I just like having her in my arms, talking to me like she always does.

Maybe it's a sign of yet one more disturbing mental sickness of mine, where hearing Melissa praise or mildly berate her boyfriend actually gets me good and hard? Yeah, it probably is. Might as well add that to the pile of red flags then.

I know she told me a ways back what The Boyfriend — *She always refers to Jack as THE Boyfriend* — did for a living, but God knows I wasn't listening. For some reason or another, some comment of hers led me to assume he worked at the United Nations building, doing super nationy-type stuff like ironing creases out of the flags or making sure the UN council members' nameplates in the Big Talky Room are in order and perpendicular to the edge of the desk. But I don't remember what the reasons were.

Yes, it is so called the Big Talky Room.

My hand creeps lower down her back, into her jeans to feel her bum. She's got some lacy number on under there, nothing my fingertips recognize, but it's full-bottom coverage and not the thong or g-string butt floss she knows I prefer. I tug at the waistband with my Kung-Fu Sex Grip.

"What do *you* think, Chester?"

"About your underwear? It's soft. Snug. Feels clean, too."

"No, about The Boyfriend."

"What do I think about Jack? I guess it might depend on whether Jack knows about me yet. Does Jack know about me?"

"Doubtful."

"So, you think he's a clueless idiot then? Jack doesn't know jack?"

"That's not what I mean. I'm just good at keeping secrets." She nuzzles in under my ear, a tiny bite upon my lobe, and all I can smell is her irresistible aromatic blend of sweat, pheromones, and Lever 2000 pomegranate-infused body wash.

"Well, for the record, I think Jack's a douche."

"He's not though. He's a nice, sweet guy. He's good to me. And what do I do? I reward that sweetness by screwing around with *you* every two weeks."

"You don't need nice and sweet, Mel." Yes, she does. If anyone deserves nice and sweet, it's Melissa. "You really don't. It's bad juju." I tug at her t-shirt until she helps me pull it off over her head. I pull mine off too.

"So, what I need is someone to kick me when I'm down?"

"Or when you're *going* down, am I right?"

Usually I can get an appreciative reaction from Melissa from virtually any sex joke in my repertoire, and she'll typically fire an even better one right back at me. But this time she buries her face a little more into my neck instead. "Chester. The Boyfriend's moving. He's leaving Manhattan for an opportunity in Osaka."

"Osaka? Is that the jockstrap factory on Staten Island?"

"No, Japan."

"He's working for a jockstrap factory in Japan?" She flicks my nose with her index finger, and I'll admit it actually feels pretty good.

I ask, "So what's the *bad* news then?" I do the one-handed bra unclasp and release the hounds. If I was one of these babies, I wouldn't want to be locked up all day either.

"He wants me to come," she says, sitting up now and pulling away from my grabby hands.

"So do I. *Entendre!*"

"Clever. But you mean, *double* entendre. There is no single entendre."

"There isn't?"

"I don't think so."

"That's stupid. Now, bring those double entendres back over here." I pull her back in, and squeeze, trying to get both of her nipples in my mouth at once.

There's a severe lack of both talking and/or pleasure moaning from her. I stop only momentarily, and with boobs in mouth, look up at her to make sure she's still present.

She's looking right at me; a little *too* present for my lasciviousness. "You sure there's nothing on your mind tonight, Chestnuts?"

Playfully, I push her down and collapse myself on top of her. "Nope," I mumble, with my face buried in her breasts.

"Riiiiiight."

"What, *riiiiiight*?"

"You're just being less communicative than usual," she says.

I move down, and give her bellybutton a much-needed tonguing, tasting her ridiculously sweet tummy sweat.

"And I keep pushing it," she continues. "And any normal guy in this exact scenario would say, '*Listen, casual sex partner of mine. Can we keep all the relationshippy bullshit out of this? I've got a boner down here that is in serious need of some rather immediate de-bonering.*'"

I pull her jeans down, slowly at first past her perfect, shapely hips, before giving them the old Magician-Yanking-the-Tablecloth-Off treatment. Abracadabra!

"I mean, it's not like I'm your *girlfriend*, right?"

And, that's it.

With her toes in my mouth, I finally stop. There's that G-word. Damn, why did she have to use the G-word? It's like pressing my face into the window of the Magnolia Bakery in the off-hours when I just want a fucking cupcake. And I really want that cupcake right now, man.

And then, in both timely and untimely fashion, the in-suite phone rings and my one free hand strains to reach for it. "Hello?"

"Mr. Eddy, this is the front desk. Your credit card is not going through. It appears to have been cancelled."

I say, "Uhhh—"

Maybe it's a sign that I have a burgeoning criminal mind and the innate instincts of a serial killer, but within two seconds, I've already got my next four moves mapped out in my head:

1. Hang up the phone
2. Finish going to town with Melissa
3. Find the absolute nearest back exit from The Kitano Hotel
4. Head on down to the Magnolia and grab a cupcake

I hang up the phone, and Melissa asks, "What did they want?"

"Huh? Oh, he—uh...he just wanted to know if I've ever read any Michael Crichton," I say dismissively. "You know: *Sphere? Jurassic Park?* Say, have I ever told you how much of a turn-on an interrupting phone call can be?"

"But all you said to him was, *Uhhh*—"

"—Uhhh?"

"Forget it. I get the message. I can tell you are obviously not in the mood for chit chat."

"I most certainly am not, milady." Especially if said chit chat is going to be the continued hammering home of her non-girlfriend status. "Say, do you think there's ever been a porno made called Jurassic Pork?"

"I'd think that would be way too obvious for someone to have overlooked by now."

"Yeah, probably. I tell you though, dinosaur porn is going to be the next big thing. Think about the possibilities! What do you imagine a triceracocks would look like?"

"Surely these thoughts of yours could be put to better use right now, don't you think?" Melissa flops onto her belly and shakes her little ass at me. My fingers wriggle up under her sheer black panties; her gossamer bum fuzz tickling the palms of my hands. Like a stretching cat, she arches her rear up in the air.

I squeeze.

Melissa moans a little.

The phone rings again. *Again?*

I squeeze harder. Melissa moans a little less. The phone keeps ringing. *What's with this guy?*

I bury my face between her cheeks. Melissa clears her throat like she's flipping through a gardening magazine she's already read three times before. And I can still hear that fucking phone. *This guy at the front desk is killing me!*

Reaching for anything, I grab the wooden Zen garden tray from beside the bed and chuck the whole thing — *rocks, sand, and that stupid miniature garden rake* — at the phone, knocking the receiver onto the floor. That'll show him.

Standing on top of the bed, I remove the rest of my own clothes, tossing them into the pile of sand on the floor, and then commence jumping up and down over Melissa like I'm King Kong and she's an inordinately horny Fay Wray. I know: Very Zen of me.

As I'm scratching my armpits and Ooo-Ooo-Ooo'ing, I slowly become aware of the ever-so polite knocking at the door. Melissa grabs ahold of my apehood, but only gets as far as the intensified door banging will take her. "Should we get that?" she asks, saliva dripping from the corners of her mouth.

But before I can mutter a "Fuck no," a key card opens the door and there's the concierge standing in the hallway not looking at all like he appreciates a good monster movie. A Japanese family with a couple of kids happen to be passing by our room and decide, *"What the hell, let's stop right here and get a good ol' look at some real American pole smoking. Sorry kiddos, but this will probably scar you for life. By all means, keep on looking though."*

I pick the Zen garden tray up from the floor and cover myself with it. This on its own has definitely got to be worth a few slanderous cultural effronteries.

"Konichiwa," I say, bowing politely.

***

Mel ends up paying for the room and the damages, and is also swell enough to inform me "Konichiwa" technically means "Good afternoon." Thank you, boyfriend studying Japanese so he can whisk my favorite girl off to The Land of the Rising Sun. In my defense however, it was probably around One o'clock in Japan when I uttered the phrase, so I think it should still count on a technicality.

We end up staying the night in the hotel — *'Cause really, where else am I going to go anyway?* — but the sex doesn't happen. With my arm around her, we watch the snow come down out over Park Avenue, talking until we fall asleep.

She confesses work just hasn't been the same since I got fired two months ago. She actually admits that she misses me. BOSS has been away somewhere for the last two weeks (re: upgrades), and there's simply no one left there who's been any fun at all. In her heart, she knows she doesn't really want to move to Osaka, but claims she does like The Boyfriend enough to actually consider it. Especially since it sometimes feels like she's never going to get a break on Broadway any time soon. She took a singing gig at a shady jazz lounge in Queens, but she'd only performed three times before the place went out of business. She also tells me she had hand-foot-and-mouth disease last week, for some reason or other. Sounded pretty disgusting, too, I'm not averse to mentioning.

Melissa talks about her "Someplace," that one spot in the city where she'll go when she's feeling lonely or blue. Her Someplace is an innocuous tiny bench on Grand Street, where she likes to sit and people watch; there's always sweaty dudes playing basketball in the courts across the street, and she gets just enough of a whiff from the East River to put her in some sort of relaxed, fugue state. She admits she's found herself there a lot more lately.

Her Someplace sounds kinda corny.

Mostly though, I still just want to tell her I love her. But I never do. Even when she's eventually snoring in my ear, I still can't say it.

The city lights reflect blindingly off the snow outside, pouring between the curtains and onto the bed like prison bars, trapping my feelings inside of me.

Holy shit. Now *that's* corny.

You're Desperate and I'm Right Here

TBH, I rarely wash my hands after using the bathroom. And if I do, it's never with soap. You don't know exactly what kind of shit those bitter bathroom attendants might be putting in the soap dispensers.

Without a kiss, Melissa left for work this morning from the hotel; her footprints visible in the pile of Zen sand still scattered on the floor. I get out of bed, and step along her tracks to the door, maybe just to see what it feels like to walk away from Chester K. Eddy. I don't feel anything, really. Do *they* feel the same?

Collapsing back onto the bed, I stop and think about what I've got left. Nowhere to live. No money. No auditions I'm hopeful for. I can probably forget about drinking at Philly's too, considering the size of the tab I've been running up.

And now Melissa is thinking about leaving the city with a boyfriend she's not even one hundred percent committed to.

I wrap myself in the unstained bedsheet. I feel like a ghost, but not an actual ghost of course, because a real ghost is transparent and made of ectoplasm; everyone knows that. Or they look like Bruce Willis. But hold on; I'm *trying* to be transparent, aren't I? Isn't that what unfiltered honesty is all about, anyway? Does being super honest equate to being a ghost? Am I reading too much into this? Do I need an online dictionary to properly define my feelings right now? Anyways, I've always been more of a *Die Hard* Bruce Willis guy, myself.

So, do I want to be transparent? Or do I want to actually exist?

Boy, Charlie Brown has really Charlie Browned himself this time, hasn't he?

But what does the real Charlie Brown keep doing? He gets back in there, because he'll never learn when to give up. He jumps back into the ring, not because he's a hero, not due to noble actions of any sort, and not because he's a born fighter, but simply due to the fact the guy's a total moron. He's an absolute glutton for punishment. He's taken so many footballs to the head and uppercuts to the chin from that bitch Lucy, he can't even think straight anymore.

I raid the minibar of all its contents, dumping bottles of Jack Daniels, Efes beer, three kinds of vodka, soda, orange juice, candy bars, and some potato chip brands I've never heard of into my satchel. This shit is going to add up, but if Melissa doesn't find it amusing — *She's not going to find this amusing, is she?* — then The Boyfriend can always pitch in. Of course, if he doesn't, she might just dump his ass right there, so this is probably the best thing I can do for her, correct? Let's go with that.

I might as well grab the phone charger from the charging station while I'm at it too. Right? Right. Done.

In spectacular fashion, I drain one of the 50ml JD's before leaving the room, tossing the empty bottle into the unflushed toilet.

***

Downstairs at the front desk, I'm in the midst of apologizing to the concierge for any and all inconveniences, and just as any highly offensive ringtone is known to do, my phone immediately goes off. The concierge — *Not giving me an inch in the apology acceptance department, clearly reliving my antics from last night* — is now throwing up in his mouth a little upon hearing,

"Fuckie suckie! Me fuckie suckie!" blaring from my pocket.

After pausing for a moment to consider if 2 Live Crew ever won a Grammy, I say to him, "You know what? I'll just see myself out." I walk out onto Park Avenue, partially regretting having missed the opportunity to ask if the room fee might've also included a free nuru massage.

I'm still so stuck on my secret feelings for Melissa that I don't even check the number. I simply assume it's her calling. I say, "Before you freak out about the additional charges, Mel: don't worry, okay? I will definitely be sharing some of this shit with you."

"Mel?" asks a gruff man on the other end, who is most likely not Mel Gibson. Probably not one of the Spice Girl Mel's either.

"Sorry?" I say.

"Is this Chester Eddy?"

"Do you mean, Chester *K.* Eddy?"

"What?"

"Can you speak up?" Now I'm just messing with the guy.

"Who is this?" he asks.

"Didn't you already ask that?"

"Is this the right number?" he asks.

"What number do you *think* this is?"

"I don't have time for this."

"Ha! You didn't ask a question. You broke the chain, which means you lose."

There's silence on the other end for a couple of seconds, and all of Park Avenue around me seems to get louder.

"Listen, I'm not really in the mood for games here," he says, without much amusement.

"How about we start from the top again? Let's pretend you just called."

"That sounds an awful lot like a game. Listen, someone named Chester Eddy responded to a casting call I placed. Are you him?"

Another audition? A potential job? Am I desperate for work? "Yes, I am." Man, I love perfect timing. "Chester K. Eddy at your service. And with whom am I speaking?" *Professionalism dial up to Ten, Chester! Crank it!*

"Glenn Workman. I'm the director for *Willows*." I recognize his name. Small-time director. Ambitious, though famous for over-bloating any presupposed hype for his work.

The production does not ring any bells, but there's a fairly good chance I may not have been in a terribly lucid state when I sent my resume. I blink into my phone as though it can appreciate my confusion. "Well first of all, I should be completely transparent with you, Glenn. I am fairly drunk right now."

"Christ. Do you know, on average, how many actors I call a week who answer the phone drunk?"

"I'm not at all good with estimations. But I'll say—I'm the *first*?"

"*All* of them," he says. "You're all a bunch of drunks."

"Is it still considered an *average* if you're talking about one hundred percent?"

"Why do I do this to myself?" Glenn lets out a troubled sigh of whoopee cushion proportions.

"Hey, you called *me*, man."

"I'll be straight with you here, Chester. My assistant literally just quit on me and I can't be bothered to actually read any of these terrible resumes on her desk."

"Trust me when I say, there's no need to read mine. It's pretty spectacular."

He ignores me and continues, "They just kept piling up here so I'm starting from the top."

The phrase, *"You're desperate and I'm right here"* echoes in my head again. Yeah, I definitely need to use that. "So, if you're starting from the top of the pile, that would mean I was the last person to send a resume?"

"I suppose so. Does that make a statement about your ambition and perseverance? Or lack thereof?"

Yes, it obviously does. "No. Not at all."

"I do like your headshot though," he says. *Aww, Glenn likes me!* I can't remember which headshot I might have sent him, but I hope it wasn't the one where I had the infected bee sting on my eyelid. With some of Melissa's makeup on, I mostly just looked like fat Vince Vaughn. Still. "Can you come in tomorrow for an audition?" Hopefully Workman's not looking for a fat Vince Vaughn, but it sure does sound like he's at critical mass here. Or maybe he simply doesn't care. Either way: good for me! I love the smell of desperation in the morning.

"What play was this for again?"

"Willows."

"As in, *Wind in the*—?"

"No, it's the—"

"The stage adaptation of that fantasy flick with the little dude and the baby?"

"Certainly not."

"That guy was in Star Wars too, you know. Played one of the outer space teddy bears."

"The full title is, *When the Willows Speak They Sing in Unison*."

"What the *what*—?" That is a mouthful of terrible. It's like some nerd asking if you can smell the fruity aroma of the red wine, but the best you can tell is that it's cinnamon Pepsi. I can't help from snickering. What are the chances my resume is the *only* one on that pile? But standing outside The Kitano Hotel, with the realization of just how little I've got going for me at the moment, gives me just enough life back in the ol' system to jumpstart my bravado. "I've got a proposition for you, Glenn—"

"I didn't call you so *you* could make *me* an offer."

"How about this: forget any potential audition. Chances are fairly good I would blow it anyway. Extraordinarily, too. Plus, I don't know if I'm the right guy to be playing a little person."

"It's not—"

"However, it *does* sound like you need an assistant? Depending on how desperate you are — and, let's be honest, if you're calling *me* first then you're pretty fucking desperate — maybe you want me to take over with sorting through resumes?"

Pause. "You want to take a personal assistant position?"

"Sure I do."

Even longer pause. "Instead of coming in for an actual audition?"

"Again, Glenn. Trust me. My audition would be memorable for all the wrong reasons. Like, I'd say all the lines with a racially offensive accent."

Deep sigh. I love the deep sighs, as long they're not mine. "Why the fuck not, then?" he says.

I love the Why-the-fuck-nots, too! Everything's coming up Chester, isn't it?

He tells me where the theater is and asks, "Can you come in right now?"

"How do you like your coffee, Mr. Workman?"

Not Going Down Like the Titanic (Put A Gilmore Girls Mug on That)

TBH, I actually owned a VHS copy of *Titanic* back in the day. Not super proud, but it did get me over to a girl's place one night, where she let me — *Consent!* — stroke her inner thighs while we watched the movie on a school night in her parents' basement. That makes it worth it. Even if she *was* talking to someone else on the phone for most of the movie. Don't care. Still worth it.

You see what a little basement accessibility does for your kids, Stuart and Lorraine Eddy?

Usually when I have an audition, I go in super prepared. I'm punctual, I walk in with confidence, have a couple of contrasting monologues memorized, and I'll always know exactly what it is a casting director is looking for. That's just the kind of guy Chester K. Eddy is: professionalism at 110%. You don't get many chances in this town, so you've got to be aware of the importance of not blowing them.

Today, however, I'm going in at a slightly different angle. This director is desperate, and I've already convinced him he needs me, so it's a minibar-sized bottle of whiskey and a satchel-full of stolen hotel luxuries for me.

I've never had a spring in my step until now, but I'm certain this must be just that. Like floating on the clouds. Or perhaps the booze on an empty stomach only makes it *feel* like I'm floating; though honestly, I don't know if I can count the number of times I've kicked off a morning with nothing but whiskey, but I do know I've never felt quite *this* good.

It's that feeling of having nothing. Where starting from the bottom is the best place to be when you're about to get your life back on track.

I'm in a total *End-of-the-80's-movie* moment, where the jock's just passed his final exams after macking on his hot tutor and learning a valuable lesson about honesty and respect, when I over-exuberantly scissor-kick clear across the sidewalk and onto the street — *I totally nailed it, too* — knocking an incoming bike courier onto his ass. I'm quick to say, "My fault! Sorry, my fault!" but only because my keen, detective-like attention to detail spotted the courier's wallet pop out from wherever, and I wanted to get him back on his way before he noticed it lying there too.

See? I do have the innate instincts of a serial killer.

He's not even out of my sight before I snatch the two fives from the wallet — *What, that's it?* — and discard the faux leather remains into a large planter behind me. Ten bucks still gets me a greasy two-egg breakfast at a nearby diner, with a coffee to go, and a one-way subway trip to the Upper West Side for my meeting with Glenn Workman. Lookit me, being all professional-like.

Theatre One Hundred is an innocuous building on West One Hundredth Street — *Come on, who's naming these places?* — that has housed such esteemed and well-received productions as "Bottom of the Ninth Century" (because baseball + armies of Danes = a solid one-week showing), "The Invagination of Anders Beaver" (NOT what you're thinking, you sick puppy), and the stage-adaptation of "From Justin To Kelly," starring neither Justin nor Kelly.

Workman greets me in the lobby. He's young, probably even younger than me — *But I know I look young for my age, so he's probably thinking I'm younger than him. Unless, of course, he looks old for his age? Never mind* — and he's slim, trim, and, even though he's only wearing jeans and a black tee, he's dressed like he planned this outfit weeks in advance. Still, I'll be honest here, Glenn Workman has one of those faces you just want to punch: the sort of slitty eyes that are meant for sizing others up; tiny nostrils situated beneath the kind of upwardly-pointed nose meant for identifying bouquets of pomace brandy at an East Village party brimming with subpar glitterati; a mouth you'd expect the most turgid of language to spew forth from; an air of pompousness about him.

And a rat tail. A fucking rat tail haircut.

I hold the coffee cup out for him. "Sorry if it's on the cold side, but I had no idea how long it would take to get here. I've never been to the Upper West Side before."

"Never?" he asks deridingly. Like West One Hundredth Street is the center of the New York arts scene.

"Never," I proudly confirm. "I mean, what's up here, really, besides the worst slush puddles in the city and that creepy apartment where, not only does Yoko Ono live, but where they filmed *Rosemary's Baby* too. Remind me to one day explain my theory that Yoko and Rosemary are actually the same person. It'll make total sense when you hear it. Trust me, your head will spin."

He dismisses me, and gestures around the lobby, boring me with the details of its grand design. *A feat of modern classic architecture! The Umpteenth Wonder of the World!*

"Is there a working terlet in here, Mr. Workman? I really need to take a piss."

"Sure there is, but first, I want to show you the façade."

Ooo, the façade. Tell me more! Obviously, as an actor whose career is in near critical condition, I'm going to have a killer hard-on for architectural details, aren't I? Please don't waste any more of my precious time in getting me out there to see that façade!

Workman takes me out to the sidewalk, where the entrance to Theatre One Hundred is the only patch that isn't shoveled. He places his coffee cup down on the front step and begins to not-so-briefly describe the minutiae of this magnificent edifice, to the point where I have to bullshit him about my being too cold out here: "It's my abnormally higher levels of estrogen that give me the lower skin temperature of a nineteen-year-old girl," I say. Followed by, "But really, the inside of the theater is truthfully the most *theatery* part of the theater, where all the magic happens. Ipso facto: I really just want to dig my teeth into the meat of it all. Of particular interest would be the men's room, if you please?"

"You realize," he begins. "That examining the nearly unseen details of something is the true key to knowing everything about anything."

"That sounds really cryptic."

"I'm not trying to be cryptic, Mr. Eddy. I only want the best from my personnel."

"Honestly? I'd truly be at my very best if I didn't pee my pants today." I motion toward the lobby. "May I?"

He gives in, and wags his hand at the door, commanding me to enter. I do examine the nearly unseen detail of the fact he left his coffee cup sitting on the step, and I wonder if he only brought me outside in the first place just so he could cleverly dispose of the shit coffee I brought for him. Mental note.

***

After relieving myself, Glenn Workman takes me inside the modest 300-seat theater, before showing me the office, where both he and his assistant —

Allison, I learn her name was — worked; there's a desk here for each of them. To my surprise there actually is a shit-ton stack of paper on the assistant's — *on MY* — desk. "That is a lot of resumes," I say.

"Isn't that what I told you?"

"You never really know what someone's idea of 'a lot' is. I mean, I might say I've gotten a lot of ass in my time. As a totally random and hypothetical example. But what *I'm* likely to consider a manageable amount of sex, someone — in this case *you* — might be all, '*Oh my god, no more vaginas please!*'"

Insert brief, but agonizing pause here.

"Listen, Mr. Eddy—"

But as long as I don't keep talking I should be just—

"Unless you're into boys, I suppose. Then I guess you might be all, '*For the love of all that's real, hold off on the meat popsicles,*' right?"

"Mr. Eddy, I don't think—"

"Well, not *boys*. Men. I meant men." *This is not getting any better.*

"Mr. Eddy—"

"Please, Glenn. My dad is Mr. Eddy. Just call me Chester, okay?"

"Is this how you talk to everybody, Chester?" he asks, in all seriousness.

"I think so. Usually. But I'm not a psycho, if that's what you're worried about. Not really." For the record, psychotic diagnosis via an online BuzzFeed quiz does not hold the same cohones as a professional medical opinion. "Is that going to be a problem?"

Workman exhales from his nose slowly like he's an air mattress with a hole in it. "No," he says after some contemplation. "Actually, I think we're maybe more alike than you think."

"You just said the word 'think' twice in the same sentence. But do tell."

He breathes back in, even slower. But Glenn Workman doesn't say anything more; he just stares through me.

"You had no intention of telling me, did you? One of those 'You'll see...' comments people like to throw around to raise eyebrows. Like a little revelatory lesson I'll learn in the near future; where I'll stop whatever I'm doing and shout out, 'Whoa. *That Glenn Workman fella was fucking right, wasn't he?*' And then everyone on the subway will just stare at me."

"I was merely meditating upon our similarities."

"See? Now you're doing it again. Being cryptic."

He shrugs his shoulders innocently, and moves back toward the door. "I should let you get started on sorting those out," he says, gesturing at the stack of resumes. "By all appearances, it doesn't seem as though Allison ever separated these by roles. *When the Willows Speak* has five different parts I'm looking to fill."

"So, if I sort these by role, it's really just five smaller piles, and not quite as daunting as I'm making it out to be, is that right?"

"Depends on your idea of *daunting* really," he says with a smirk. At least I know this dude is semi-capable of appreciating my sense of humor. He's still got the kind of face that begs for some punching, however. I'll hold off on the punching for now.

"Well," I say. "Pitter patter, let's get at 'er, then."

"If you still want the job, that is. It doesn't pay well, but if the show's a hit, it could be good for you."

That pile of resumes is practically hitting the bent ceiling fan above our heads. "You're desperate and I'm right here," I tell him, singing the words to a tune I just made up.

Glenn pauses, then asks, "What's that from?"

"Just a little something I'm thinking about. A work in progress, if you will."

"Definitely sounds like a work in progress." He disappears from sight, before I can decide if his comment was an insult or not.

I look at the tower of paperwork on the desk, and see my own resume sitting right there on top. On it, I've specified I'm submitting for the role of *Matthew Willows,* which does not ring any bells for me. Someone has drawn a Wilford Brimley mustache on my headshot, and I assume it was Glenn Workman — *Probably visualizing me in full makeup for my future casting of the dashing Matthew Willows* — but then I notice this someone has also snuck a drawing of a crude penis sticking out of my ear. *What the fuck, Workman?*

But every other headshot in the pile has also been defaced: mustaches; eye patches; cartoon scars; blacked-out teeth; clown wigs. You name it. Every actor in this pile looks like a homeless pirate who's just robbed a novelty hat store.

Maybe Allison the former assistant did it? I don't know. Maybe she knew she was quitting and had this dastardly plan of capricious vandalism mapped out all along? If this is the case, she really could have used a few tips and tricks from Chester K. Eddy on how to be an A-list, shit-tossing, work monkey. This is pretty amateur stuff, right here.

And as I flip through the resumes, fondly reminiscing over the not-quite-technically criminal escapades Melissa and I would cook up, I see it: Melissa's resume. I helped her write it up too, so I recognize my handiwork immediately. Her own headshot has been defaced with a beard right out of the

Civil War, a pair of square-framed glasses, and the word *Lunchmeat* written over her shirt. Those glasses look good on her, too.

It appears as though she submitted for the role of *Madison Willows* — *Matthew's wife? Step sister? Sexy neighbor with the same last name?* — and I wonder just how close we could've gotten to achieving our oft-talked about ultimate dream of acting together in the same production.

Melissa's resume wasn't all that far from the top either, which probably also says something about her ambition and perseverance being close to on par with my own.

***

Seventy-five minutes later, I've got six piles of resumes sorted: one pile for each of the five parts in *When the Willows Speak They Sing in Unison*, and one pile for resumes that didn't include a preferred role or that were submitted for the wrong play entirely. You'd be surprised how many actors will just throw a resume at everything out there, hoping some of their drunk shit will stick to the wall. I guess it's like fishing in the not-so-great Monona though: the more hooks you cast, the more likely you're eating a six-foot sturgeon for dinner.

I couldn't find a writing instrument of any sort around this desk — *Could it be in the drawer that's mysteriously locked without a key? Looks like we've got a mystery on our hands, gang!* — so, I've placed the following items on top of the piles to indicate which is which:

-Gilmore Girls coffee mug = *Madison Willows*
-Crumpled ball of an old Subway wrapper (Which still smells

like...tuna? Who am I kidding; all Subway sandwiches smell exactly the same) = *Matthew Willows*

-A stale Cheeto that's already had the cheesy dust licked off of it = *Melville*

-A water bottle, in which the bit of water left from just long enough ago has started to grow a layer of fur on it = *Martha*

-Old cassette tape with a worn label that reads: "Salad Cream demo" = *Miss Lee*

-Mousetrap I found on the floor in the corner, and it wasn't until I'd already dropped it on top of the resume pile that I noticed a rat tail dangling out from the spring-loaded bar (That rat was likely so hopped up on Cheeto dust he chewed right through his own tail to escape) = *You're Auditioning for the Wrong Play, Moron*

Next, Workman instructs me to find the ten best actors for each role. Twenty for the two leads. I'm starting to have flashbacks of doing actual work in actual jobs; bosses *telling* me what to do, rather than asking. I already don't like it much.

Remember that spring in your step, Chester! Where's that spring in your step?

I tell him, "I have no idea what your play is even about. So how exactly am I supposed to decide on the *best* actors?"

"How did I select *you*?"

"Well, I mean—"

From somewhere behind him, Glenn produces a copy of the script for his play. "Here you go. Read this. Then just pick who you want and call them," he says clearly. "Set up times for them to come in to audition. Preferably ASAP.

If they don't answer, leave a message, but then bump them down the list and out of the Top Ten. Twenty for the lead parts! Find the next best fit and contact *them*. Rinse and repeat. Got it?"

"Sounds easy enough," I say, and notice Glenn is staring fixedly at the rat tail in the trap; he's probably envious of its proportion and pageantry.

But really, I start questioning the whole process here; I mean, is this how my *own* auditions worked? Some barely-independent, half-functioning assclown with no previous experience and who was cleaning toilets at the Times Square Popeye's a week earlier got to decide who was or wasn't going to get an audition, basing his entire decision on whether or not the girls' headshots have any visible cleavage or if the guys aren't anyone they know who they owe cash or drinks to? I do come across a couple of dudes who fit that very description, so, you know: right into the wastebasket with you! *You're never finding me, Thomas Richmond!*

So, first of all, obviously, I don't read the script. No surprises there. Then I start with the Madison Willows pile. I want to add Melissa's resume to my Top Twenty Madisons, but I fight the urge; hoping some distance from me is just what will bring her closer. To be honest, if someone else confided in me this exact same strategy for winning their girl, I'd have told them they were utterly delusional.

So, yes. I know.

But Melissa and I are different from any hypothetical star-crossed lovers I've got wallowing inside my head, living made-up lives.

This is different.

So, I pull her resume from the pile and toss it. I even recycle it, in a metaphorical act of giving her past experience and education a different life in the future. *Is that a stretch? That feels like a bit of a stretch.*

Still, the part of me that's already missing her voice, dials her number once more.

Voicemail again. I listen to the whole thing too, even though I'm fully cognizant of the fact I'm too much of a pussy to leave her a message. I just like hearing her voice. *"Hey, it's Mel — blah blah blah — Oh, look up there. A unicorn!"*

Maybe unicorns *can* fly though. I've never really thought of it from her point of view before.

Once I've called and booked audition times for seventy actors — *In one day? Shit, how hard was I working here? I should be asking for a raise already. But imagine how long this would have taken if I'd actually read that script?* — I run the schedule past Workman, with all ten auditions for the role of Martha booked for tomorrow. I fully expect him to tell me I've screwed up somewhere — *"Are you nuts? We can't hold auditions on National Pizza Day!"* — but he doesn't. He actually thanks me for bailing both him and his production out of the dire situation left after his last assistant walked out on him.

"T'was easy, Mister W. No problem, really. What else should we tackle? Put an APB on that missing key for the desk drawer? Maybe check out the façade again?"

"I think we'll call it day, Chester." He glances down at his watch. "Are you eating?"

"That might depend on if you're paying. I might not look it, but I'm broke. And also, technically homeless right now."

"Actually, you *do* look homeless. That's why I was asking."

"It's the SisQó hoodie, isn't it?"

"I don't even know what a SisQó is."

"Aw, c'mon. *The Thong Song*? It's basically the granddaddy of booty videos." I give him a quick twerk show for his personal pleasure. Not sure if he's appreciating my flare, however. "To be honest, you can't really get full value for my twerking under these cheap office lights. It's best enjoyed at night, on a busy sidewalk; preferably outside a club's queue and after a few drinks too many."

He stares at me oddly now, and I'm really not sure what to make of the silence that's found itself wedged between us, much like the swimwear selection and the badonkadonks in the SisQó vid.

Eventually, I say, "So, you said something about eating?"

"There's a great little place around the corner," he says, flicking off the light in the office.

I just shrug and go along with it. Glenn Workman and I walk back out to West One Hundredth Street. The early evening's setting sun is already disappearing behind the George Washington Bridge; the day's blue sky beginning its wonderful pastel transition into night.

I can't help but get a creepy sort of vibe from Workman, but I sure as shit ain't going to say anything before he spots me a meal.

Jeffrey Dahmer & The Pork Sliders

TBH, I had a major thing for Daphne Blake in Scooby Doo as a kid; though I guess most guys probably did. For me, it was those lavender tights she wore. As an eight-year-old, the purple legs mystified me; as an adult, they just get me all worked up.

We're at a little diner in the Upper West Side called The Upper W — *Seriously, are these places being named by stay-at-home Pinterest moms?* — and Glenn and I are waiting for our meals. It's chicken parmesan for me with a deep-fried pickle on the side, while he's just broke some sort of record for ordering the World's Most Boring Burger: "Just lettuce. And can we toast the bun a tiny bit? Not too much though!"

Yikes. It's no surprise really that Workman would have been here dining alone with his dry lettuce burger if I hadn't agreed to tag along.

"Thanks again for treating me," I say, just to get something out.

"My pleasure. And this might be a good chance to get to know you a bit better," he says. *Glenn Workman, you've just earned yourself +1 Creeper Points.*

"Did you and Allison eat out together much?" There must be a way I can sniff around for clues that might help indicate what's normal behavior for this guy, and what might simultaneously help *me* avoid being chopped up and later having someone discover my body parts stuffed inside a freezer. Sure wish I'd retained more information regarding Jeffrey Dahmer's modus operandi, and less about his failed career at the chocolate factory.

"Not so much, no. We did see each other a couple of times — you know, *extracurricularly* — but it never really worked out."

She didn't quit, did she? She's been hacked to pieces and is locked up inside that desk drawer, isn't she? Glenn takes a moment to look back toward the kitchen, maybe wondering when our meals are coming, and I take the opportunity to slide his fork and knife closer to my side of the table. *It's the Great Homicide, Charlie Brown!*

I dig further, with a shrewd attention to detail, not unlike Columbo, or the McGruff the Crime Dog, at the very least. "Is that why she quit?"

Glenn stares out the window, out onto the street where a police car idles at the red light, and he strokes his rat tail. "I don't think I was really the right...*fit* for her." *Ding! +5 Creeper Points.*

"You're doing that ambiguous comment thing again, Glenn." I give his elbow on the table a light nudge, and I joke, "Was this a sex thing?"

"Yes, it was."

Wow. Just like that. No hesitation. "What? Really? You know, it seems like it's *never* a sex thing. You don't know how refreshing it is to hear that."

Cue Glenn Workman's serious face. "Refreshing? Have you ever heard of the SAA?"

"Is that the one where groups of nerds gather to recreate Medieval sword fights and banquets?"

"Certainly not."

"That's a relief. 'Cause there's nothing sexy about Renaissance fairs. I imagine they're all pretty filthy down there." My eyeballs point under the table to my man-balls for reference. "Not exactly a hotspot, unless you're really wanting to get Medieval crabs, you know what I mean?"

"The SAA stands for Sex Addicts Anonymous."

"You had a sex addict working for you and you let her just quit?"

"Allison wasn't the sex addict. *I am.*" *Congratulations, you've reached 1000 Creeper Points. Come claim your prize!* "And I have my first meeting tonight."

Not many things are a bigger buzzkill than when you think you're talking about a hot nympho, but it turns out to be Kevin Spacey buying you dinner instead. "You haven't even been to a meeting yet and you're already telling me about it? Doesn't sound like you're being too anonymous about the whole thing."

"You should come with me, Chester."

Uh, NO I definitely should NOT. "Who, me?"

"Like I said, I suspect we're more alike than you think."

"Well, although I can happily admit that, yes I do enjoy sex, I don't know if I'm quite ready for some ten-step program."

"There's twelve steps, actually."

"*Twelve* steps? That's practically a marathon."

"There's no requisite timeline for meeting the steps. The only requirement is wanting to curb your addictive sexual behavior. At least, that's what I've been told."

As far as I know, I don't have an addiction to sex. I mean, I'm not into the real kinky stuff, like autoerotic asphyxiation, strap-ons, or vacuum cleaners. Just give it to me straight, that's what I'm all about. "I like a good pair of glasses, but I wouldn't say I need the girl to wear them in order to get off."

"What else?" He's got a look in his eye, like a kid in the candy store who's just been handed a fifty. *Go on, Glenn. Go fill up a bag with those fucking marshmallow strawberries and bananas.*

I think about my parents' pool house: Chester's Mack Shack™ I called it.

And I think about my frenetic hankering for that bedroom in the basement. Daphne Blake. The Designing Women. The View. Melissa and me and our surreptitious trysts within the bowels of the Deutsche Bank offices. Her voicemail messages. The way she pronounces the word *unicorn*. No one can hit a hard *C* as soft as she can. Her tiny, pointed chin. The slight curve of her clavicle, like the edges on that fine china your grandmother wouldn't let you touch. I can't help it, but even her explaining the pros of moving to Japan is a goddamned turn on.

"Unicorns," I say to Glenn. "Unicorns get me worked up too. Glasses and unicorns. Unicorns wearing glasses."

"If unicorns and glasses are your weaknesses, then you've already helped yourself toward Step One: *Admitting you're powerless to the addictive behavior that's made your life unmanageable.*"

"Unmanageable? Well, I can still get my ass out of bed every morning and make it to auditions."

"Is that making you happy?"

I think about what he's asking me, but the only issue weighing on my mind at the moment is whether glasses on a unicorn would sit *above* the horn or below it. I'm having a difficult time visualizing it. *Should I sketch this on a napkin? Maybe the frames rest upon the horn? Maybe unicorns have their own special unicorn optometrists?* But as I consider the details, I make a *Hmm-IS-that-making-me-happy?* face for Glenn and his stupid question to chew on.

I realize now that I'm not being completely honest here. I've just fully ruptured my brand-new, super terrific MEcret-free lifestyle choice, haven't I? And all it took was a sex-addicted dude rocking a rat tail and paying for my chicken parm.

Finally, I just ask: "Do they typically serve food at these sexaholic meetings?"

"I don't think so, since there's likely a few people who get turned on by food."

"Maybe they'll have desserts?"

"Chocolate's an aphrodisiac, you know."

"Breadsticks?"

"Certainly nothing so stiff and lengthy."

"Finger foods? Pork sliders?"

"*Pork sliders?* Are you kidding me?"

Finally, the waitress brings our plates to the table. I keep asking Glenn for details about the sex meeting. "Maybe some coffee though?"

"Maybe coffee," he says.

"All right. Count me in."

The waitress turns and is about to walk away, but asks, "Two coffees then?"

"No," I tell her. "We've got another date after this."

Major Richard Power

TBH, I actually find skin tags sort of sexy. I'm not even sure why myself, especially considering that, if pressed, I'd have to admit they bear more of a likeness to penises than vaginas. Still beats an ugly mole with a big hair in it.

"Well. If I had to put my finger on it, I guess it was when I ran out into the street naked with my VR headset on and I whipped my penis around out front of the Applebee's on senior's night when I knew I *really* had a problem. I'd gotten into virtual reality, and was torrenting pornographic downloads for my system. But one night I was doing it in the garage and the garage door was open. I guess I just forgot. And I wandered out into the street, doing who knows what wearing this VR headset and nothing else but my white tube socks. I was so cranked up I didn't even notice the chill. The restaurant was just around the corner, and the cops were pulling up just as I was rubbing myself against this old lady, and I remember thinking: *I think I've crossed a line here. I think I need some help.*"

"Thank you for sharing, Andy," says the emcee. She helps Andy down from the podium, rubbing his arm like he's an injured child on the playground. "Everyone, let's thank Andy for his story."

"Thank you, Andy," says the room of roughly fifteen.

Jesus, there are some fucked up people in here. My styrofoam cup of cold coffee is still full because I can't pull my attention away from these freaks long enough to take a sip.

Everyone claps politely for Andy, even though he's just admitted to some horrible, horrible shit. Turns out this is actually Andy's fifth week at Sex Addicts Anonymous; he just hadn't had the courage to share his story until tonight. A common theme, apparently. If I was one of the other screwballs here, I probably would have been assuming Andy was only coming for the free beverages at this point. I slap him chummily on the leg when he sits back down beside me, and give him a good ol' "Fuckin' A, bro" for his troubles. He's visibly sweating through his shirt.

After our meal at The Upper W, after I realized Glenn Workman wasn't a serial killer, but a sex addict — *And to be honest, I'm not sure just yet which makes me MORE uncomfortable* — Glenn and I made our way a few blocks north to this impeccable church basement. It's actually pretty nice in here, not that I have a lot of other church basement exposure to compare it to. There're some fancy urns on a shelf which seem to be displayed more prominently than they should be. *Are they empty? Or are there people in there?*

Glenn still gives me a bit of that creeper vibe, but I'll admit I've eased up on him a smidgen; he actually made me chuckle a couple of times at dinner. He told me some joke about Nepal, which I can't even recall now, but I laughed like I was drunk. Well, like I was drunker than I already was, that is.

So far tonight I've met Walter (*Mr. Sex in Cars*), Sheila (*Ms. Impregnated by a Super Soaker*), and Hamish (*Mr. My Shit's So Obscene I'm Not Even Going into The Explicit Details of it All Yet, But Trust Me, I'm One Doozy of a Sexual Superstar*). I don't presume any of the names they've given have been real, and I'm still thinking about what pseudonym I'm going to use when my turn to speak comes up. Lance? Brad? Maybe more of a cool code name, like Bullet? I make a little gun with my hand and blow the tip of my index finger. Nobody fucks with a guy named Bullet.

"Who would like to go next?" asks the matriarchal emcee running the show. Man, she's probably numb to all of this by now. Like Doctor Ruth. Or any good proctologist worth her weight in dead gerbils. I wonder how she tells her grandkids about what she does at night?

Glenn doesn't even hesitate in putting up his hand.

"One of our two new members? Great." She motions him to come on up to the podium. I begin to clap, but quickly realize no one else is. I feel I'm fairly justified in wondering about SAA clapping procedure and protocol. I'm sure they clapped for Sheila when she went up to speak about who put the sperm in her super soaker — *it was her neighbor* — but I don't recall any applause for Walter before he opened up about his preferences toward make and models, and which seats in a car are actually the best seats for sex, bearing in mind there are specific discrepancies which are wholly dependent upon whatever sexual position is being deployed. Maybe it's a chivalry kind of thing, but then wouldn't that be sexist in a way? And isn't sexism a pretty major part of all of this?

Honestly, I have no idea. I've never felt so uncomfortable in my life.

Glenn says, "Uh. Hi, everyone. My name is, Tobias."

And everyone else says, "Hello, Tobias."

Like a cult, kind of.

Hello, Walter. Thank you, Walter.

Hello, Hamish. Thank you, Hamish.

Just like a cult.

"You're likely all wondering what it is that brought me here tonight."

"There's no wondering — no judgement — in this room, Tobias," the emcee says.

"So, okay. I run my own business. Recently, I hired a young woman as my assistant. She was cheery, and pretty, and eager to get her own career off the ground." He shuffles around nervously back and forth. "I think she liked me, too. I mean, *she* was actually the one who asked *me* to go out for a bite to eat after work. We only had dinner out a couple of times before I thought it'd be a good idea to make some moves on her. At work, I'd rub her shoulders. I'd hold her hand a bit too long when saying good morning or good night. I even made suggestive poses in the doorway, or dug my hands into my pockets a bit further; deep enough to touch myself." He makes a concentrated effort to keep his nervous palms flat on top of the podium; he focuses on keeping them in one place. "But I never thought of her as vulnerable, or as someone who wouldn't be able to turn me down because she was afraid of the cost to her career. I just *liked* her. And I couldn't stop myself."

Glenn ceases talking now, but he makes no indication that he's done. Still, he isn't saying anything more; just staring off into the void of the back of the basement where a bunch of kids' colorful crayon drawings of angels, baby Jesuses, and Arks — *all of which are under smiling rainbows* — are taped to the wall.

Cautiously, the emcee asks, "Is that as far as it went, Tobias?"

"No. No, it wasn't." I can see him running all of these events through his mind. Probably wondering if there's any way he could turn back time and take it all back. But also, maybe wondering if he really regretted any of it at all.

And I'm left sitting here next to sweaty Andy, with the straight-up realization that life can be pretty fucking serious at times.

And some people actually *do* hurt other people.

How have I never noticed this before now?

"Chester?"

And I'm fairly confident I'm not a full-on sex addict, but it's probably pretty likely the potential is there. And also, I do have tendencies to not treat others as well as I could. Men *and* women. And that I really just look out for Number One. And—

"Chester?"

"Huh—?"

It's Glenn. And he's using my real name? Come on! I'd narrowed down my made-up name selection to either Haywood Jablomey or Major Richard Power, so he's just gone and wrecked that plan for me. "Did you want to say something too, Chester?"

I want to say, "*What the fuck, Workman?*" But instead, I choose to stand up and I slowly look at all the sad faces around me. "Uh, yeah. Thanks, *Toby*." We switch spots; Glenn returns to his plastic fold-up chair and I step up to the podium, finger lodged warmly within my left nostril. I've got a good one in there, just begging to be dug out. They're all watching me pick my nose, and I don't care a bit. These folks wouldn't be here if they hadn't already been doing worse acts than this.

I have no idea what I'm about to say. But of course, all I'm really hoping for is that I don't embarrass myself too badly.

And I say, "It's good to see so many of you sexual deviants out tonight." *Ugh. Here we go. What do you think this is, Chester? Some sort of kinky, degenerate comedy club?*

Blank stares.

"So, my name is Chester K. Eddy. You probably know my brother, Ace Eddy. The hockey player?"

Still mostly blank stares, but I notice a few eyes exploring the peripheral of this gathering, each hoping they're not the only one who has no idea what this maniac is talking about.

And yet, the Charlie Brown in me just keeps trying. "Number Eighty-Nine? Left Winger for the Islanders?"

One person actually gets up now, with his fingers he gestures a *V* in front of his lips to indicate he's heading outside for a smoke. But I know he's got no plans at all for coming back in here as long as I'm still talking.

"None of you watch hockey, do you?"

The guy making for the door yells back, "Islanders suck!" *Aha! Finally, some life in here.*

"Yeah, they do pal. I'm with you there. But seriously? Some people — mostly those annoying, self-righteous Canadians — give me a hard time when I say I don't like hockey. But everything happens so fast in that sport, I don't know what the hell's going on. Where's that puck, anyway? You expect, after a few beers, that I'm going to be capable of following a little black rubber ball?"

Someone in the room calls out: "It's not a ball, it's a disc."

"Like a frisbee?" Someone else asks. I think it's Hamish. *Fucking Hamish. Maybe if you took just five seconds and stopped trying to stick your penis into whatever hole you come across, you might start to notice things are happening in the world.*

"No, it's tinier than a frisbee."

The emcee is in the midst of raising a hand, but I stop her before she can join the group in delaying my point here. "People, please. *Please.* I have the sex podium here!"

I refocus my thoughts, wondering why I was ever talking about my brother in the first place. "Listen. I honestly have no idea how I ended up here in this church tonight with all you people. Today was my first day at a new job, and this is just where it went. You've all had days like that, right?"

No answers, but I wasn't really expecting any. I'm more just pausing for effect.

"So, Sex Addicts Anonymous, huh? I don't know if I'd really consider myself a sex addict, per se. I mean, I suppose there are certain questions I could seriously ask myself. Like, have I masturbated in bed while my girlfriend was sound asleep next me? Sure I have. Have I banged a homeless person? Yes, I totally did. But in my defense, I didn't know she was homeless until *after* we finished up behind that dumpster in the Meatpacking District; when I offered to walk her home and she pleasantly informed me we were already there, and did I want to stay the night? Do I have Delphic erotic fantasies or non-genital fetishes? Maybe not as many as you folks apparently do. But sure, I guess I've got my own weird stuff going on. I have a thing for glasses, for one. I've had dirty thoughts about the Designing Women. I jerk off into youth-height urinals. And yes, I admit I sort of like the feeling of my sweaty balls sticking to my inner thigh. I don't know. That's probably a thing."

Giving the small gathering a quick scan, I can tell I'm not losing anyone else at the moment. It's a good bunch; though I'm sure they're mostly hoping I'm going to whip it out right here and swing it around.

"But, I guess what I'm really thinking is: sex is weird, isn't it?"

Nearly every head nods in unison.

"Like, everything these days is so intensely sexualized. But we're still conditioned to be made to feel like a bunch of dirty, trenchcoat-wearing pervs at the bus stop about it. Everywhere we look though, it's just sex, sex, sex. It's everywhere, and in everything. Like extension cords. You know how with extension cords you have a male end and a female end? Makes sense, right?

Plugs into holes. Just like sex. It's fucking hot. But what about a garden hose? Why do we still refer to it as having a male and a female end? The male end has a giant hole in it! I'd be freaking out if my dick looked like that! Also, the water comes out through the female end of the hose. Wouldn't you say that's disturbing?"

Some woman who's been all-too quiet tonight raises a hand. "Well, electricity comes out through the female end of an extension cord too."

"Jeez, you're right."

A guy from the very back — *And I mean the VERY back; he's slid his chair right into the darkest corner* — speaks up now too. "And seatbelts have male and female ends too."

"Point for you, weirdo guy in the back. But keep your hands out where I can see them, please. Do you see what I mean, though? Everything is so friggin' hyper-sexualized. And do you know why? I'll tell you why, and I'm not going to blow sunshine up your asses; I'm just going to say it straight: it's because people are perverts. I am, you are — well, *you guys* are for sure — and everyone else out in this city tonight is a big ol' raging perv."

"And light bulbs too," the same guy at the back interrupts.

"Please, dude," I say. "We're moving past the examples already. Keep up."

It feels like somebody suddenly cranked up the heat in here; I unzip and remove my hoodie so I can breathe again. I lay it over the top of the podium.

"And yeah, sometimes it's all too much depravity and we need help. But sometimes it's manageable and we don't. We'll just give it a shot on our own. I tried changing my own fortunes recently. I invented what I've coined *The Honesty Movement*, where I'm basically spilling all my personal secrets to people who don't really want to hear about any of them. I was hoping it would be the thing to turn my life around, but it's only been four days, and so far, my movement is going about as terribly as it can. But I've got to keep trying because, well—actually, I have no idea why I have this need to keep trying. Maybe it's because I think others will be impressed by my tenacity?"

I start to fade out a little. I remember how Glenn picked my brain earlier about my secrets, and I *didn't* tell him the truth; I just made up some bullshit about unicorns wearing glasses instead.

I feel a bit woozy actually, and need to brace myself on the podium.

"But there's this girl I like, you see? And I mean I *actually* like her. It's not like my Daphne Blake cartoon fantasies, and it's not because of the kinky stuff or the secret office sex — *hands where I can see them, guy in the back!* — I just really, truly like her. Maybe too much." I use my hoodie to wipe the tear from my eye. "Sorry, there's a lot of dust in this room. Might be from all the urns over there. But People Dust is *good* dust isn't it? You don't just wipe that shit up with a microfiber cloth. You dump it in an ugly vase and keep talking to it like they're still in the room and nothing weird ever happened."

Fuck it. I'll just wipe my whole face clean here. "Where was I?"

The emcee says, "You said something about liking this girl too much?"

"Oh yeah. It's true: I do like her too much. But she told me she was thinking about moving away. It actually hurt when she said that to me. So, I know I like her too much because it shouldn't hurt like this. At least, I've never felt anything like this before. Crabs and STD's don't last forever, but a broken heart sure does. Well, I suppose some STD's do last forever, but I need to generalize here for the sake of my argument. Does anyone here have an STD?"

Only a single person puts his hand up.

"Just one? Good for you guys. Well, not so good for *you*, sir. But I expected way more hands than that. That's great."

The guy who raised his hand asks, "Can we just get back to talking about your girlfriend?"

"Melissa? Oh, Melissa's not my girlfriend," I clarify.

And then, a woman in the crowd speaks up; she sounds like an angel echoing inside my head. "You are incredibly brave, Chester. Each one of us in here needs to be brave in order to find the courage to share the things we do. And you're no different. Your Honesty Movement is really no different than the honesty we share here in the group." Yep. Just like an angel. And a sexy, throaty angel at that.

"Thanks," I say. "That really helps."

And then she opens those ruby red lips, runs her tongue stud along her teeth, and stares me down while mimicking a blow job — you know, the classic high school mime your best bud Freddy showed you in the boys' room, where he held his fist to his mouth and pumped his tongue in and out inside his cheek, which is actually really disturbing when you think about it now in retrospect. Freddy was really a bit too good at that.

Anyway. This girl here is an angel all right. The kind of angel who's in bad need for some broken halo mending.

"That helps a lot," I say.

Three Thumbs Way Up

TBH, I've used toilet paper rolls to cut my turds up into more flushable sizes. Apologies for that image. Though if it's any consolation, this is maybe the most disgusting thing I'll be admitting to. *Maybe.* In my defense, I have heard of people claiming to own "poop knives." Take that tidbit and do with it as you please. There's your lifehack for you. The Poop Knife. Go sell *that*, ShamWow Guy.

Okay, I can fess up to a lot of terrible things I've done in my life. Many of which are painfully clear by now. And I know they're terrible; how could I *not* know that? So, it's no surprise really that I put the moves on the girl who was only looking to curb her raging libido through the safety of Sex Addicts Anonymous. I mean, here's someone — *Ariel, her named turned out to be* — who couldn't stop sneaking into and attending high school graduations while wearing absolutely nothing under a stolen graduation gown; someone who would stalk lingerie stores, hoping to get invited to a three-way with couples who were just looking to spice things up; someone who would spread canned tuna fish on her nipples and let her cat lap it up.

And then I come along, drone on about a girl I love, wipe a few tears on my hoodie, and proceed to take advantage of Ariel and however far along she is in her ten steps to recovery and spiritual awakening. Sorry, twelve steps.

No two ways about it: I am a dirtbag.

Last night, after the meeting, Ariel and I spoke outside for a while, sharing her last five smokes. I still had a couple in my bag, but hey, she offered. The snow had stopped completely, and there was a distinct feeling in the air that seemed to indicate it wouldn't be falling again anytime soon. Ariel told me a couple of times how blown away she was by my ability to get people to talk out of turn in the meeting; how no one seemed to have any issues with yelling things at me. "That's just not how it ever works in there," she added.

I wasn't sure whether I should take that as a compliment or not.

I took it as a compliment. "In general, people do seem to enjoy yelling at me," I tell her.

Ariel was striking, but I could tell it was in a way not even *she* truly realized. Her jet-black hair, which by all appearances had been trimmed with those oddly-shaped crafting scissors, was a beautiful, disheveled mess. Her smile, though chapped and contorted, still had an unmistakable seemliness about it. Her eyes wanted to break your heart. She was slight, with small breasts and very little in the way of hips, but when I wrapped myself around her as we shamelessly sucked face behind the church, her body felt wonderfully unpredictable the way she and it wriggled around in my arms, like trying to contain the lava in a lava lamp. She wanted me to catch her tongue piercing in my teeth, but I couldn't manage.

When Ariel asked me if I wanted to come back to her place, I was — *at first, naturally* — quite careful to not take advantage. I may have mentioned this before: I am not a sexual predator. *Is it a bad sign that I have the need to keep repeating this line? It's a bad sign, isn't it? Fuck.*

And because I was smack dab in the midst of personal growth — *Yes, both emotionally and erectionally* — there were a few important steps I was cognizant of following, so as not to leap into a situation I'd almost-immediately regret:

Step 1) Be Cautious
Come on, this girl's a sex addict; she's mostly here to get help, and not

another twenty minutes — *Yes, twenty!* — of future fuck regret.

Step 2) Be Vulnerable
But if I'm too standoffish or coddling her too much, I'm really just pushing her away; use some of that classic Charlie Brown misfortune to score myself some goodwill and pity points.

Step 3) Be Mature
I'm thirty-two; surely, I've grown some since College Edition Chester K. Eddy was nailing anything that had a face? Look at me: I'm on the self-enlightened pathway to perennial sophistication!

Step 4) Be the Bigger Person
Again, is there any doubt at all that I can show I'm better than, say, any other dude who might have snuck his ass into a Sex Addicts Anonymous meeting and is now faced with the potential for some unhealthy, perfunctory, and downright incredibly debauched boot knocking?

Step 4.5) Remember what I said earlier about my predilection for damaged goods?

Step 5) Be the Dirtbag
Hit the road, Growth and Sophistication. This is happening.

So, when I later find myself at her place, with a leather purse-strap pulled around my neck to the point where both my heads are the same purple color, and she's asking me, "This isn't too much for you, is it? We never discussed safe words," I just choke out an "*All good*," with two thumbs up.

And then she gives *me* a thumbs up, right in the rusty bullet hole.

***

And here I am the morning after. Ariel's in the shower getting ready for work while I'm finding more and more teeth marks on my still-naked body. Purple-black flowers have bloomed in a variety of places, and pain is emanating from other areas that make me wonder, *What the hell was she doing down there?*

Her tiny apartment is nearly bare, aside from a few boxes piled up into a tower in the corner and the ridiculous amount of clothes thrown everywhere. It's like a freshman's dorm room in here. She mentioned that three other people live here too, but I saw no evidence, nor any indication of where everyone might sleep if they were all shacked up for the evening.

I'm not sure how many more nights I can go before I actually need to worry about where I'm sleeping next, but I'm two-for-two so far.

There's a brown cat perched atop the highest stack of boxes, and it's watching me. Staring into my soul. Judging me. Completely disgusted by my actual existence. Why do cats do this? I hate cats so much. The first thing I find on the bedside table is a double-A battery, and I whip it at the cat, simultaneously transporting both into an unseen dimension.

My head is woozy from drinking so much of that beer from my bag last night.

I can't recall where in the city we ended up, but the window's been open all night and it's fucking freezing in here, but also eerily quiet outside. I question how far from Manhattan I must be, and if I will ever find my way back.

I'm about to start rooting through her personal items piled high atop her dresser, but that's when the running shower stops. I've been busted by towel-clad girlfriends one too many times before to know when the clock is against me. And it's not like I'm about to find anything worthwhile here, am I?

Question: How many more overly-complicated sex toys, photos of ex-boyfriends, and expired McDonald's Monopoly stickers I was once hoping for do I need to uncover in my life?

The Correct Answer: None.

The Honest Answer: I can't believe I still have the need to compare myself to ex-boyfriends.

The Shameful Reality: Those sex toys really fascinate me. What is that weird knobby part for?

There's a Sex Addicts Anonymous newsletter beside the bed, so I opt for flipping through that instead. I read some blurb about abstinence and sobriety, and how these goals are tailored to the needs of each member. "*No one,*" the passage says, "*has any real desire to stop being sexual. The key lies in identifying the healthy and unhealthy addictive behaviors, and practicing appropriate abstinence from the unhealthy ones.*"

It's strange how closely the SAA literature will compare being a sex addict to an alcoholic. Oh, and I'm disputing any insinuation that I have an alcohol problem too, by the way.

I try to think about what behaviors of mine are unhealthy for me, but all I can come up with are things that aren't my own fault. All the parts I've auditioned for? All the hanging auditions? Melissa being with another guy? I don't like any of that very much. Feels like it's all fairly unhealthy. In fact, the whole world is against me, really. *Yes, it is. Don't even try to convince me otherwise.*

I turn the page in the newsletter and the first line of the first paragraph, the very first thing I see because the font is bolded, reads:

Is the whole world against you? It's not.
Maybe it's only you against yourself?

Oh, you're so fucking deep and introspective, Newsletter.

I actually say "Pshaw!" and I toss the paper across the room, right into an open box of dildos in the corner I hadn't noticed before now. *How does one not notice something like that? I am really off my game here.*

Just as I start wondering where Melissa might be this morning, Ariel flops down on the bed beside me. She's wearing nothing more than a pair of sky blue panties with some sort of print on them; her tiny boobs jiggle like a shallow dish of Jell-O. She's on her back, staring up at the crooked light fixture above us that's missing all the bulbs, rather than snuggling up into me. I'm already missing Mel's pre-coital cuddles.

I don't say a thing, but she goes ahead and launches right into telling me how she used to be signed up on every dating site imaginable, but she deleted all of her profiles months ago. Said she was fed up with the whole scene. Apparently, the men out there aren't really doing any favors for girls like Ariel.

"Like I said. They're all a bunch of perverts," I remark, repeating what I said at the meeting last night.

"It's the opposite, really."

"For example?"

"Okay, well, one guy brought me to some fancy hotel room, strictly to tell me all about his dad and his sick snake and his terrible job and his disappointments in finding love. I wouldn't say he was handsome, but he was sweet and sincere. All we did was drink rum and cokes until we passed out. In the morning, I left before he woke. I ate my continental breakfast downstairs, and walked back home. I never saw him again after that."

"Really? He actually had a pet snake?" Ariel nods, as incredulous a look on her face as the one on mine. "And all the other men were just the same?"

"Yeah. I mean, you sign up on Tinder and you expect to get real freaky with strangers, right? Am I not correct in assuming this to be the case?"

"I've never been on a dating site, but that's certainly what I'd use it for."

"Exactly. And I fully imagine that's what ninety-nine percent are doing on there. So why is it I only seem to find that one percent? The mama's boys who want you to cuddle with them and pursue something serious and meaningful together."

"Ugh. Beats me. But that sounds terrible." *My greatest lie in an attempted life of honesty.* I shuffle away from her a miniscule bit.

"Tell me about it. It's so draining. I've gone out for dinner dates, and exhausted myself from ducking into the bathroom to text topless pics to the guys who are out there waiting for the dessert to come. I'll return to the table and stuff my wet panties into their shirt pockets. But my shit just scares them away. Plus, I find I'm buying new underwear every couple of weeks."

"Honestly, you're better off without. The guys, not the underwear."

"Yeah." I catch her hand slipping between her legs, and for a moment I think she's masturbating. But she's only adjusting the crotch band of her panties. "You know what I did though? Just before going to the SAA meeting last night, I downloaded all the dating apps again. Because I've realized there's really no other ways to meet people in this city. It's impossible to actually talk to someone in a bar these days. And lesbians are way too much work for me."

"Tell me about it."

"I mean, I'm still going to the meetings, but I'm finding it gets harder and harder to follow the steps."

I suppress the urge to make the all-too-easy *You know what else gets harder and harder?* line, and keep it to myself. Still makes me smile though.

"So, all I'm left with is: Maybe it's *my* fault?"

"*Your* fault? Nah. That's like saying all my bad luck is *MY* fault."

"Right. Bad luck. But you can't really compare bad luck to sex addiction. That's not the same thing. You can't blame bad luck on a person's flaws and frailties, can you?"

"Huh. You're right. It probably *is* my fault." Ariel stares at me, a befuddled look on her sharp face. "Can I ask what you're abstaining from?"

"Abstaining? I don't watch television. But that's just because I can't afford cable or Netflix."

"I don't mean television," I say.

"Okay. Well, I'm also trying my best to not steal things anymore. I used to be quite the kleptomaniac."

"Maniac? That seems harsh. It's not like you're some sort of unbalanced schizoid. No, what I meant was the sex stuff. The SAA literature talks about abstinence and sobriety."

"Oh," she says, becoming suddenly very quiet. "We're not obligated to share our personal goals."

"Come on! It's ME! We go way back, don't we? Who could you possibly ever trust more than Chester K. Eddy?"

"I'll be honest, I totally forgot your name. I've been going to these meetings for seven months now. Tell you the truth, I'm not very good at staying sexually sober for long. Or anything-sober, really. Everything I tell myself I'm going to abstain from, I just cave. I stole a bottle of vodka from your bag last night."

"You did? When?"

"While you were sleeping. I finished it in the bathroom just now. Not to mention, I drank a forty ouncer of Jim Beam right before the meeting, which ended up with me bringing you here to my place. I drink so I don't have to think about sex, but then I have no control over myself and end up making poor decisions and having sex. It's a vicious circle. The hen or the egg."

"Chicken," I correct her, though I don't even know if Ariel's using the saying in the right context. Truthfully, I've never actually understood the *chicken-or-the-egg* discussion. I don't know; my brain's just not wired that way. I get a headache whenever I think about it. But I nod like I understand nonetheless.

"Sure," she says.

"Though I don't see why more people don't use dinosaurs and dinosaur eggs as an example instead. They're so much cooler than chickens. Maybe it depends on whether you believe in the existence of dinosaurs or not?"

"Uh, right."

"Have I told you about my dinosaur porn idea?"

"Dinosaur porn? That's been done to death."

"It has?" *Alas, poor Jurassic Pork. I knew thee well.*

"Never mind," she says coldly. "My point here is I shouldn't have made out with you behind the church after the meeting, but I did. And I definitely should NOT have brought you back *here* last night. But, what can I say? I have a soft spot for fragile and insecure men."

I look around the room, with a small glimmer of hope that she's maybe talking about someone else. But she definitely means me. I still find the need to clarify, just in case. "You don't mean ME, do you?"

"I find that after having sex, I usually want to just get up and run away from the guy because I feel guilty and ashamed."

I puff my chest out like a horny peacock. "I guess that says something about me, huh?"

"I almost left in the middle of the night."

"Just like that?"

"Yeah. But I stole your vodka instead. Why have you got so many hotel-sized beverages in your bag anyway?"

"I like to think of them as child-sized."

"Child-sized vodka?"

"Yeah. That doesn't sound right. How about fun-sized?" She shrugs her shoulders in a display of not really caring. *Fun-sized it is.* "I can't believe you thought about just leaving me alone in your own apartment."

"To be perfectly honest, it's taking everything I've got to stay here right now."

I poke her naked breast gently with my pinkie finger. "Well, you can't go out looking like that, milady."

"So," she starts, ignoring my roaming hand. "I've decided I'm going to get back on *PlentyOfFish* and try to land myself a sex freak."

"That's the spirit! You go, girl!"

"A real BDSM creeper."

"You're the true modern woman. Grab your life by the girl-balls."

"And I'm going to keep trying to go cold turkey on men who just want something serious."

"Guess that puts *me* in the clear then."

Ariel looks at me, with that look I've probably seen a million times already. She says, "You're kidding, right?" *Why do they always give me that look?*

"ME? I'm not that guy! We're having a serious talk about sex addiction and I'm here squeezing your nipple."

She's not even blinking. It's eerie.

"You really think I'm that guy? I mean, yes, sure. It would be nice if maybe you were nuzzling that little face of yours into my neck here — *What's this part called? The nape? I've heard nape somewhere before, though I guess it's usually describing a woman's neck. Do dudes have napes?* — but I mean, honestly? I do sometimes get relationshippy feelings for my friend; you remember Melissa, right? I mentioned her once or twice last night."

"Once or twice during our hump fest, even."

"Well, whatever. But what's so bad with snuggling anyway? Snuggling gets a bad rap."

Ariel sits up now. She reaches for a purple bra from the bedside table and puts it on. "I'm just not a snuggler. Well, I am but I'm not."

"You are but you aren't? What does *that* mean?"

"You know when you start dating a chef and you think, this is going to be great! A full egg breakfast every morning; four-course dinners every night. I'm never eating ramen noodles or microwaved pizza pops again! Well, it always turns out that coming home to cook after being a chef all day is the last thing they want to be doing." Ariel gets off the bed now and takes a button-up shirt that hangs from the top of the open closet door, and walks into the bathroom with it while saying, "It's the same with being a professional snuggler."

I call after her, "I'm sorry. What—?"

From the bathroom she says, "Snuggling. It's my day job."

"How the fuck is that even a thing?"

"It's alternative therapy. Some folks just need a hug."

"So, people pay you to hug them?"

"Sure, they do." She comes back out of the bathroom now, fully dressed with a cardigan pulled over her shirt and cotton pants on.

"You just show up at their door and, what—? You snuggle on the couch?"

"Or the bed."

"And there's no funny business?"

"Not allowed."

"So, it's like prostitution without the happy ending?"

"There are no happy endings in prostitution, Chester."

"Tell that to the ones *I've* been with."

"Yeah, I'll be sure to ask around the next time I'm hanging outside a Jersey gas station at two in the morning. Besides, my clients are mostly men over sixty. Trust me, funny business is the *last* thing on their minds." She ties her hair back into a tight ponytail, which immediately puts funny business on the forefront of my mind.

"Men over sixty? Those guys are the *biggest* pervs! Plus: hello! You're a sex addict."

"They're just sad and depressed and are lacking companionship in their lives."

Then the reality of what it actually is hits me: "They're desperate," I say.

"And you're right there."

"I guess so."

"Trust me when I say I know what that's all about." It's also right now I realize Ariel is at the door, dressed to snuggle (professionally, that is) and I'm still sitting near-fully naked (in only my thin pair of cartoon baby hippo socks with holes in the big toes) on her stained sheets.

"What's the matter, Chester?" she asks, oblivious to my feelings.

"I think I just want to be held right now."

Whatever air she has inside her blows out. "I gotta get going, man."

"Can we just cuddle for a few minutes, Ariel? Please?"

"Dude. I know I'm fucked up, but you've got some real serious issues. And my name's not Ariel. It's Jasmine. Disney princesses are another one of my fetishes."

"Me too. Man, Snow White was the hottest one, wasn't she? She could have done so much better than those dwarfs. Wait, is it *dwarfs* or *dwarves*?"

"Did you even see Snow White?"

"Does the porno version count?"

"I wouldn't think so."

"Then no."

I think it was called *Blow White*. Honestly, some of those porn titles aren't even clever. They'll just stick a suggestive word in there and not even think about it. So lazy.

Somewhere, *Jurassic Pork* is telling me to just shut up already.

Sugar Hill: Where My G-Ma Be Cribbing

TBH, I swallowed a large stone when I was twenty-two. I'd heard about a party down at the Monona shoreline. A throng of high school grads were gathering there, so naturally my assumption was that twenty-two-year-old Chester K. Eddy might really impress these unsullied partiers with some true veteran carousing. Didn't happen. And made more obvious by the fact I couldn't manage to mooch a single beer and that I ended up swallowing a rock for attention. It's been a decade and I still haven't seen it resurface. I think about that stone inside me every so often, and ruminate on whether or not it's going to cause any serious problems at some point.

So, with the snuggler itching to make her exit/escape, I clearly needed to prioritize a few items. Here are the Top-Three Things I Needed to Take Care of Before Leaving Jasmine's Place:

#3: Clarify whether or not the Little Mermaid was technically a princess (I hadn't seen the family-friendly version of that one either, so a public poll may be in order)

#2: Find some underpants because I simply could not find mine anywhere (Jasmine tossed me a pair of crusty, threadbare Silver Surfer boxers that some dude had previously left behind. The fewer questions I had, the better. And she chucked a balled-up pair of pink socks at me too, free of charge, in case I needed some without holes)

#1: Figure out a mature way of agreeing to mutually not see one another again after this moment (Her approach was saying she'd call me, and then disappearing faster than I had time to realize I'd never given her my number in the first place. And I guess that settled that.)

So here I am now, outside her smelly, cinder block apartment which appears to be situated uncomfortably on the corner of Harlem Circa 1972 (on a bad day) and Downtown Beirut (on a good day).

I've got to say though; these frilly pink socks are actually pretty cozy on my toesies.

There's a van parked outside the building with "Fuck the Police" spray painted on the side in black, seemingly by an angry child. I notice there also happens to be an angry adult in the passenger's seat and he's staring me down. Staring me down hard. He's got a teardrop tattoo below his twitching right eye.

"The fuck you doin' here?" he asks me, about as politely as I imagine he's capable of asking anyone anything.

When I first came to New York I was the same cocky asshole I am now, but I was a cocky asshole who was out of his element. When I got lost five minutes after disembarking from the Greyhound, I asked a local yokel for some directions. And wouldn't you know it? New Yorkers are really the most pleasant people when you ask them something honestly! From then on, whenever I didn't know how to reload my Metrocard, or which unmarked off-Broadway theater I had an audition at, or which Swedish massage parlors were the ones that give the happy endings, I just pretended I was a tourist and asked someone. I still do it now out of habit.

Even if there's an apparent convict in a van with the words "Fuck the Police" spray painted on the side.

I say, "Excuse me, my good man." *Oh yeah. This is a fine start.* "Would you be so kind as to tell me how to get to the Upper West Side? I seem to have gotten lost."

"The fuck you mean?" he says. I could be wrong, but this gentleman seems just a little less angry already.

"The Upper West Side? You know, they've got cool brunch spots and vegan restaurants and the Museum of Natural History."

"The fuck?" I'm unsure if there's some kind of criminal code that prevents him from beginning any sentence with anything other than *The fuck*. Do I ask him as much? Probably not, but we'll see where this goes.

"Listen," I say. "I got stupidly lambasted last night and woke up in the bed of some freaky sexaholic with a thing for Disney. Actually, I'm unsure whether it was her bed or not, now that I think about it. But I also have no idea where I am, and you, fine sir, are giving me those *Lay-of-the-Land-Expert* sort of vibes."

He's just staring at me.

"Go on; tell me I'm wrong," I challenge him.

Is that a smile forming at the corner of his mouth? It's shady in the van, so I can't really tell if it's actually a smile or if maybe his lip was slashed in a prison yard knife fight.

Finally, he says, "You in Sugar Hill, y'know?"

"Sugar Hill? I've never heard of Sugar Hill. Well, except for that Wesley Snipes flick."

"This's that."

"This is the movie?"

"Uh huh."

"I'm sorry, but that doesn't make any sense. I mean, you're saying *THIS* is that movie. But that isn't logical. Like, is Wesley Snipes here right now? 'Cause

I don't see him anywhere. I think what you mean is *THIS* — where we are right now — is the real-world place that the fictional film was based upon. Don't you see how what you're saying might be misconstrued and made more confusing?"

There I go. And now he's gone back to looking straight-up pissed again. My problem now is I can't take my eyes off the tattoo. It's just sitting there, like it was a piece of spinach caught between his gold teeth. Or, more accurately, like spinach puree dripping down his cheek instead. *Actually, I suppose the metaphor doesn't have to be spinach at all. Why am I stuck on spinach? But as long as I don't say anything about it—* "I've heard teardrop tattoos can either signify you've killed someone or that you were raped in prison. Is there a way I can tell just by looking at it? Say from about this distance?"

Another bit of fine work, Chester K. Eddy.

"You saying I been violated, motherfucker?" The entire van shakes a little.

"No, no. I was just curious if there's a difference. It's my insatiable thirst for knowledge, y'see? Also, the advertisement on your van here: I'm keen to know if it's meant to say *FLICK*, but your *L* and your *I* got a bit too close together and now it looks like *FUCK* instead. I do that all the time, and then I look at it and go, *Whoa. I better re-do that shit.* I can't imagine writing it with a can of spray paint would be any easier. On an unrelated note though, Sugar Hill sounds quaint. What's the rent around here?"

"Man, nobody afford rent in this city."

"Tell me about it, Jailbird. But Sugar Hill sounds like somewhere my grandma would live."

"My G-Ma *does* live here."

"Our G-Ma's should really hang out more often. Sounds like they've got a lot in common. Charming neighborhoods. Handsome and gregarious grandchildren. Likely a large plate full of those cookies with the jam in the middle." I open up my satchel and brusquely dig around through the stolen hotel minibar contents as efficiently as I can. I think I hear a gun cock from inside the van. "Listen, I've got Diet Mountain Dew and Jack Daniels in here and I'm ready and willing to exchange them for decent directions. Pick your poison."

He smiles a sparkly, gold-toothed smile. See? You just gotta know how to talk to the yokels.

***

Okay.

So, my G-Ma — *I'm definitely calling her G-Ma from now on too, even right to her face, I totally don't care* — always told me to not judge a book by its cover. But that's bullshit, because everybody does that. Except the pseudo-intellectual hipsters who look at art from a distance with their heads cocked slightly or update their Facebook statuses with the most incessantly banal and vexatious posts concerning their opinions on The Decemberists, Daylight Saving Time, non-US politics, and their own personal liquor collections. It doesn't matter what *they* think.

In this case, however, my G-Ma was absolutely correct. How else could I have so soon found myself sitting next to a guy named Bullet — *See? It WAS a cool name!* — in the driver's seat of a van that smelled straight-up awful, like a bad combination of scented markers, dolphin droppings, and the *Grown Ups* movie franchise?

Bullet and I are each knocking back a bottle of JD, while we discuss the forces of nature that have unceremoniously brought us to our specific points in life. I tell him all about Melissa, my spiraling acting career, the booger picking, and my weird, pointy toenails. And him? Turns out he actually *was* gang-raped while incarcerated, and given his teardrop tattoo by a portly fella named Oliver Dung. *Hey, no judgements here, Bullet. No judgements.*

Bull — *He told me I could call him Bull, but that I couldn't call his BULLshit. See? Funny guy too!* — explained how he was put away for trivial reasons he didn't wish to talk about. When I boldly asked him if he had any pre-slammer dreams whilst growing up on the mean streets of Sugar Hill, he confessed to having regrets over never writing children's books.

"You should do that then," I tell him, swishing the last few drops of whiskey around the bottom of the bottle. "You should start writing that shit today. Right now."

"It's not too late for me, Galahad?" *Okay, I may or may not have told him my name is actually Galahad: the awesomest of all the knights. It's a victimless crime.*

"Trust me, it's *never* too late. Would I still be slumming it up trying to get on Broadway if it was too late for me? Hell no, bro. To give up on art is to watch art die. And I don't want to see art die." Plus, I'm literally no good at anything else. So, the reality is I have zero options at this point. "How about you?"

Now there's a real tear forming in his eye, and the dude actually says, "To the victor goes the spoils!" No kidding. He yells it out the fucking window.

And — *since a part of me is frankly still nervous for my life* — I shuffle over the opposite direction a little. "Uh, yeah. Just like that, Bull." Why is he yelling shit like that out the window? This dude is unhinged.

"The fuck do I write about, though? Give me an idea, Galahad."

"Just take something from your life. Well, I'd probably avoid any of the prison stories if I were you, but there's plenty of other things to draw upon. And maybe lose some of the F-bombs too. How about a talking van?"

"Nah."

I nod my head toward the back of the vehicle. "You could write about the smell back there."

"Can't write no story 'bout no smell. Maybe an animal? Kids seems to like animal stories."

Looking out my window, into the driver's side mirror, I see the spray paint on the side of the van and it gives me an idea. "Flick," I say.

"Flick?"

"Yeah. Picture this: it's the 19th Century. A young Edgar Allan Poe — chimneysweep by day and worker at the musket factory by night — lives on a steamship. The conditions are terrible, and a family of head lice takes up residence on Edgar's scalp. The youngest, Flick the Louse accompanies Poe on all of his whimsical adventures." With my arms, I imagine a big, bold Broadway marquee. "You call it: *Flick the Poe Lice!*"

"I don't think Poe did any of those things."

What are you, Bullet? A history buff? "It's fiction. And it's only *one* idea. We're spitballing here, Bull."

"It's fucking terrible. And shouldn't it be Flick the Poe *LOUSE*?"

"Let up, dude. I wasn't really aiming to get into proper group nouns here."

"Well, if it's the title, then it's gotta be accurate, motherfucker!"

"You're not exactly making any great strides over there."

Out of nowhere, Bullet flings his 50ml Jack Daniels bottle out the window, and it explodes against the building's front stoop; blue sky and stark white snow reflecting off the tiny glass shards in an incredible rainbow display. Beautiful, that is if I wasn't shitting my pants right now.

On the dashboard of the van, I spot the two cans of Diet Mountain Dew sitting together next to a small pile of ammunition. How does one tell if bullet shell casings are empty or not? That's not a life skill I've ever picked up. "You know what," I tell him. "I'm just going to leave you with that Dew there — in fact, keep 'em both! — and be on my way. I'm not sure if you're really in a listening mood after all."

"The fuck, man? I know I sometimes have violent mood swings, but I thought we's tight here."

"Were we's ever tight? We's just met twenty minutes ago! I'm just not sure if we's looking for the same things in this relationship anymore, Bull. Plus, I really need to get to work. It's my second day at the new job, you know?"

"A good first impression is key, yo."

"Tell me about it." I give the vehicle a tap with the back of my hand. "How about a lift to the theater then?"

"I'm not allowed to move the van."

"Not allowed?"

"I'm waiting for someone."

"You've been waiting for someone this whole time?"

"Truth."

"By any chance, is this someone your G-Ma?"

"Nah. But if this someone came here and saw you sitting in the van, you probably not making it to work today. Know what I mean, Galahad?"

"You know, I think I'll just walk. That brisk November Manhattan air is really something special. Especially on a Wednesday." I hand him what's left of my bottle of JD. "Here. You might as well finish this, too."

As I hop out of the driver's seat, the bottle whizzes by my head, shattering on the road.

And I run.

Like the fucking wind, I run. As far away from Sugar Hill as my skinny legs and frilly pink socks will take me, hoping to hell I'm headed in the right direction.

Rat Skulls in The Snow

TBH, I've shit my pants once or twice. And I'm not talking about when I was kid with a weak stomach and I blew out my o-ring every time I had chicken strips at the Burger King. I'm talking about as an adult. You feel something in your loins is off but you think you can still squeak out a fart and before you know it there's a warm wetness down there and a very telling, non-discreet stink to it all.

It might have been more than twice though.

I don't recall Glenn Workman telling me what time I should show my face today, but I'm going to assume he meant *before* Happy Hour. I try to pick up my pace, but only enough so I don't stand out. Everyone makes fun of that idiot who's clearly late for something; frantically running through the city with that psychotic sort of *My-Life-Depends-on-My-Punctuality!* look in his eyes. I make fun of those idiots. Constantly. Never get enough, actually.

Unfortunately, when I eventually do get to One Hundredth Street, I realize I'm on the wrong side of Central Park and have to huff it through the snowy trails, which seem to only be populated by folks in hospital scrubs and those dog-walking babes burdened with the balancing act of having both amazing bodies and butter faces. I'll oftentimes make an extra effort to smile at those ones. It picks them up; makes them feel a tiny bit better about themselves. *See? I'm a great guy.*

A fairly good person, at the very least.

Questionably helpful, perhaps? I'll find the appropriate category eventually.

This one coming my way now throws a gap-toothed smile at me as we pass one another. And I toss a winning grin back her way. Yeah, she's definitely going to start her ten-hour shift behind the yellowed window at the immigration office on a real high. The old self-esteem boost might even get her laid tonight, as long as the dive bar she frequents is dark enough.

Finally, I make it over to the west side. There it is! The glorious façade of Theatre One Hundred! Glenn's cup of coffee from yesterday is also here, still sitting on the front steps. I pick it up, shake it around a little (it's near frozen; the icy bits rattling around like it's a McDonald's fountain drink), and take a sip. Maybe I'm too drunk to give a shit, but I chug the rest of it back. I wouldn't go so far as to call it terrible coffee — *I mean, it HAS been sitting outside for twenty-four hours* — but I can admit I've guzzled worse before.

Just as I toss the empty cup onto the road, the front door opens, and there's Glenn Workman standing in stupefied amazement.

"Chester! You haven't been waiting out here all morning, have you?" he asks.

It's been like two minutes. Still, I try to look like I'm fresh off the boat and don't know any better about how this world I'm barely a part of actually works. "Uh...yeah. Sorry. I was knocking for a while but then just assumed you weren't in yet. Figured I'd wait for you out here."

"Do I need to be questioning your ambition and perseverance again?"

Of course you should. Always. "Never! I'm the go-gettingist of the go-getters."

"I guess I should have mentioned there's a back door, Chester. You should use that when coming and going."

No, I am not about to make a back-door joke. I'm better than that. "I'll bet there is," I say. That doesn't count as crude innuendo, does it? I'm too subtle for even myself sometimes.

Still, Glenn just ignores me and asks, "What happened to you last night? I saw you outside after the meeting, sharing a smoke with Ariel."

I shrug my shoulders like I have no idea what he's talking about. I don't know why I do these things; it's just reflex. Glenn continues to explain how he didn't want to interrupt Ariel and I, so he went back inside for a few minutes. When he came back out, we were gone.

"Yeah, about that," I start.

"You didn't sleep with her, did you? Chester, that girl has serious emotional problems!"

"And I *don't*? What happened to two negatives making one positive?"

"Well, I'm not about to assume I really know you or your emotional problems all that well yet."

"It won't take you long. Trust me. I'm an open book. I'll pretty much tell anyone everything, if they give me five minutes. I could do it under four, too."

Glenn looks at his watch. It's one of those square, plastic digital numbers from the 80's, that may or may not transform into a tiny robot. "We've got at least five minutes before the auditions will start showing up." I almost forgot I'd scheduled the Martha auditions for today! The first of which was at 12:30, so I can at least begin narrowing down what time it might actually be right now. He kicks some snow off the steps and sits down, patting the empty space beside him. "So, tell me about these problems of yours."

As I sit, I notice a dead rat on the curb, mostly sticking out from the snowbank; its black tail rigor mortised into a crooked question mark, and the hair and skin missing from half its skull so the big nasty teeth look even more like one of those inner jaws/second mouths of the aliens from Aliens. "I guess

I just don't want to be *that* guy," I say, pointing to the rat.

"That guy *does* look pretty miserable," Glenn comments, stroking his own rat tail for effect. "I don't blame you."

"I mean, I'll be the first to admit I'm a lot like a rat to start with."

"Because you carry the Bubonic Plague?" he jokes.

"I doubt it. Though seeing a doctor probably couldn't hurt."

"You're an invasive species?" he continues.

"On a technicality, maybe."

"You've been subjected to various forms of experimental scientific research?" *Okay. We get the joke, Glenn.*

"There's money in that, isn't there? Might have to keep that idea in my back pocket. No, I mean I'm an opportunistic survivor, Glenn! Just like a rat."

"Really?"

"Sure I am. Look, I have basically nothing going for me in my life right now, but I keep pushing. I keep scraping at the walls and scrapping for every inch."

"Might I remind you: you only got this job because I was in a fix and desperate."

"Sure. But my survivor mode kicked in and I actually landed a *different* job from the one you were originally offering me."

"But not the one you wanted."

"Still."

"And, some might argue, it's actually the *lesser* job."

"Still," I say again.

"Still," he says.

I eye the rat in the snowbank; its skull is actually whiter than the snow. I decide to press on. Keep scrapping. "Rats are also hard workers and easy to train. As am I. And they're highly social animals, like me. But look at him now: all alone in a snowbank. I don't want to be that guy."

"He's alone because he's dead, Chester."

"Alone because he's *dead*, or dead because he's *alone*?" And how far am I from either of those undesirable states, really? Well, at the very least, I don't believe I'm carrying any diseases or pathogens. That's something. "Have you ever noticed the kind of people who like to keep rats as pets? Usually they're raging weirdos, right? Lots of dark, baggy clothing. More than a little socially awkward."

"I can see that. Kind of unfuckable?"

"Oh, *completely* unfuckable."

"And maybe they like *Game of Thrones* a bit *too* much?"

"God, I hate *Game of Thrones*. I mean, I get it already; incest, castration, everybody dies. It's basically the Trump administration." *Okay, that was an easy setup, but I could have used The Wall as an example, so I'm not THAT obvious.*

Glenn leans back a little, sizing me up, not so unlike any number of the gold-digging tramps who have pestered me at Philly's Bar. God, I miss that place already. "What?" I ask him.

"I'm just realizing that it's taking a conversation like this for me to get to know you better. Remarkable, isn't it?"

"Very."

"But there's more than that, isn't there? It's not just about being a dead rat, right? I mean, we're all dead rats eventually, Chester."

Is this getting too deep? I don't really want this to get too deep. What I want is to say, *"Dammit, Glenn. Can I just get some work done here already?"* But instead, I consider for a moment the number of jobs I've lost suddenly

from saying/doing the very first thing that comes to mind. My Top-Three
Botched Jobs Due to Social Ineptness might include:

#3: Tim Pitty's: This was a crap bar in the Lower East Side. On only
my second shift, I showed up to work drunk, wasting no time in yelling
out, "Who wants to chug straight from the taps?" Things went from
Zero to Shitshow in about eight seconds. Using my best judgement —
Wait, Chester K. Eddy has a best judgement? — I didn't even show up
to work the next day, or ever again.

#2: Big Brothers and Sisters: Here I did some office administrator
work. Now listen, I pride myself on my very professional email
etiquette (face-to-face is an *entirely* different story), but for a whole
week, for some reason, I decided to personalize the company's slogan
("The Power to Change Lives") in my email signature for everyone I
contacted; not one person noticed until Doreen — *Fucking Doreen!* —
had the gall to randomly select one of *my* emails to use a screencap for
in a meeting about office courtesy and respectfulness. Everyone in that
meeting saw my signature ("The Power to Change Doreen's Vibrator
Batteries") on the giant projection screen. And then it was hello pink
slip.

#1: The Deutsche Bank: I don't have to bring up the porn again, do I?
They've probably still got a 24-hour Geek Squad on the job, trying to
wipe that computer clean.

Where was I? Oh, yes. I was about to say something else, but I stopped
instead and really thought about what it was Glenn was asking me. Sure, I'm
feeling a lot like that dead rat over there, but what's really on my mind is that

nagging feeling that the world is against me. Why else would this colossal tidal wave of hopeless love, human excrement, and highly questionable sex acts be smashing upon the shores of the Isle of Chester K. Eddy so suddenly?

So instead, I tell him, "I seem to have hit a giant wall here, Glenn. More impenetrable than anything Trump ever promised us. Fuck, and I thought I was going to be less obvious than that. My Honesty Movement was supposed to free me, but it's only given me more crap to figure out how to deal with. I'm up to my eyeballs with unresolved dilemmas."

"Nothing is ever really so insurmountable."

"Fuck that, Glenn. It's like—like. Uh. Shit, my metaphors seem to be off at the moment. What's the toughest obstacle you can think of?"

He thinks. And I can tell he's putting some real effort into it. And he comes up with: "The *American Ninja Warrior* obstacle course?"

"There's gotta be something more incredible than that."

"That surfer girl who had her arm bitten off by a shark? She was surfing again like a month later."

"That *is* ballsy. No, I mean something of mythological proportions."

"Like the Labors of Hercules?"

"There it is. Yup. I feel like my life right now is akin to the Labors of Hercules."

"Right. 'Cause you remind me of Hercules so much."

"Hear me out, Glenn. Jeeze. You're very quick to dismiss, you know that?"

"I'm not really all that familiar with the story though. Enlighten me."

"What, I'm going to just list off the Fifty Labors of Hercules? You brought it up! Why don't you Google that shit?"

Glenn pulls his phone out, and with the astonishingly adept speed of a high-school kid researching new Air Jordans, he's on the Wikipedia page for

The Labors of Hercules in roughly 1.5 seconds. "Well, first of all, it says here there were *twelve* labors, not fifty."

"Twelve? Pfft. That's not so hard. I already feel like he had it easier than me."

Mumbling to himself, Glenn reads, "Hercules had to slay the Lernaean Hydra—"

"The what?"

"He had to capture the Ceryneian Hind—"

"The *hind?* I don't know what that even means, but it can't be any harder than finding a cab on 5th Avenue at five o'clock. Which I've done *multiple* times, thank you very much."

"He cleaned the Augean stables—"

"Seriously? The great and mighty Hercules had to mop up some cow shit? I've had worse jobs than that. Hercules can't compare to me. That guy was a pussy."

Here. I'll prove it. *Presenting! The Twelve Labors of Chester K. Eddy:*

#1. Start a successful Honesty Movement = *failed*

#2. Get a bank account like a real adult = *failed*

#3. Don't be an idiot and get kicked out of my brother's apartment = *failed*

#4. Survive a night in Sugar Hill = *done!*

#5. Convince Melissa to dump The Boyfriend = *working on it*

#6. Keep Melissa as far away from Japan as possible = *I'm getting to that...*

#7. Prove my love for Melissa = *how the hell do I do this?*

#8. Find the balls to admit I'm not a douchebag, but that I'm just infatuated with my best friend = *can't I be both? how does this even count as a labor?*

#9. How many more do I need here?

#10. Uh…take care of that ringtone on my phone, maybe?

#11. Forget it

"Listen, Glenn. It doesn't matter if I'm better than Hercules or if I'm not. My point is: I've hit a wall, it sucks, and I'm sort of sad about it, okay?"

"That's fair, Chester. That's totally fair."

"And I'm grateful you've given me this job. Really."

"The job you didn't want? You're welcome."

"Also, I promise I won't blow it. Even though it's still early days and my track record for blowing employment emphatically says otherwise."

"Just be that opportunistic survivor you were talking about, and you'll be fine. But how about we just get inside before we freeze? I can't feel my ass anymore."

"Me neither. Also, my pants are soaked."

I don't know; as weird and creepy as he is, maybe this Glenn Workman fella will turn out to be alright.

We head inside and I first make a stop at the bathroom to change out of my wet clothes. I ask Glenn if there are any pants in the theater's costume closet I can borrow. The next thing I know, I'm being handed a pair of old-timey striped convict pants, white sailor bell-bottoms, mom jeans, and some lavender ballerina leotards. "Take your pick," he says.

It's pretty bad when your best option is to look like a sailor. Like I just got back from Pearl Harbor. Christ. Say what you will about dying alone in a snowbank, at least it's not this embarrassing.

I think the dead rat is shaking his head at me. *Tsk tsk, Mister Eddy.*

Where's a WWII Kamikaze when you really need one? Just kill me now. Go ahead and fly a tiny explosive airplane right into my life.

My Type Comes in Stereo

TBH, I don't really know anything about Japan, other than what's considered to be overtly stereotyped and likely quite a bit racist. Here's a super-condensed list of things I know relating to Japan:

- Kamikazes in World War II (already covered)
- Ninjas (apparently not an American invention. Who knew?)
- Godzilla (see also: Son of Godzilla, SpaceGodzilla, Mechagodzilla & Mothra)
- Mickey Rooney in *Breakfast at Tiffany's*
- Wildly confusing game shows
- Tentacle porn
- Super Terrific Ultra Bubble Kawaii (a laundry detergent brand that Mel swears by, which she can only find at a peculiar bodega in SoHo)

Granted, this sample size is perhaps not enough data to base an informed opinion about an entire country upon, but this is what I'm choosing to work with. So: Fuck Japan.[1]

As I sit in the theater in my sailor pants, after checking my phone for new texts from Mel that aren't there, and then deciding to read some old ones instead (like, *"Just saw a pigeon carrying a horseshoe—WTF??"* or the always popular, *"You'll never believe where I'm shitting right now"*), I decide

---

[1] The Fuck Japan Amendment: I'll give you guys props for the tentacle porn. You've got something pretty special happening there.

I'm going to pop on over to the Deutsche Bank after work to visit her and tell her as nicely as I can to Fuck Japan.

Fuck Japan hard.

"Do *what* to Japan?" Glenn asks.

"Oh, sorry. That was meant to be my inside voice again," I say.

"You do that a lot, I've noticed. I hope it doesn't distract from the rest of these auditions today."

Dude, I'm already distracted. You're lucky I'm at least sitting still. "Of course not!"

But I mean, waiting to hear from women is the worst. Here's the thing: they never seem to call/text when you're *really* waiting to hear from them. It's agonizing.

I haven't heard from Melissa for more than twenty-four hours now, and it's killing me. Sure, we've gone longer than this without communicating before, but she wasn't contemplating a move to the far east with some douchebag named Jack.

Okay, benefit of the doubt. I've got to remember I'm growing here. Maybe Japan's not so bad? It's not like I really know any better.

No, screw that. I'm definitely doing the ol' Deutsche Bank Pop-In after I get out of here.

We've got ten actresses booked for the Martha auditions today, and have seen seven of them so far. The first six were TERRIBLE. Absolutely amateur. They fidgeted on stage like they were afraid of us. They couldn't project. They had no presence. One of them was chewing gum and another read her monologue from her iPhone. Still another even had the girl-balls to prepare a fucking Shakespeare monologue. Shakespeare! *Wherefore art thou, common sense and the illusion of straight up professional courtesy?* How do you say, don't quit your day job folding graphic tees at the American Eagle in iambic pentameter?

I might not get a whole lot of work myself, but I at least know how to *appear* professional. *Excuse me while I pick another booger out of there.*

The last one was okay but she stated she doesn't do plays that are of an "Ungodly Nature." Turned out she'd only been in Manhattan for three weeks now and was generally pretty clueless about the "Ungodly Nature" of pretty much all Broadway shows. Case in point: she happily boasted about the tickets she purchased to see *The Book of Mormon* tonight, to which Glenn and I just eyed one another sinisterly. "Enjoy the show," Glenn said to her as she gathered her bag obliviously.

After this, Glenn looks at his audition list and calls out, "Chelsea McMahon?"

Chelsea McMahon comes out onto the stage, and I immediately remember her from her headshot. Silver-blue eyes and pointy elf ears poking out from dirty blonde curls. She's got these amazing honeycomb melon breasts too, which really should have been in that headshot, now that I'm seeing them. Her resume is really doing a disservice for her. Strangely, she's actually decided to come in barefoot and is wearing ripped jeans and a *Slayer* t-shirt, all fashion choices that are typically frowned upon for auditions, but I don't care at the moment since there's never been a pair of jeans that has fit a woman better than these are fitting Chelsea McMahon right now.

Glenn is looking over her resume, and Chelsea patiently remains quiet and unmoving up on stage. Waiting for us to give her the go ahead. I know as an auditioning actor, you're supposed to wait until you have the director's total, undivided attention before beginning, but I'm sure sometimes those asshole directors are just sitting there whispering about why they can't find that show they saved on Netflix or that amazing clam chowder they ate the night before. Just to make you sweat.

I lean in to Glenn and whisper, "You know, I still don't have a clue what this play is about."

"Didn't you read the script yet?"

Of course I didn't. "Just the good bits," I tell him. I only remember now that Glenn had given me a copy of the script for *When the Willows Speak They Sing in Unison.* Glenn Workman might have written the play himself, but that doesn't mean it's going to be any good.

"What did you like about it?"

I ask him, "Why do all the character names begin with M? That's really confusing."

"Hmm. I guess I never noticed that."

"This is why you need an editor or a writing partner, before you start whipping the thing together and throwing it out there into the world. People are going to judge you, Glenn."

"I spent *seven years* on this script, Chester."

I've never spent seven years on anything. "Can you give me a bit of background on this Martha character?"

"Martha is Melville's wife."

"That helps a bunch. Thanks." People have told me it's hard to do sarcasm while whispering. I have completely debunked that theory.

"Melville is a game hunter. But Martha's ultra-competitive, and wants to kill more deer than her husband. Also, she slept with Matthew, like pretty much every other woman in the town."

"Yikes. She IS competitive." I look back over to the girl on stage, imagining her hunting quarry; motionless and in silence, waiting for the right time to unload her Elmer Fudd cannon into a grazing deer. "Do you think she's related to Ed McMahon?"

"Martha?"

"No." I nod my head toward Chelsea. "Her."

"Who's Ed McMahon?"

"Come on. Really? The old sidekick from *The Tonight Show*?"

Welcome back, confused facial expression. "You mean Steve Higgins?"

"Who's Steve Higgins?"

"From Jimmy Fallon. *The Tonight Show*."

"What? No, not *that Tonight Show*."

"Leno?"

"*Carson*, you idiot."

"Chester, do you seriously expect me to know anything about one old dead guy who sat on a chair beside another old dead guy, telling jokes about the Space Race and *The Man from Uncle*?"

"And *that's* how you choose to summarize the Sixties? With moon landings and *The Man from Uncle*?"

"How about Austin Powers?"

"Um. Not a real dude, Glenn."

I look over at the stage and Chelsea McMahon is still standing there; still cradling those breasts like one of those massive 24-count cartons of eggs. And yes, the instinct is to go with the Newborn Baby metaphor, rather than the Carton of Eggs metaphor, but I don't like clichés and, also, babies absolutely terrify me. I know what she's thinking though: *"Boy, these two guys are intense. In particular, the younger, handsomer one, who really seems to be aggressively lobbying for me. He's probably got an ass-load of power in this city, and I probably wouldn't even care if he had some weird Golden Girls or Designing Women thing, which might actually be a turn-on for me, now that I'm thinking about it. I wonder if he's single? Also, that other guy has a rat tail? Really?"*

I wink at her, and she waves back politely.

Glenn says, "When you're ready, Chelsea. Go ahead."

She clears her throat and takes a pair of red glasses from her back pocket, sliding them over her pointy ears.

Oh man, those glasses. Look at the corners on those crimson frames. The way her glasses catch and reflect the theater lights are making them the headlights and me the deer.

Chelsea begins her monologue but I don't even know what she's saying. When I eventually get over the glasses thing, I've immediately gone ahead and gotten distracted by the Ed McMahon thing. It's always something with me, isn't it? I'm starting to think maybe I've got some low-grade ADHD, though it seems to mostly be my own thoughts that distract me, rather than YouTube and shiny objects.

I lean back in closer to Glenn and say, "You know, I remember hearing a rumor that he never actually died."

"Who died?" he asks, mostly keeping his eyes and ears on Chelsea.

"Didn't die, I said."

"Who?"

"Ed McMahon."

"Now he *didn't* die?"

"It's only a rumor."

"I'll be honest, I find it difficult to follow you sometimes, Chester." He leans forward in his seat, a little farther away from me, attempting to refocus on the girl on the stage.

She's got some monologue I've heard a dozen times before; seems to be a popular one for young actresses to use. I don't know; something about how it's difficult to open up to her best friend about feelings she has for some guy she's not entirely sure is even real. How do you not know if someone is real or not? Sounds like a problem no one without prescription medication has ever had before.

Sometimes I think about auditioning with a monologue written specifically for a woman. I feel like I could totally kill it.

I lean forward in my seat now, too, and whisper to Glenn. "The rumor is he never actually died, and he's just wandering around Mexico knocking on doors and telling people they won the Publisher's Clearing House lottery. The same people, over and over."

"Who?"

"Ed McMahon. He's lost his mind and is wandering around Mexico."

"*You've* lost *your* mind."

"Maine, that is. Mexico, Maine. Bet you didn't even know there was another Mexico, did you?"

"Chester—"

"As a kid, Ed McMahon worked there as a carnival barker."

"Can you please just shut up for a minute here?"

"What?"

"Shut. Up."

Shut up? All I'm wondering is if this girl is related to Ed McMahon. That's somewhat relevant to what we're here for, isn't it?

Okay, fine. Maybe it isn't relevant at all.

But still.

I feel a lump of dried ear wax fall out of my inner ear; now it's just sitting there, cradled in my antitragus. Yes, I do so know the proper names for the parts of my ear; but it's only because I once auditioned for the role of Doctor Lauchlan Twindler, disgraced Manhattan ear, nose, and throat specialist, and I actually took my career seriously at the time so I did a little bit of research for it.

I used to clean my ears with Q-tips until a walk-in clinic doctor told me they can actually do more harm than good. He said to just leave the copious amounts of wax alone and eventually it should all dry up and fall out on its own. Q-tips were a scam? I wondered what else I had been believing all my life. But I haven't cleaned my ears for over ten years now, and everything's hunky dory. Now I'll just feel the tickle of a crusty wax ball fall out, and I pick it from my ear and flick it across whatever room I'm currently taking up space in.

So instead of continuing to bother Glenn Workman with a short history lesson on Ed McMahon, I remove the ear wax and toss it somewhere into the seats behind us.

Before I know it, Chelsea's taking a slight bow on stage. Man, I can't believe I tuned out the girl's entire monologue.

"Thank you, Chelsea," Glenn says.

"Thank *you*," she replies, but looking directly at me. "Anything else before

I go?"

If it's not obvious by now that I'm a clueless, one-track-minded idiot, I blurt out, "Are you related to Ed McMahon?"

"Ed McMahon's my dad," she says with an easy breezy smile.

I lay an *I-Told-You-So* slap on Glenn's arm — The one he's currently burying his face into — and ask Chelsea, "So what's the truth? Is he really alive?"

"*Is he alive?* What kind of a question is that? I just talked to him last night."

"Does he live out this way or back in Burbank?"

"What? My dad has a Volkswagen dealership in Walla Walla, Washington."

"But did he ever have a hidden camera show called *TV's Bloopers and Practical Jokes*?"

"Uh, no."

"With Dick Clark?"

"Who?"

Okay. We're done here. Jeez, have I really just been going on about Ed McMahon for the last five minutes?

"Feels like twenty minutes, actually," Glenn Workman says to my surprise. "You were talking with your inside voice again."

"Oh. Sorry."

Glenn turns to the stage. "Thanks again, Chelsea. That'll be all for now."

She gives us an unsure wave as she exits, prompting me to check the last two names on the audition list: Emerald Thesaurus and Strawberry Trotter. You'd think I'd remember scheduling a couple of girls with a couple of names like that, but I most definitely do not. I don't recognize their headshots either — *Okay, yes, I do recall being half cut yesterday morning, though I choose to not let alcohol be a roadblock in my life, thank you very much* — but there's nothing here that makes me feel like I owe them the next six-and-a-half minutes of my life. I just can't get Melissa off my brain and it's actually, literally, paining me the longer I sit here.

There's a buzzing sound somewhere coming from something electrical; these overhead spotlights are giving me a headache; my tongue's dry; my forehead feels clammy; there's bugs crawling beneath the skin on my arms. I brace myself on the back of the seat in front of me.

"You okay?" Glenn asks.

"Woozy," I say. "I think I just need to grab some air outside."

"All right." Then he calls out, "Emerald Thesaurus?"

Over top of obnoxious, clomping footsteps I hear, "It's pronounced Emm-*rayde* Tee-*soar*-ooo."

Oh.

My.

God.

Shitting.

Gods.

I bolt out the door as fast as humanly possible so as not to see what it is Glenn is about to be dealing with in there.

***

Okay, so the fresh air might be good for me, but it's these mini bags of some unpronounceable brand-name hotel potato chips I had in my satchel that are truly killer. I think they're sour cream and onion, but I can't tell for sure. They're so exquisite, in fact, that I dropped a handful as I was front-loading them into my face like a fat kid eats Skittles, and a big chip landed close enough to the dead rat that I should have let it go, but I totally didn't.

That one might have been the best one too. But I could have just been over-compensating.

There were five mini bags in my inventory of Adventure Supplies — *Yes, Adventure Supplies is what I'm calling it now* — but they've disappeared in an embarrassing amount of time. I mean, they *were* mini. Still, it's enough to give some life back to my body.

West One Hundredth Street doesn't have much to look at, aside from some scruffy dude piling trash bags on top of snow across the street, or the familiar glowing orange and green of a crackling 7-11 sign. But I'm content with sitting out here for now, rather than heading back inside. Man, this job-working thing is hard! I'm beginning to think maybe I'm not really cut out for regular employment. I mean, what do people get out of this? The point of it all is lost on me.

Question: If I could have one job in this world, what would it be?

Answer: Easy. Weatherman. I could be wrong all day every day and still be employed. "It's the weather! That shit's unpredictable!" And seeing as how I'm already wrong more often than not, that seems like a pretty slick deal.

Still, as I shake my noggin clean and head back inside, my phone finally rings: "*Ah, me so horny! Me love you long time!*" It's Mel! It's got to be! My Righteous Moment of Me has arrived!

And I don't care what anyone says, 2 Live Crew wrote some damn catchy jingles.

"Chester K. Eddy?" the woman's voice on the other end asks.

Not Mel.

You know what? Fuck 2 Live Crew. They're nothing but a filthy one-hit wonder bedaubed in overtly controversial smut and parental advisory warnings.

Just like me.

"Is this Chester K. Eddy?"

"You can drop the *K*. I try to avoid being associated with Philip K. Dick."

Pause. "That doesn't even—Never mind. This is Chelsea McMahon."

I intentionally blank for dramatic effect. What is it with me and wanting to make this poor girl sweat it out? "I'm sorry?"

"I had an audition literally ten minutes ago. *McMahon*? Don't you remember McMahon?"

"Yeah, it's starting to ring a bell—" Of course, she might just be assuming I've got some sort of serious drug problem. If only my shitbaggery was that easy to explain. "What's up? You're probably wondering why I was wearing sailor pants aren't you?"

"I couldn't see your pants. You were sitting a few rows back from the stage."

"Oh, never mind then."

Insert uncomfortable silence here. "Why were you wearing sailor pants?"

"Well, if you MUST know, Miss Nosy. I had a one-night stand with a freaky sexaholic cuddler who had a Disney princess fetish, and—You know what, just forget it. It's a long story."

"Thanks for bringing it up then."

"Did I?"

"Listen, Mr. Eddy. I just wanted to apologize for my audition. I know I blew a couple of lines back there, which I'm sure you noticed."

I totally didn't. "It's true. I totally did."

"Ugh. I'm so humiliated."

"Don't be. But try and remember to not say '*blew the lines*' around us theater types. An embarrassingly large percentage have embarrassingly large drug problems. No need to get any of them all worked up thinking about that embarrassingly large baggie of coke stashed back in the office."

"You?"

"Not me, no. I mean, I wish I could even *afford* a baggie of coke! Nope, it's nothing but clean living for Chester K. Eddy." *If we don't count all the other weird shit I've got going on, that is.* "As for the audition? Don't worry about it. They aren't all that important, really."

"What?" The speaker on my phone crackles with her shrill outcry. "Of course they are! Auditions are *everything*. How else am I going to land the part?"

"You mean that part in some shitty project you never really wanted in the first place, and now you're ass-deep in the inane B.S. that's basically *every* project *ever*. Does it ever cross your mind what all those extras might be talking about in the background of restaurant scenes in movies? I'll tell you: Nothing. They *want* to be talking about how they're regretting their life choices, and how they really should have gone to meteorologist school like their dad wanted. But can they admit that to dad *now?* No fucking way. That's what they *want* to say, but they're not saying anything! They're just mouthing words to a fake conversation and laughing without actually laughing because they're instructed to not make a sound. Told to move their mouths like goldfish. All that background noise is a pain in the ass for the sound editors to dub in post-production, you know?"

The silence on my phone says, *I have no idea what it is you're talking about.* And I can't blame her, really. That one got away from me a bit. "But I'm not trying to be an extra in a movie," she finally says.

"You'd be much better off if that was the limit of your ambition. 'Cause otherwise you get stuck in this cycle of doing one bad gig after another, assuming it's all leading somewhere — to something major and meaningful — but it's not. It's just not. It never was, and it never will be."

"Boy. You are super negative, you know that?"

"I didn't used to be." Maybe Chelsea McMahon reminds me of me, when I was at the beginning of my career. What I was, before I became older and broken and jaded and merely in the infantine stages of man-boobs. "I used to be just like you, Chelsea."

I'll assume this next silence means she's pausing to think about it.

However, this seems like an unnecessarily long pause. My phone is getting hot on my ear.

Then, finally, she says, "I can see that. But I think that's how it always goes, isn't it? If movies have taught us anything."

"I try not to glean too many life lessons from the movies," I say. "Except for maybe *Hot Tub Time Machine*."

"So, the past and the future are pretty big things for you?"

"To be honest, I'm more of a present-tense guy. What about you?"

"Me? I think about the future a lot. Like where our political climate is headed. Having children. Or finding success on Broadway."

"Success on Broadway? So, I'm basically Future You! Only with smaller cans, I hope."

"Much like the sailor pants, I couldn't see your cans from where I was standing," she says. "But I'll assume they're smaller."

"Trust me, they're much—" With my free hand, and out of view from anyone, I cop a feel of myself. I don't even know where I was going with that statement. "Never mind."

Then she has the girl-balls to ask, "Can I make a suggestion for the play though?"

"It's not really within my power to make changes, if that's what you're asking. This is sort of Glenn's baby. And I learned the hard way that you never stick your thing in another man's baby."

Awkward long pause #3, is it now? This is going excruciatingly well. "I hope that's a joke."

"Yes. Totally a joke. I don't know about you, but boy-o-boy, *my* face is sure hurting from all the laughing I'm doing over here."

"What I was going to suggest was, maybe you'd consider changing the Martha name to something sexier? If she's going to be this crazy hot hunter chick, maybe back it up with a better name? Martha sure isn't ringing any five alarm fire bells."

"What would *you* change it to?"

"Nora, maybe?"

"Nora? You haven't thought about this at all, have you? Also, Glenn seems to like his characters' names to begin with M's."

"Misty then?"

"Too vague."

"How about Melissa?"

All of a sudden, there's a buzzing inside my head again. *I feel clammy, dizzy, like...*

"I said, how about changing the name to Melissa?"

...like I'm going to—

"Chester?"

I hit the snowbank hard, and the last thing I recall seeing is that gnarled, dead rat face. No doubt grateful he died here like this, instead of ending up like me.

The First Rule of Honesty Club & Other Advice from Dad

TBH, I'm aware there are unwritten rules when it comes to conventional audition protocol, but I mean, if someone can't be bothered to write it all down, then I'm not going to go out of my way to rein it in. I know I shouldn't show up for auditions in costume or with props, but I totally do. Even super bulky and elaborate props, like miter saws or a lemonade stand. I've brought a handgun — *A fake one! I'm no psycho, thank you very much* — before too, which is definitely a no-no. I've looked at my phone, and even answered it during auditions. I've also totally gone out of my way to disrupt other actors' auditions too. You know that person in the background during news reports who keeps doing stupid things to get attention? That's me. I make up backstories for the roles I'm auditioning for, and I work some of this new material into the monologues ("I'm Doctor Lauchlan Twindler, disgraced Manhattan ear, nose, and throat specialist! And goddammit, don't you try and tell me I've never BMX'd in Bolivia or donated sperm to Eddie Murphy!"). I've even kissed the reader, which is when someone is reading lines with you for your audition and the scene involves a kiss or some close, physical interaction. I've overstepped my mark and gotten right in there and planted a few — *Some with tongue, if I can get away with it* — but more often than not it's just made the casting director annoyed and uncomfortable. The readers have always enjoyed it though. Pretty sure.

Consciousness returns, and I find myself on the floor of Glenn's office. I'd be willing to bet this babyshit brown carpet likely contains decades worth of Frito dust, dead skin, and rodent droppings. The crooked ceiling fan is whirring awkwardly above my head.

The shadow of Glenn's weird little Michael Jackson nose looms above me. "Welcome back, sailor," he says, with a tinge of pervy ominousness.

I don't think I'm wrong in admitting my immediate instinct is to: A) forget I'm actually wearing sailor pants, and: B) check to make sure that: C) I'm not naked from the waist down and: D) my fly is pulled right up to where it should be, so that: E) I don't have to call the cops, especially since: F) how do you call the cops anyway? is that a 911 thing?, and besides: G) I likely have: H) no real ground to stand on, and: I) no alibi, or what's probably more likely still: J) some outstanding fine with the city I still have yet to pony up.

Okay, so I don't really know how to make proper, intuitive, alphanumeric lists. It's not a skill I ever learned. Sue me.

But still: the fly is up and the pants are on good and tight. *Whew.*

With a nervous chortle, I say, "Oh, heh. You called me sailor because I'm *wearing* sailor pants, right? I almost forgot there."

"What happened to you during those auditions, Chester?" Glenn asks as he helps me sit up. "You should have seen those last two. They were *worse* than terrible."

"Emerald Thesaurus and Strawberry Trotter? Terrible, you say? That's surprising."

"Strawberry auditioned with a puppet."

Do. Not. Tell. Him. You. Are. Actually. Sorry. You. Missed. That.

Like. Legitimately.

A fucking puppet. That's awesome. Not even I have had the balls to audition with a puppet. My puppet would probably have been a gerbil. See how they like it the other way around for a change.

With one shaky hand on the desk, I pull myself up, rattle my head back together, and have a seat. The piles of resumes are still there, the various roles designated by their assigned random found objects. "I'm just—I mean, the truth, Glenn, is that I've gotten really uncomfortable around this friend of mine. Just thinking about her makes my brain go all weird."

"Weird as in, you think she's trying to kill you?"

"What? No, definitely not that weird."

"I see. She doesn't approve of these questionable directions you're suddenly taking in your life?"

"You think these are questionable directions?" Of course they're questionable directions! I'm so thirsty right now I literally just considered unscrewing the cap from the water bottle on the Martha pile and downing its last few drops of years-old, furry, brown water. "My decision-making process is not that bad, is it?" *Yes. Yes, it is, Chester. You know you kinda, sorta want to lick that stale Cheeto while you're at it, don't you?* "This girl, I just mean— what I mean is, I *love* her."

"That's sweet, Chester. Love can be powerful, can't it?"

Cue the vomit in the back of my throat. "Yeah. It can, Glenn. And the real problem is that I just can't seem to tell her as much."

"But what about your Honesty Movement? Shouldn't that *require* you to tell her something like that?"

"For some reason, this appears to be falling outside the rulebook. You know, like, *The first rule of Honesty Club is you don't talk about Honesty Club.*"

"That's very contradictory. Seeing as how you've basically told everybody everything."

"Except for her."

Glenn breathes out slowly — *and totally judgmentally* — from his nose. "Do you really have a rulebook?"

"Well, no. Obviously, that would require far more ambition than I'm prepared to dredge up."

Now he plants himself on top of the desk; that creepy vibe coming at me like wavy stink lines from a cartoon skunk. "Listen, Chester. Love—it's a complicated thing."

"No need for this right now, Glenn! I'm pretty sure I already had this talk. The one you're supposed to have with your dad in the eighth grade, but instead you have the pleasure of hearing it whispered to you in the corner by your pervy uncle at Thanksgiving."

"That's not where I was going with this. But thanks for comparing me to your pervy uncle."

"I won't deny it, there's some definite similarities there, for sure."

"Was your uncle cheating on your aunt too?"

"Was he *what* now—?"

"You want to know *my* truth, Chester?" *Oh please, Glenn. Haven't you shared enough truths with me already? We only just met, didn't we?* "My truth is that I don't think I love my wife anymore."

Huh? "Jesus, you're married too? Exactly how many secret problems have you got hidden away in there?" In a real *Think-McFly-think* moment, I knock my fist on Glenn's skull for emphasis.

"I'm in love with a different girl, who's not my wife."

"Not your ex-assistant? Allison, I think her name was?"

He shakes his head.

"There's *another* girl? What is up with you and the ladies, Glenn? I'm actually kind of impressed. Now *there's* some honesty for you."

"Chester, listen. Let me tell you something my father told me a long, long time ago."

"You know, the way you phrased that, all I can think about is that scene on Cloud City where Vader cuts Luke's hand off."

"Weren't they on the Death Star?"

"So help me, Glenn Workman, if your art house hipster ass is trying to out-pop-culture-reference me right now. It was fucking Cloud City, all right. That place where they had dinner with Darth Vader and all the weird little pig men were running around? What were those pig men called, anyway? Great, now you've got me thinking about what the pig guys in Star Wars were called."

"It wasn't me who brought up Star Wars, Chester. I was only about to—"

"Mynocks? No, that wasn't it..."

"I only wanted to share some advice that my dad—"

"Gluggnocks? That doesn't sound right either..."

"Chester!"

"Ah, shit. Sorry, Glenn. You know, when I'm in the moment like that, anyone who's talking to me sounds like a grown-up in The Peanuts. Just another one of my Charlie Brown moments, I suppose."

"Listen. All I wanted to say was my father once told me that if you're doing something for a girl, you'd better be honest with yourself about it."

He's really giving me fatherly advice right now, isn't he? "I don't even know what that means."

"It means—well, it means essentially what you think it means."

"Don't say *that!* I have *no idea* what it means. I just told you as much."

There's the judgmental breathing from the nose again. "Just don't lead her on. That's all."

"You know, your dad gives pretty terrible advice. But it's still more advice than my own dad gave me." *Yes, Mister Stuart Eddy, that's a pretty low bar you set.*

"I think maybe you just need some real food and sustenance in you, Chester. You can't survive much longer on your diet of Doritos and Jack Daniels."

"Are you offering me dinner again? Because — and I'm being totally honest again — I don't think I can watch you eat another dry lettuce burger."

"Chester, I don't really want to be that judgmental guy in your life—"

"I'm only supposed to have *one?*"

"—but you're trying me, pal. You're really trying me." He fishes out his electric green velcro wallet, tears the thing open, and tosses a ten my way. "Go get yourself something to eat. I'd love to give you more so you could change out of those pants and that disgusting hoodie, but that's all I've got on me."

Snatching up the bill, I say, "Thanks, Dad. Maybe we could go out shopping later?"

"Don't push it, okay?"

Because theater-regulation bell bottom props apparently don't come with pockets, I stuff the money into the front of my pants, like I've just given myself the lap dance of a lifetime. And this, as I squirm around in my chair, is when I notice the top resume on the Madison Willows pile (the one marked by the Gilmore Girls coffee mug; Lauren Graham's *I'm-not-believing-this-family-dynamic-for-a-second* smile on it): it's Melissa's resume. The very resume I could swear I'd tossed into the recycling bin when I organized all of these in the first place yesterday.

I did toss it, didn't I?

And was that only yesterday? Christ, I'm living one exasperating existence, aren't I?

I move the coffee mug off the top, and there's my girl: the eyes of a freshly born star, hair like the Black Stallion's shimmering tail, and the kind of mouth that produces the sort of quality filth you'd never believe. She once told me to go down on her like she's "Day-old Jell-O salad at a coronation parade." Now, maybe I don't fully comprehend that phrase, but I still think it's the dirtiest thing I've ever heard. And the intention was nice.

I take the pile into my hand, and give the resumes a flip though; counting them as I work my way to the bottom. Twenty-one. Yep, one more than I had here yesterday.

But still, I passive-aggressively mention: "Hey, Glenn. This pile of resumes here—if I had to estimate, it looks as though there's one too many. Didn't you ask for twenty?"

"Is there not twenty there?" he says, perhaps a tad more passive-aggressively than me.

"Hey, I've won thirteen different guess-the-number-of-jellybeans-in-the-mason-jar contests in my life, so I feel like I've got a pretty good track record." Holding up Melissa's resume, I give her a healthy shake. I can still smell the ink from the Deutsche Bank photocopy machine we made out at on our lunch break. "But I thought I trashed this one?"

He squints from across the room, trying to recognize the headshot. "Beats me. Maybe you *thought* you did, but subconsciously you wanted the girl to audition? She's got that look though, doesn't she?"

Yep: eyes, hair, mouth. Trust me. I know.

"I guess we'll just have twenty-one auditions for the part," he says, sort of being dismissive about it all. "Don't worry about it."

"Consider it not worried about," I gleefully confirm, barely under my breath. I decline to tell him that I'd know for certain whether or not it was me who called Melissa.

Glenn actually whistles to himself as he exits the office. Who whistles to themselves anymore? Possibly just lewd construction workers, serial killers, weirdo college roommates, and all people over the age of Seventy. I'm not yet fully committed to ruling out the possibility that Glenn Workman is a serial killer — *All signs pointing to the singularity of sex addiction* — but the whistling still raises a few questionable red flags.

Yep, I am definitely going to pop-in to the Deutsche Bank once I'm done here. Maybe I'll ask Melissa to audition for the play? Maybe this will be the thing that brings us together? Maybe I'll treat her to a nice ten-dollar dinner, split two ways. And maybe I'll even tell her I love her?

Maybe don't get too far ahead of yourself, Chester K. Eddy.

How Many Fights Can I Pick in Thirty-Four Minutes? Place Your Bets

TBH, I get caught up watching YouTube videos of people — *Likely doctors, but in a lot of cases, likely not* — squeezing pimples and popping cysts. It's incredible the amount and variety of puss, blood, juices, and gases that can come out of the human body, from these strange little alien bumps and sacs. The videos where they pull super-long ingrown hairs out, unreeling them like a firehose off one of those big spools, are like found money. I once knew a guy in college named Melvin Blackhead who had pimples all over his face, and I tried my absolute hardest to come up with a joke he'd likely never heard before. I couldn't do it though, which at first had me assuming it was a sign of my sweetness and innocence coming to the forefront, but then Melvin started seeing some disgusting chick named Tiff Whitehead and I just couldn't stop myself. I brutally lambasted the two of them, verbally blasting the vilest of shit from a megaphone while standing in the snow beneath Melvin's dormitory.

Was this a story about growth? I'd better get back to that.

As I approach the ominous 60 Wall Street building — *Quick, take a guess what the address might be* — home of the Deutsche Bank, with a satchel full of supplies I've earned from my adventure so far, I get a feeling: that this is my righteous moment. In terms of stages within The Hero's Journey, I'd say I'm snuggled right in there between Apotheosis (the *Armed with New Knowledge* stage) and The Ultimate Boon (the *Finally Getting the Shit I Want* stage — if I remember my Joey Campbell studies correctly). My quest is nearing its end! I just need to get inside that building, find Melissa, and tell her everything.

Then I've won, right?

Though maybe this is more like a video game; one of those classic side-scrolling dungeon crawl numbers where the levels are really just all the same garbage over and over again, until you finally get to Boss Level: the same garbage again but with a bigger version of one of the dudes you fought earlier. And this time it requires some stupid, non-intuitive trick to beat. Either that, or you just keep hitting it a LOT.

Let's go with the video game analogy; it feels less like post-secondary studies. But first—that smell...is that waffles?

LEVEL I
THE NECKBEARD

You've got to be kidding me. There's a fucking *Wafels & Dinges* truck outside the Deutsche Bank now? This sure as hell wasn't here before I got fired; I could have been eating waffles dunked in Belgian chocolate fudge every day for lunch?

And why has Melissa chosen to withhold this information from me? Probably The Boyfriend's fault, right? He wants to keep waffles from me too, doesn't he? That guy is really starting to stick in my craw.

I ask how much it is for a waffle and the dude in the truck looks at me like I just called his mother a raging whore. It doesn't seem to take much to set off people working on Wall Street. Even if they're just running a food truck. He points a meaty finger above him and says, "What, you can't read the menu?"

"Of course I can read. I just presumed — perhaps incorrectly — that you might have intimate product knowledge here."

"And I presume people can read. So, who's the more presumptuous?"

I stop myself. "You know what, I don't even want to argue with you right now." The worst thing I can do is pop in on Melissa while I'm in a bad mood. I look up at the menu. Who the hell knew there were so many different options for street waffles; and toppings for said street waffles.

And then he goes and interrupts my focus: "Would you hurry it up, pal?"

Blow it off, Chester. You don't want to get all worked up by some street vendor who probably flunked out of culinary school. It's not worth the argument! Let it go.

I don't even turn back to him; just keep my eyes on the menu. *You've got this, Chester!*

"I could be reading my damn book here," he says, flapping something around in my peripheral.

But I still don't say a word. *Give me a C! Give me an H! Give me a—*

"It's not hard," he badgers. "You pick a picture you like and read the big number beside it. It ain't fucking rocket science."

Okay. Fuck it. I throw eye daggers at him, like I'm Dwayne Johnson with evil wizard powers. "Hey, if you'd just told me how much it was for a waffle in the first place, we wouldn't be in this bit of a social pickle, now would we?"

"You know what? I don't even care anymore."

"I'd be willing to bet you *never* cared."

"I'm closing up shop for the night, pal."

"Who are you, the King of fucking Belgium? You've got product and I'm a paying customer."

"Belgium doesn't even have a king."

"Belgium does so have a king! It's a monarchy!"

"They've got a president, fuckwad."

"Oh, my Christ! Your fat ass is sitting in a food truck selling Belgian waffles, and you don't even know that the country you represent is a constitutional monarchy!"

"I represent America!"

"The only thing you're representing right now is the uneducated, knuckle-dragging, unindustrious, choad-chomping, neckbearded shitbags of America! Which is likely still a pretty large assemblage, so good on you!"

He slams the window gate down without a word, and for some reason, not caring at all that his napkin dispenser and box of plastic forks are still outside.

Well, that wasn't exactly my finest display of maintaining the cool.

Somebody on the sidewalk yells out, "What did the waffle guy do to you, asshole?"

"All I wanted was a waffle!"

"So, you call him a neckbearded shitbag? Classy."

"Hey, HE started it!"

"Real mature," he says, walking away. "Nice pants, by the way."

I thought people were supposed to like sailors?

I really don't have an argument left in me — *Have no fear, it's nothing an 11-floor elevator ride won't soon fix* — so I simply grab up all of the plastic forks and the napkin dispenser and add them to my satchel's growing inventory. And I'm officially calling that a win.

LEVEL II
THE GAY-PLUS GATEKEEPER

The building security requires you to show your ID, but Ryan is the same guard who worked here when I did. And good ol' dumbass Ryan is the same guy who sold me naked pictures of his girlfriend eight months ago, so we're still good. He lets me go on up to the 11th Floor, where things seem suspiciously quiet. But it's like six o'clock right now — *I remember Melissa and I bolting out of here every day as early as possible, always trying to break our own record* — so I shouldn't be all that surprised by the metaphorical tumbleweeds blowing by.

There's a new receptionist here, much hotter than the previous one, but she could probably cut it out on the lipstick and the hand jewelry a tad. I tell her I'm here to see Melissa, only to be informed Mel's already left for the night.

"Are you serious?" I ask, for no reason other than I seem to enjoy creating all-new — *and hilariously inappropriate, I might add* — confrontations with total strangers.

Her eyes dart around a little, though I can't tell if she's following an insect or trying to avoid eye contact with me. "Why would I joke about something like that?" She goes back to clacking on her keyboard. I can see she's typing a message to someone.

"Did Melissa say where she was going?"

"Nope. Home, I assume." The wooden nameplate on the desk only says H. MCCOSKEY; all in capital letters. My cubicle here had *chester e.* on it — *not in caps* — so I wonder where the discrepancy must have come from. Plus, shouldn't the first *C* in McCoskey at least be lower case? There must be someone with an English major around here, or a graphic designer at the very least, who has a say in these kinds of things.

I'm so thrown off by this friggin' nameplate, I don't immediately register her answering me. "What's that?" I ask.

"I said she went home. Like, ten minutes ago," H. MCCOSKEY repeats while typing something else.

Ten minutes ago? Melissa probably walked right out the door while I was arguing with the Waffle Nazi, and didn't even see me outside. "Did she leave with anyone? Did anyone pick her up? Like a boyfriend type of anyone?"

"Believe it or not dude, not all of us girls talk to each to other about everything," she says. "And to be honest, I don't even like her that much."

"You don't even—? What the hell are you talking about? *Everybody* likes Mel."

She gives me one of those faces, like I've just blasted some F-bombs in church.

"I challenge you to find a single reason to *not* like Melissa."

"I mean, she's kind of a bitch for one thing. Don't you think?"

"You take that back!"

Finally, she turns to look right at me. "Who are *you*, anyway?"

"Listen here, young lady." *Jesus. Did I really just sound like my grandpa right now?* "First of all, I'm still a little riled up from a slight disagreement with a waffle vendor outside. And secondly, it's very rude to be Facebooking with someone else while I'm here trying to ask you things of extreme, and utmost importance."

"You're not really asking me anything important, though."

"You could fake *some* interest, at the very least."

"So, *who* are you again?"

"Chester K. Eddy. I used to work here."

"Wait. Are you the guy who got fired for downloading gay porn on your computer?"

"Hey, there was *normal* porn too!"

"Are you saying gay isn't normal?"

"That is NOT what I meant. You're putting words in my mouth. I'm a champion of the LGBT Community."

"It's LGBT+ now, you know."

"*Plus?* What the hell does that even mean?"

"Well, the acronym keeps having new letters added. At the moment, it's up to LGBTQQIAAP. Stands for 'Lesbian Gay Bisexual Transgender Queer Questioning Intersex Allies Asexual Pansexual Community.' But they've just shortened it with a *Plus*. LGBT+."

"Why not just call it LG+? Or just Gay-Plus? That sounds pretty good, actually. I'm going to start calling it Gay-Plus from now on."

"Listen, I'm not going to get into a whole thing with you here. But you're not allowed to just make up new acronyms for recognized institutions. That's not for you to decide."

Amidst a sleeve of tattoos on her left arm, I notice a small, black triangle of ink on the inside of her wrist: a surefire sign of lesbianism. Either that, or it's hip these days to intentionally get paradoxical symbols tattooed on your body in order to confuse the general populace. Could be; I'm really not hip enough to know otherwise. The hippest thing I've done lately was watch all nine seasons of *Scrubs*. Why does everyone hate Zach Braff so much?

I dismiss her with a wave of my hand. "These things are all getting way too complicated," I say. And then I quickly downshift into Pleading Mode. "Come on. I took a train all the way from the Upper West Side down here to Wall Street; the very least you could do is let me leave a note on Melissa's desk for her."

H. MCCOSKEY writes something else now; giggling a little to herself with eyes all aglow. With my sharp, junior detective skills and jungle-panthery, hunter-like senses I notice her type 'SHIFT+' into her message.

"You're telling your friend there about Gay-Plus, aren't you? You're gonna start using *my* new terminology, and take credit for it, right? Then I bet you'll go and slip it into your spoken word poetry at the speakeasy."

"No, I'm just telling my girlfriend about how this guy at my desk right now doesn't know shit about us or our feelings."

"Oh, that's wonderful. 'Cause obviously *I'm* the bad guy here, right? If you think you can make me feel bad for coming up with a better buzzword than you, then you and the dyke parade best think again. Do they still have speakeasies, by the way?"

"Dyke is a derogatory term. Unless you're self-identifying."

"That is totally un-fucking-fair!"

She chooses to ignore me now, and continues her online chatting.

"Hey, I get it. You want to hate on men? You want to have casual sex? You want to wear loose clothing? You don't want to shave your legs and arm-pits? You want to wear a bikini when you're seventy and your body's all wrinkles and flab and faded tattoos and other signs of bad mistakes? Great! That's your choice as a woman. That's your own identity. Roar, goddammit, roar! But do not, I repeat: DO NOT give me the burdened and persecuted sob story. I mean, Rosie O'Donnell's certainly got it harder than you, but I'm trying to be unbiased here." For all the shit I say about Rosie O'Donnell, I think that if I actually met her one day, I'd probably only ask for her autograph. *Exit to Eden*, any*one? Hello.*

Now she picks up her laptop and swivels away from me in her chair, but I can see that her camera light is on. I also spot the words "SAILOR PANTS" — *Yes, in All-Caps.*

I wave nonchalantly to her unseen partner, then lean in closer so she can see me better. Because that's *just* what she wants. "What's really not fair, ladies, is how you're treating *ME*; some poor schmuck who's just trying to stay afloat and keep his head above the surface of proper social cues and conduct."

H. MCCOSKEY giggles a little.

"Also, since we're here, I'd like to take note of the fact that gay women get to use the 'gay' or 'lesbian' tag, while men only get 'gay'. There's your inequality right there."

She continues to ignore me in favor of more snorting, chortling, and keyboard clacking.

"I'll also have you know that, as an actor, I've played a handful of gay characters in my time. Two handfuls, actually. Lots of lispy accents, you know? I'll bet you didn't know that Doctor Lauchlan Twindler, disgraced Manhattan ear, nose, and throat specialist was secretly gay, did you? I'm practically type-cast, which may or may not be saying an awful lot about my masculinity right now."

Still nothing.

"Aw, fuck it." I dig a small, crusty booger from my nostril and flick it at the computer screen. And just like it would do in a movie, for maximum effect, it hits the little camera directly before bouncing off into H. MCCOSKEY's rainbow coffee mug, of which is likely filled with some new age herbal tea that can only be pronounced in clicks, and a squirt of feminist cocktail.

How's that for proper social cues and conduct?

LEVEL III
THE BIGFOOT SIGHTING

Not sure why they've got that girl at reception, since I managed to simply walk away from H. MCCOSKEY without her even noticing. Right back into the old office.

Though maybe she was just happy I left? Hmm. Could be.

There are still a few schmucks wrapping up around here (ie: downing their hidden caches of scotch, deleting their cookies — *Sure wish I'd known how to delete cookies when I was here. Wait, what does cookie-deletion actually do? Anyone?* — and leaving obvious traces of purposefully-unfinished work on their desks so their morning supervisors think balls are being sufficiently busted around here).

I pass my old cubicle and there's some disheveled dude there with a cast on his foot, trying to get his crutches nestled comfortably into his armpits. Stumbling and bashing his shoulders and wrists into cubicles, he looks like a baby flamingo attempting first steps. His name slate reads, simply: LESTER. Dude doesn't even get a last initial. Another editing discrepancy. It's completely appalling! Does no one care about professional consistency and proper office synergy anymore?

I crank the palsy-walsy up to eleven and dive right in: "Lester! What's up? You're not heading home already, are you?"

He's also got what I would refer to as a Molester Mustache. *Yeah, you know EXACTLY what that looks like.* "Excuse me? Do I know you?"

"Do you *know* me? What the hell, bro? When you broke that foot, who was the first one to run over to help?"

"My dad was, actually."

"Are you sure you weren't just hoodwinked by the all-too-natural fatherly vibe I've got going on? It wouldn't be the first time."

"So, *who* are you?"

"Chester K. Eddy. I used to work here." I tap the desktop gently with my hand. "Right at this very desk, as a matter of fact."

"You're the guy who got fired for downloading porn on your computer, aren't you?"

"That's me!" Man, I must be some sort of epic legend around here. I don't bother asking Lester if he can either confirm or deny that statement. *Let me have my moment!*

"The legend himself," Lester smirks. *See? Hot damn!* "Some people around here say you're like Bigfoot—" *Darn right, they do.* "—You know, 'cause Bigfoot doesn't know dick-all about society and runs around the woods naked, shitting and jerking off into rotted tree stumps."

"I'd say that's a pretty unfair comparison." *Nearly accurate, but still unfair.*

"And this desk wasn't *yours*, by the by. I requested it be removed and hosed off or turned into wood chips."

"You don't make wood chips out of MDF core and laminate, dipshit." *Here we go again. I'd say buckle yourself in, but you've probably already jumped from this moving vehicle by now.* "And, *BY THE BY?* Who are you, Geoffrey Chaucer?"

He mocks me with one of those classic high school *Lookit-me-I'm-imitating-a-big-dumb-nerd* faces. "Oh yes. Just let me pen some texts about the Middle Ages over here. Can someone pass The Canterbury Tales?"

I want to kick those crutches right out from under this guy. But I don't, and I probably would have two months ago, so there's some more growth for you. My growth is coming fast and hard. That's right, you can put that on a t-shirt. Do people still put things on t-shirts? I mean, as it is, you can buy pretty much anything you want, as you want it these days. Why make more work for yourself?

He asks, "So what *ARE* you doing here, Bigfoot?"

I point at Mel's desk with my chin. "I came to see Melissa. But I've been informed she left already."

"And yet you're still here."

"How very observant of you. I thought I'd be the proper rogue gentleman and leave a weensy love note on her desk. Hey, can I use *weensy* without the *teensy*, or do they have to be paired up? I don't see why they can't be mutually exclusive."

His eyes become serpentine slivers; hands grip the crutches a little tighter. Molester Mustache twitches slightly. "A love note?"

"You don't mind, do you?"

"Me? Nah. But I don't know if her boyfriend would be so blasé about it."

"Jack?"

"Or whatever his name is. You just missed him too. Came by to pick Melissa up."

I don't think I was ever one hundred percent believing Jack was a fictional character, but I was also not entirely convinced otherwise. No doubt, there was a part of me that wanted to assume Mel was merely pulling my leg; that she secretly loved me in return, and was also too chickenshit to admit it.

But the best women are the ones you need to win over, aren't they? If the Hallmark Channel taught us anything, it's that the perfect girl (in Hallmark's case, one of those *Party of Five* girls who couldn't find any other work) doesn't simply fall into your lap. She's not waiting for you; you've got to find *her*. And work that shit.

I sniff at the air, like some creepy-ass, secret-alien-on-Earth private investigator from any series on the Space Channel you keep hearing is good but it really just looks like the worst show ever created.

Side note: Here's what I would do, if I could do anything I wanted. I would seriously buy the Hallmark and Space networks and amalgamate every series and movie on there into just one single show and then fire it off to North Korea and see if that won't make them realize the U S of A is totally not worth even a microsecond of their time. I'd be an American hero!

The sniffing around for clues is getting me nowhere however, so I try a different approach to getting the information I want out of Lester. "I'm sorry, but before I so rudely interrupted you, I believe you were saying something about what this boyfriend looks like?"

"No, I wasn't. And you didn't interrupt me, you were just sniffing like you've got a drug problem."

"Well, maybe you could amuse me, Lester. Would you say he's bigger than me?"

"About the same size, I'd guess."

"Good to know." Not very helpful though, as it's highly unlikely I'd be proficient enough to take someone my own size in a fistfight, if things came to blows, that is. "Handsome?"

"Would Melissa be seeing someone who wasn't?"

"Of course she wouldn't. Let's move on to the wardrobe then. Where might he land on the d-bag scale? If a ONE is what your grandfather was buried in and a TEN is an Ed Hardy shirt."

"He really seems like more of a sweater vest and chinos guy."

"Chinos? Like he's in a GAP ad from 1995?"

"Pretty much."

"That's appalling. Is his hair on point? Can I at least assume it's trendier than mine?"

Lester tilts his head, trying to gauge if I've chosen to follow a trend that wasn't merely something inspired by a condom poster above the men's room urinal.

But he doesn't have time to say anything on the matter before I blurt out, "Hey. I've been nearly homeless for two days now. When am I gonna find time to style this mop?"

"Define *nearly*."

"Basically."

"So, literally."

"Yes, I'm literally homeless. Why you gotta be so judgmental, Lester? I don't think I've ever met anyone so judgmental before, man. I mean, it's not like I'm rocking a rat tail or anything."

"Maybe you *should* be."

"Come again?"

"You might have a better chance with Melissa. I mean, she must be into that. Why else would her boyfriend have a ponytail?"

"A ponytail?"

"Yep."

"Jesus."

"That's what I thought too. Though maybe it is more of a rat tail, now that you mention it."

Stop me if I've used this one before, but:

Oh.

My.

God.

Shitting.

Gods.

A cold, clammy sweat immediately hits me, and this is exactly when my stomach chooses to punish me for being in love with my best friend. My own stomach! *How could you do this to me, pal? After all the good shit — Not counting the last three days — I've done for you?*

So anyway, I'm calling it a victory due to the fact that even though I vomit up *something* from my insides — *It looks like watered-down tapioca pudding with Rice Krispies and chili flakes in it, if a visual description is warranted* — I *did* however manage to get some on Lester's feet. Onto the one foot in the cast with toes exposed, and the other that's wearing what appears to be a vegan Doc Marten. So, bonus.

LEVEL IV
IN THE BOWELS

As if sitting on the porcelain throne and wondering exactly what the hell it is that's blowing out of your ass isn't bad enough, try doing it while also considering the fact your lady love is actually diddling your new boss, and a sexaholic with a rat tail to boot.

Glenn even told me earlier that he was in love with someone who wasn't his wife. And of course, I also recall seeing Melissa's resume back on the audition stack, after I was certain I'd tossed it out. It makes so much more sense now.

It's all coming together, just like a good Scooby Doo mystery. But more Daphne and less Scrappy Doo, if you please.

Call it good timing, good fortune, or good ol' divine intervention, but pretty much the exact second in which Mr. Lester McDoucheCrutches — *Hey, that's good; I'll have to go back and use that one as soon as I'm done here* — told me that juicy nugget about The Boyfriend, something in my bowels immediately tried to kill me. I bolted for the bathroom so fast I think I ended up in the women's room by accident. I mean, there's even fresh flowers beside the sink in here. Smells like there's some fancy soap in these dispensers, too.

I'm fairly confident I managed to keep everything in before my ass hit the toilet seat, but something tells me these Silver Surfer boxers are not long for this world. If I remember my Marvel Comics lore correctly, the Sentinel of the Spaceways' appearance heralded the imminent destruction of all that's holy by some massive planet devourer who liked wearing really tall, weird-ass helmets.

So, in the spirit of Norrin Radd, the Silver Surfer, I really should have seen this coming.

But I didn't, and now I'm sweating profusely — *That awful, cold, clammy sweat, not the fun orgasm variety* — and gripping this bar on the wall awkwardly and unconfidently because I'm not completely certain what orifice I'm about to unload out of next. I must have ducked into the handicapped stall, now that I think of it, since us regular schmucks aren't so lucky to have one of these bars. Sometimes I think I'd like a bar to grab onto as well. Is that so much to ask? I'm working just as hard in here as they would be. Likely even harder though, since I'm not the one who's paralyzed from the waist down. Christ, why is the grip on this metal bar rubbed down so much? What are these chicks doing in here? Maybe I'm not working nearly as hard.

Conveniently, my brain is now choosing this time to realize I didn't bring my bag into the bathroom with me; it's probably still out there on one of the cubicles. Fuck.

I can't recall anything questionable I might have eaten earlier — *Though a steady, three-day consumption of coffee and booze is likely not the ideal diet* — but if I'd actually gotten a waffle from that neckbeard waffle guy, I'd definitely place the blame there. Screw it. I'm going to blame him anyway.

One final burning burst of something rotten later, I give myself a courtesy flush and reach for some TP.

And there's no toilet paper. Of course there isn't. Because that's just how my Wednesday is going, isn't it? I'd use some of the napkins I stole from the waffle truck — *Because that would be so awesome in a totally serendipitous way, now wouldn't it? Though something tells me our protagonist has not been written with that kind luck and fortune on his side* — but again: no bag here.

To top it off, my moment of utter futility is suddenly broken — *nay, wholly annihilated* — by the worst sound I can think of.

You know, for maximum impact, this might be a good time for another quality Top-Three List. Okay. My Top-Three Favorite Sounds to Hear from the Other Side of a Wall:

#3: Roaring applause (ideally after my character has just exited the stage, and I've knocked the audience dead with my bang-on performance of Snooks Keene in the revival production of *Moose*

Murders)

#2: The crying of just-dumped twenty-somethings (I can't count the number of times I've had through-the-wall conversations with girls who've just been left in a tear-filled, ugly-crying heap by their boyfriends. Okay, it was only the one time, but that was some honest-to-goodness vulnerability we shared that night)

#1: Sex, any kind (a no-brainer)

Alternatively, my Top-Three *Least* Favorite Sounds to Hear from the Other Side of a Wall:

#3: My parents discussing my career prospects and educational future (they both seemed to agree I was a lost cause, but seemed to want to argue about it anyway)

#2: Melissa taking a call from The Boyfriend less than two minutes after I had my penis inside her (I don't know; call me old fashioned, but that just seems rude)

#1: The squeaky wheels of a wheelchair entering the bathroom while I'm in the handicapped stall with shit running down my leg and no toilet paper on hand (of course, this is what's happening right now. *Keep it coming, Wednesday. Don't let up on me now*)

There's a lot of mumbling and swearing under the breath — *in addition to my own mumbling and swearing, just to be clear* — as this incoming wheelchair inches closer and closer to my hiding spot. Sometimes you don't have to look: you can just sense by the way the air is moving, the way it's being displaced around a room, that an approaching body is extremely, morbidly,

Kirstie-Alley-On-A-Good-Day obese. The No-More-Please-For-The-Love-Of-God bending of wheelchair metal is a dead giveaway too. This handicapped behemoth parks her chair directly in front of my stall and, after sucking in air like an eighty-foot blue whale consumes helpless krill, she says, "How long you gonna be in there, love?"

Love? Like anyone could have any reciprocal compassion for this wandering Death Star on wheels.

I very nearly blurt out a "Calm yo tits, bitch!" but I'm quick to remember we're in the ladies' room. Where are my ladylike manners? Also, not sure if I could pass off my deep voice as feminine. Though if I *was* severely handicapped, could my extremely-masculine-thank-you-very-much vocal cords not just be a side effect of my handicapped-ness? Perhaps not enough on its own to score me a free pass into the disabled stall, but maybe I've got more than one handicap?

Anyway, instead of saying anything, I opt to act my way out if this. I'm an actor, remember? I know it hasn't factored too much into this story so far, but now's my moment to shine! *Get into that spotlight, Chester! You've got this.*

So rather than answering directly and respectfully like any reasonable person trying to acclimate to society, I simply grunt out a series of very untactful yelps relating to severe, abdominal discomfort. But to be honest, I truly believe if this *was* for an audition — *Say, either for constipation cream or anal leakage diapers* — I would have totally nailed it. Totally.

ME: "Ungh! Herrrgh! Huuurrrrffffch!"

ANAL LEAKAGE DIAPERS DIRECTOR (*Who's Very Nearly Given Up on Making It Big with His Artsy Jim Jarmusch Rip-Off Films*): "Where has *this* man been hiding? It's the second coming of Sean

Penn! Post-*She's So Lovely* but pre-*Hey, I'm a novelist!* Sean Penn, that is."

And...scene!

A few quick raps on the stall door, and she asks: "Things all right in there?" I can very nearly feel the salvo of saliva, spitting from her mouth hole, and bulleting against the door.

Still, I continue to choose grunting over polite human contact, prompting this person to apparently opt for trying to get into the next-biggest stall in the bathroom, one which was certainly *not* designed for bodies the size of small moons, much less in wheelchairs too. And I'm not averse to admit that I imagine the whole procedure is likely quite comical. So, what do I do? Naturally, I pull out my phone and try and get a picture, of course. Melissa would slap me if she heard about this incredible situation I've found myself in and I *didn't* get a picture as photographic evidence.

I have to be super careful though — *tactful, one might even say* — and make sure my phone's on silent and the shutter sound is off. Done and done.

This is going to be classic.

So classic.

Reaching my phone down under the stall door, I can nearly see the image on the viewer: but it's like a solar eclipse in the bathroom lights, or like when they want to show you just how enormous Godzilla is and you only get a glimpse of a big, scaly, green leg appearing from behind the Flatiron building and stepping on a tour bus, bits of bodies being squeezed out of the windows and onto 5th Avenue.

Whatever. I'll snap a few in succession real quick, and hope there's a nugget in there somewhere.

So, ready...set...and...

The flash goes off. "Shit!" I yelp.

I panic, and my thumb presses down on the *Snap Photo* button hard enough to set it off multiple times now. "ShitshitshitshitshitshittySHIT!" I'm lighting up the bathroom like I'm a tunnel rat blowing my cover in the Vietcong. *I don't even know what that means. Man, I'm so panicked, even my metaphors are freaking out here.*

There's some indecipherable yelling, and meaty fists slamming against the bathroom stall, like I've just enraged Sloth from *The Goonies*.

The stall door bursts open now; her arms — *likely jacked to Carrot Top proportions from having to self-propel her ass around town* — nearly peel it from the hinges.

What else is there to do at this point but jump off the toilet and bolt from this handicapped stall and out of the women's room with shit on my leg and my sailor pants and Silver Surfer undies down around my ankles? *In the most grown-up and respectful way, of course.*

Well, yeah. That goes without saying.

But I've been sitting on the crapper so long now my legs have gone numb and fallen asleep, so the moment I stand up is also the very same moment I hit the tiled floor face-first.

This has turned into a classic moment all right. As in, a totally classic Chester K. Eddy moment.

My only saving grace is that I — *though malnourished, hungover, teetering on the edge of consciousness, and mostly inactive for the majority of my adult life* — am still slightly more mobile than the bride of Jabba here. I hike up my pants, peel myself off the floor, and burst out of the women's room. For some reason, I'm also screaming, "Hey, I'm handicapped too, you know!"

I only catch sight of this beast in my peripheral, but it's no less terrifying. She's still screaming bloody murder and likely reaching for the rapist spray buried within fat folds. Someone once told me there's a rapist somewhere out there for all of us, but sometimes people are wrong. *Come on, rapists: hands up if this is for you. I didn't think so.*

In my head though, as I'm scrambling for freedom, all I'm hearing is the last words my brother said to me when he kicked me out of his apartment: *"You're an idiot, Chester. And it's about time you start figuring out how to function on your own."*

I should really call my brother back, shouldn't I? I think he'd really be impressed by exactly how much I've gotten my shit together.

Ace Eddy scores again.

The BOSS Level (Dick Butt vs Robot)

TBH, women have to put up with a lot of annoying shit. If I was a woman, I'd totally wrap toilet paper around the inside of my pants instead of using a pad. And I'd put fresh makeup over yesterday's makeup so I wouldn't have to wash the old stuff off. That seems like a bitch of a hassle.

Okay.

Let's try to put most of what just happened behind us. I mean seriously, if this *was* a video game, I would have chucked the controller against a wall long ago. Remember when controllers used to be connected to the game stations with a cord? You ever try chucking one of those, forgetting it's only got so much slack, and then it springs back at you before it even connects with the wall?

Anyway. Mr. Lester McDoucheCrutches is nowhere to be seen when I get back to Melissa's desk. Probably still in the men's room washing vomit off of himself; trying to get in under that cast to get his foot clean. Turns out I *did* leave my bag here, which is definitely something positive. The best thing I can think of doing is leaving a note behind for Mel. I grab a bottle of Wite-Out from her desk supplies (always kept immaculately tidy and sorted) and then decide what to write my special note on.

I've got it! I even yell out 'Eureka!' which I'm certain no one outside of Jimmy Stewart movies has ever yelled out loud before. From my satchel, I pull out the Zen garden rock I swiped from The Hotel Kitano. Looking at it now, it even appears sort of heart-shaped. So, I'd say this is a pretty fucking special sentiment I've got happening here.

I work out in my head what I plan on writing, accounting for the size of the rock and the thickness of the Wite-Out brush tip, and I come up with:

I'M A
DICK BUT THE
TRUTH IS THAT
I LOVE
YOU.

I don't know; period at the end or no period? I'm always confused as to what might constitute a sentence and what's simply a note. Also, should I be calling it a *full-stop*? I've heard full stop is technically more accurate, but that's only from those annoying jerks who think they know everything and just *looooove* correcting you.

Screw it. It's a period, and I'm fucking putting one on there.

But I don't get my note finished because I'm rudely interrupted again. *Again!* And this time it's a doozy. It's her. The Brainless Office Shit Supervisor herself: BOSS.

I've done it. I've made it to the BOSS Level! She's just as I remember her: a tall giantess (maybe six-three?) with the big Elaine Benes hairstyle, the Botoxed lips, the dead-black mole sitting right in her sorta-mannish chin cleft, the printed scarf around her neck from the Alicia Silverstone *Hang Yourself with an Endangered Animal Collection*, and the too-tight, Wall Street power suit pants that never fail to show off a little VPL.

She smells like a fresh magazine too, but not the kind with perfume samples inside; it's more like *Modern Dog*.

Confession time: four times a year I get giddy at the newspaper stand, waiting for the Cuban guy in the Bart Simpson *Don't Have A Cow, Man!* hat to put out the new issue of *Modern Dog* because the cover blurbs on that magazine are THE BEST.

Like: *"Need New Apps for Your Dog?"*

Or: *"Why Does He Keep Licking That? (And Should He Keep Going?)"*

And let's not forget the classic: *"Gimme Some Yum-Yums!"*

This world is officially totally insane.

Also, sub-confession time: does it count as loitering if I'm not actually taking the magazine into hand and flipping through it? 'Cause the Cuban guy with the Bart Simpson hat has a propensity for whacking me with a broomstick every time and yelling/spitting "No Loitering!" in my face. I mean, I only ever look at the cover, which he's *already* displaying. I'm just saying. I think I win on a technicality.

What was I talking about here?

So, smell aside, don't get me wrong: BOSS isn't too hard on the senses; she's actually sorta sexy. But an ugly personality will always put a damper on pornstar lips. I don't care what anyone says. You can quote me on that.

"Chester K. Eddy. So wonderful to see you again."

I literally cannot tell if she's being sarcastic or not. I mean, in many ways, yes it *would* be nice to see me again, I'd imagine. Obviously. I get that. However, under *these* circumstances — *Being here after hours, stealing office supplies to write love notes on stolen hotel rocks, and, oh yeah, I don't actually work here anymore because I was fired for, well, I don't really have to go over the Why's one more time, do I? Seems fairly unnecessary* — it doesn't feel so obvious. Maybe she *is* happy to see me?

"What brings your horny little pimply-bonered ass back here, Mister

Eddy? Popping in to take a jump on that trampoline of yours?"

Scratch that. She is most definitely *not* happy to have me here. "First of all, BOSS, is '*trampoline*' meant to be some sort of sexual metaphor, you know, like the town-bike one we've all heard a million times?"

Pause. "And second of all?"

"I never really had a second of all. No, wait! *Pimply-bonered ass?* That doesn't make any sense when you think about it. Do I have boners on my ass? 'Cause that would be gross. AND mostly uncomfortable."

"Amusing," she says in her least-amused tone. She motions to the rock in my hand now. "Were you going to toss that through my office window? Perhaps smash up some equipment around here?"

I look at the rock in my hand, and all I'd managed to spell in white correction fluid was:

I'M A
DICK BUT T

Yeah. I am a real dick butt sometimes, aren't I?

"It's a rock from a Zen garden, not a fucking grenade. If I was going to burst in here all Bruce Willis *Die Hard* style — *Remember when he had hair? That was weird, wasn't it?* — I'd bring a hell of a lot more ammunition than a rock."

"Well, that doesn't sound very Zen of you, now does it?"

Move along, Chester. Move along. When have you ever won an argument with BOSS? Maybe that one time when you convinced her your sorta famous brother might be willing to put his face on a twice-a-week newspaper advertisement for the Deutsche Bank? But that's likely it. "You seem relaxed," I tell her. "Your skin looks cleaner. I heard you were away on vacation?" *There you go. That's better. Start a nice, buoyant conversation regarding her health and well-being. Everybody gets off on attention like that.*

"You heard I was away? You two must have better things to talk about than *me*, don't you?"

"We really don't. You are our everything." I think if I actually ran into a bear in the woods, I would totally poke the shit out of it.

"Amusing," she repeats. That's twice now she's said *Amusing*. I don't recall that ever being a saying of hers. Maybe she's been in for a vocabulary upgrade. "It wasn't so much a vacation, however. I had business in Tennessee. Still, I feel recharged and I have absolutely no desire to be pissy with you right now."

"And yet you continue to be." Did she just say she's *recharged?* As in, there's some real robotty-type stuff going on around here? My brain wants to rattle off a list of tech startups in Tennessee in order to deduce her exact whereabouts, but then my brain realizes I don't exactly follow current tech company trends. Or any trends, unless celebrity death rates count. "Tennessee? Doesn't that place have a lot of Pentecostal churches?"

"Believe it or not, I wasn't actually there for the church scene."

"Those are the ones with all the snakes, right?"

"Again, I really don't—"

"It's supposed to be good luck if they bite you. I think that's how it works. Still, seems pretty stupid to me."

"Please stop talking about church snakes."

"Well, you certainly *do* sound more imperturbable than I remember. Though you also do still sound a bit like a computer program, if you don't mind me saying. You know, one of those digital voice recorder thingies that can read your writing out loud for you, but you only use it so you can hear your computer say stuff like '*boobies*' and '*stinky dinky*.'"

She stands a little more upright, a bit more stiff. Just like a robot would do. "Are you saying I'm a robot?"

"Are you *admitting* you're a robot?"

"I made no such comment."

"Quick, what's the first thing you think of when I say: *5-3-1-8-0-0-8?*"

"I'm mostly thinking how happy I am that I had them clean out your desk."

"Wrong! Punch that into your digital calculator, then turn it upside down. That's *BOOBIES* spelled in numbers."

"You're a twenty-something, shit-disturbing moron who thinks about boobies a lot. Amusing."

"For the record, I'm thirty-two."

"Oh, Christ. Do you realize the number of things I could have people do to you, Mister Eddy? This is private property. And you're trespassing."

"I'll admit that while there is a part of me — *that unfeeling, masochistic, glutton for punishment part of me that's rearing its ugly head more and more often lately* — that's interested in hearing the finer details of said threats, I was really just about to mosey on out of here. To be honest, I only came here to find Melissa, and it appears as though I've just missed her. So, if you don't mind, I'm just gonna leave this here note behind and be on my merry way."

She sneers judgmentally at the Wite-Out-smeared rock in my hand again. Evil shimmering within robot eyes. Optic receptors, I think they're properly called. Assuming she's a robot, right? *Listen, Melissa and I put a lot of time and energy into our robot theory, so I'm just not ready to start debunking it yet.*

Aside from *Being A Robot*, here are my Top-Three Reasonably-Justified Assumptions I Have About BOSS:

#3: She's still looking around the office for her lost vintage Bionic Woman melamine cereal bowl (But she'll never find it 'cause Mel and I catapulted it off the roof of the Deutsche Bank on our lunch break; that thing is probably bobbing in the flotsam and jetsam around Staten Island by now).

#2: She's thrice divorced, and I'm pretty certain all three of her ex-husbands were torn asunder, consumed à la black widow style, never to be seen again.

#1: Her heart is black and shriveled, like one of those really hard raisins you always find at the bottom of the box. Every other damn raisin in there is plump and juicy, but that one fucking rock-hard raisin always gets you. Her heart is like that raisin. Only bigger. Like a prune, I guess. But as far as I know, there's never a rock-hard prune in the bunch. And prunes are fucking gross. So gross that no one has ever noticed when they've gotten a bad one.

She asks, "So you're *not* just hanging around for old-time's sake? Maybe taking in a lunchroom quickie? Flush a three-hole punch down the toilet? We haven't even had time to catch up."

"Sorry, maybe next time. Besides, you told me about your trip; I talked about boobies. I'd say we've covered the finer points."

She smiles, the way I'd smile when I try to visualize my worst enemy getting trampled by extremely angry and incredibly aroused elephants. "I'll tell you, that new temp they sent to replace you, he barely speaks English and is missing three fingers on his right hand, and he's still more productive than you *ever* were."

"That's super. Though he's probably just happy to not be in Pakistan right now. Even if he does have to see *you* every day. And I don't really care, 'cause I've found myself a sweet new gig anyway."

"You have a new job already? I would have lost *that* bet."

"Well, it was more like Glenn was desperate and I was right there."

"That makes more sense. Sounds like you just need a good strong drink."

"Did you say *dink*?"

"Drink, you moron."

"You're right. Maybe I'll hit one of my old haunts; one of the Midtown bars I haven't stiffed before, and just disappear, you know? And then stiff them too, I guess."

"Well..." she starts.

"Well?" I follow.

"Why go anywhere? I've got some booze right here in my office."

"You've got—?"

"Booze. In my office." She cocks her head toward the dark office behind her. "I've got an entire minibar full."

Is it wrong that at the very suggestion of a minibar my first thought is to replenish my satchel's inventory of Adventure Supplies? Well, I *am* a freeloader; I've never made much of an effort to disguise that fact. Freeloading the spare bedroom in my brother's apartment. Freeloading meals off Glenn Workman. Freeloading Melissa's love.

And especially, freeloading booze. It's basically my specialty.

She says, "So, how about it? Other than alcohol, I can't think of too much else that can take one's mind off one's problems." And then BOSS winks at me, as though I was still unsure what a middle-aged woman offering alcohol to a younger man meant. At least, I'm going to assume I know what she means here. She sure does seem a lot less robotic than she did thirty seconds ago, I'll say that.

Next, from her pocket, she withdraws a pair of glasses — *Oh no* — unfolds them — *Dear God, why me?* — and touches the end of the temple to the tip of her oily, too-red tongue — *Why is this happening? I need to sit down, or at least get a copy of Modern Dog to flip through here* — before rubbing the frames across the breast of her blazer — *Wait, is she trying to simulate her tongue licking her nipple, but using the glasses as a middle-man? This is actually very confusing, now that I'm pausing to think about it.*

"We can do this the easy way or the hard way." And for her coup de grâce, BOSS slides those glasses over her ears. Pushing the frames snug to the bridge of her nose with her middle finger. In a sort of *Fuck You* to all the times I wished computer viruses upon her or played pirated Spin Doctors songs on the office intercom system.

Fuck me, indeed.

"I've been on Team Hard Way basically my whole life," I tell her not-so-proudly.

She moves closer now, taking my once-pristine, now off-white hoodie strings with the chewed-up aglets into her hands and gives them a little tug. She pulls my deer-in-the-headlights face toward her, motor oil breath stinging my quivering nostrils. God, I feel so violated. I fear this encounter is quickly degrading into all sorts of shades of gray. And I'm getting a sneaking suspicion that she doesn't actually have beer in her office. I need to think of a way out of here, fast.

"Listen, BOSS. I realize I can talk a pretty big game, but I'll be honest here: you're making me feel just a smidgen uncomfortable right now."

Directing me to her darkened office, she bumps the door open with her ass, knocking something onto the floor in the process. She doesn't care. The combination of these massive windows and the glacial chill in here make it seem like we're suspended in mid-air above the city. She ignores the incredible view and makes her way to the stainless-steel mini-fridge she's got hidden behind her desk. *Okay! There IS beer after all!* Before I know it, she's tossing a bottle of something my way, blindly-assuming it wasn't eight-year-old Chester K. Eddy who still holds the Lake Monona Bullet Sturgeons Little League record for fewest balls caught in a season — *Of which, by the way, the record is Two Balls, and even that number was bloated due to some suspected shady backroom deals made by low-level gangsters who had money riding on local dog fights, school bus street races, and little league baseball games. I was clueless to it all though, and was just happy to have caught one. Go Bullet Sturgeons!*

Still, I catch the bottle of imported Kyrgyzstani hooch like I had money riding on myself.

BOSS provocatively situates herself on the desk, and urges me on. "Go on. Give it a shot."

Surprisingly, the lid twists right off — *They don't child-proof these things in Kyrgyzstan?* — and the smell hits me like that time I walked into the bathroom right after Uncle Eric used it, on the night he got kicked out of the Red Lobster for violating the all-you-can-eat-coconut shrimp rules. I imagine this is exactly what the streets of Kyrgyzstan smell like, not to assume anything. I'm sure they're wonderful people.

Drunk. But wonderful. Like me.

I take a gulp and try my best to pretend the swill isn't instantly cauterizing my insides. God, I'm feeling woozy already. I go to brace myself with a hand on her knee, but my aim is off and I lurch forward, knocking my forehead on the desk edge.

"Don't worry," she assures me. "This stuff is known to work hard and fast. At least in the three countries it's legal in."

From the floor, I forget trying to make a good *Working-Hard-and-Fast* comeback, and instead try to focus on just one of the multiple spinning BOSSes above me. Finally, they come together as one, and I realize she's not even holding a drink of her own. "I give up," I manage to spit out.

And then I still have the audacity to take another shot from the bottle.

"Hmm?"

"I'm not going to fight this. Just—just do whatever the fuck you want to do to me, lady. I don't care anymore." And one more gulp for good measure.

"Whatever I want?"

"Yeah, let's just get this over with. I mean, I realize there's this whole ME TOO movement going on right now — *which sort of bothers me on the level of: Why can't my OWN movement catch on? But I think that's maybe not the point I'm trying to make at the moment* — and on the one hand, I could totally throw your actions back in your face. I mean, this is exactly what you ladies have been fighting against, isn't it?"

"And on the other hand?"

"Huh?" I ask, shaking the cartoon stars away from my head.

"You're incredibly bad at this, Mister Eddy. You can't start a list and then end it at one bullet point. That's not how lists work."

"Maybe I didn't *have* another — no, wait! I remember what I was going to say." I take another look at the bottle in my hand. "What's the alcohol content in this stuff? There's no label on here. No, what I was going to say was: I'll take the hit. For shitbag men everywhere, I'll be the martyr. I'm a modern day Ghandi, or Martin Luther King — Though, in the annals of history, I'd say they're still fairly modern, wouldn't you? And I wouldn't *necessarily* call them shitbags, but I didn't know them. I'm just assuming they—WHY IS THERE NO LABEL ON THIS SHIT? That really should have tipped me off in the first place, don't you think?"

BOSS has got her face buried in her hands now. I notice, but keep going anyway.

"So, come on already. Let's just do this thing. Violate away! Where do you want me? Have you got some freaky toy you want to stuff in my meatus? Or should we go old-fashioned?"

I finally break her. "Jesus, Chester. Will you please just shut up already?" I can break anyone eventually. Even my mom's book club broke down and agreed to read and make notes on *Shiloh* the fucking beagle for me, so I wouldn't have to do it myself in Fifth Grade. What can I say? Well, there's nothing much to be said, really. "Just stop talking."

"So, I'm *not* going to be a martyr tonight?"

"No. Absolutely not."

"Damn."

"I'm not going to violate you. I never was. God, if I had any sexual interest in you at all, don't you think I would have cornered you in the maintenance closet when you worked here? I fired you for a *reason*, asshole."

"Because of my reckless porn spree?"

"Because you're an asshole."

"I'm changing my ways though! Did you know I'm currently smack-dab in the middle of a major growth spurt? An emotional one, that is. I think I've already had all my other growth spurts."

"I'm sure."

"Well, even if you were planning on turning this office into a Mario Lopez bachelor party, it would have helped if I didn't find you so repulsive."

"Right. And I'm sure these glasses weren't doing anything for you."

"Honestly? Even with the glasses, I'm pretty turned off right now." This is when she takes the glasses off and chucks them at me. I try to catch them — *Go Bullet Sturgeons!* —only to get beaned in the head.

"Asshole."

"So, if you're not planning on taking advantage of me, why am I in your office drinking illegally imported Russian grain alcohol?" There's some sort of translucent brown flakes floating around inside the bottle. Another reason having a label might be beneficial.

"It's because of your brother, actually."

I think, *Wha—?* But then I end up saying, "Huh—?" Not much better, I suppose.

"Always a master of eloquence," she ribs me.

"Okay, let me put that in technobabble for you: *Does not compute. Error! One zero one zero zero one zero one one zero one.*"

She pulls another bottle from the fridge — *Though this one requires a bottle opener. Why didn't she offer me THAT one?* — and guzzles it back like a true souse from the rough, dirty, unpaved backroads of Kyrgyzstan. Though it's fairly likely *all* streets in Kyrgyzstan are unpaved. Again, just generalizing.

"Your brother is Ace Eddy, yes?"

The bottle in my hand starts to feel heavier now. "Let me answer your question with another question: If my brother unceremoniously and not-so-diplomatically disowned me, is he *still* my brother?"

"I don't give a fuck, really. If you — at one point in your sad little life — ever called Ace Eddy brother, then you should know that he owes me money."

"*My* brother owes *you* money? It's a small world after all, isn't it? What does he owe you for?"

"It's really none of your business."

"Oh, come on now, BOSS. You can't drop an ambiguous comment like that and not cough up details. Shit like that wouldn't fly in a film or a book. That's just lazy writing. Unless you *are* going to say, but at an even more appropriate moment, so then this moment now will pale in comparison to the shocking reveal later."

BOSS looks around her office, as though there actually exists the possibility of a missing wall and a camera crew. Maybe some boom poles above us. "Do you seriously think your life is a work of fiction? You can't be that much of an idiot."

Would an idiot love the word *boom pole* so much? I think not. "Trust me. No one would want to be reading about *my* life. I'm only mildly interested myself, and that's just because I have a truculent aching for self-inflicted misfortune. You know, like Charlie Brown."

"The steakhouse?"

"Now who in the grassy knolls of Hell hears the name Charlie Brown and thinks of the steakhouse first?"

"There's another Charlie Brown?"

"Your database needs an upgrade, lady." I'm on my knees now, which is about as high an elevation as my foggy head can handle at the moment. "So, what does my brother owe you money for?"

"If you must know," she says, barely tolerating my presence now. "I won a signed Ace Eddy hockey stick at an auction. Turns out it was a fake. The autograph *and* the stick."

"It was a fake stick? Like it was made out of tongue depressors or Froot Loops glued onto a shish kebab skewer?"

She stares directly at me. The words, *You Are an Idiot* scrolling invisibly across her optic receptors. I'm sure at this point that if she had been planning on assimilating me for the Robot Uprising, she'd have thought better of it by now.

"Listen," I tell her. "I can get you a signed stick if you want. I could probably have a rookie card and a game-worn jockstrap tossed in at no additional charge if you want."

"That's not the point. I was taken advantage of, and all I have to show for it is a signed Cal Clutterbuck stick."

"I have no idea who that is. But that dude sounds cooler than my brother." *Probably would be less of a jerk to me, too. Wonder if this Cal Clutterbuck fella could use a roommate? Mental note.* "So, what were you planning on doing then? Were you going to get me drunk and hold me hostage? Like some unbelievably flimsy terrorist from an 80's movie? I hate to make the comparison again, but like Hans Gruber in *Die Hard*?" I take another drink, if only to reduce the strain on my now-cramping forearm muscles.

Then, reaching behind her, she takes something from her desk and holds it up.

It's Chase's credit card.

From the floor, I take a look around inside my bag, pushing miniature bottles, plastic forks, and a stolen phone charger to the side. But it's not there.

She nods her head toward the cubicles on the other side of her office door. "I saw this bag sitting out there and wondered, '*Now what kind of moron leaves their reeking bag of personal items behind on their desk?*' And then lo and behold: there's Chester K. Eddy dressed for Fleet Week and painting a note on a rock with company Wite-Out."

"Why were you rooting through someone's personal belongings? That sounds like grounds for dismissal to me. There's video cameras around here, aren't there?"

"There actually aren't, no. I had them removed a couple of years ago. But idiots assume they're here somewhere so nobody does anything too stupid." Conveniently, I now recollect my last day here, when I admitted to a bunch of the other stuff I did around here because BOSS told me there were cameras. Damn, she's right. Only the idiots. With an honorary mention to all the dick butts out there, too.

I try to stand, try to lift myself up from the floor now, but my arms are floppy noodles. The sweaty bottle drops from my sweaty grip. I swear I can hear the liquid burning the carpet as it gurgles out. Then BOSS rises from her desk, towering above me, just as any formulaic supervillain's nefarious plan-revealing would play out. "All I needed was this credit card and an inebriated Chester K. Eddy, and here we are. Now, let's go make a transaction, shall we?"

"Well, the joke's on you, BOSS. That card was cancelled two days ago."

"Amusing."

"No, really. Turns out my brother wanted me to figure out how to function on my own. Turns out I can't."

"You're actually serious, aren't you?"

"Am I ever not?"

She looks carefully at the card in her hand; flipping it over and back again, as though some tiny detail was overlooked. But when she looks back at me, sitting on the floor, picking my nose and blinking like a dumbass, the answer is obvious.

"I'm an open book," I tell her. "A book of disgusting truths and embarrassing honesty. Like a diary. But *my* diary, not someone else's. Someone else's diary would be the wrong kind of open book, wouldn't it? The open book adage wouldn't really work in that case. Boy, some expressions could handle being a little clearer. Like 'Bob's Your Uncle'. What the hell does that really mean?"

BOSS chucks the credit card at my head, like Colin Farrell in that shit Daredevil movie. The impact takes the wind out of me, and I'm knocked over onto my back, though it's the hooch in my stomach and the memory of that Daredevil movie itself which are the more likely culprits for the pain I'm feeling at the moment.

"You're not so honest," she says, bringing us back to my original point here. *Do you ever notice I get sidetracked a lot? Oh wait, she's still talking—* "You had intercourse under your cubicle, you discarded your snot-drenched tissues on the lunchroom table, and you left ass cheek imprints on every window and photocopier in the office. You were the most deplorable worker we've ever had. And we even had Scott Baio on the payroll for two months."

"But I told you, I've changed! Nothing but genuine veracity now! Sure, I've hit a few roadblocks recently — *and that's not including the shit I've gone through in just the last thirty minutes* — but I've been *trying*! I keep trying, even if all my changes lately have mostly been coming up looking like Caitlyn Jenners."

"You say you've been trying to be honest. But I'd be willing to bet you haven't told Melissa about your true feelings for her, have you? You spineless worm."

Ouch. The one that really smarts. There's no good comeback for that. I try anyway: "Shut up," I tell her.

Nope. There was definitely no good comeback for that.

"Just get out, Chester."

"What about my brother's hockey stick? You don't want to resolve that still-dangling plot line?"

"I'd rather see you gone, if I'm going to be perfectly honest myself."

I pick up the credit card from the floor, and gather my bag. "Do you mind if I use the bathroom again before I go? Something's really been doing a number to my stomach."

She actually, literally pushes me out the door of her office (re: cyborg strength — *though I could chalk it up to me still being wobbly from the booze*). I think I heard a tearing sound from my crotchal region, too. "Just go. And you can tell Melissa not to come in tomorrow."

"Is tomorrow a holiday? Should I be asking my new boss about holiday pay?"

"It's not a holiday, it's me firing her."

"Firing her? For what?"

"For having a shitty boyfriend. She can thank you for that."

"First of all, I'm not her boyfriend. I'm fairly certain Melissa is currently dating my weird, pervy boss, which pretty much puts the cherry on the suck cake. And secondly — *look, I did the list thing properly this time!* — she's not going to care because she's leaving anyway. She's going to Japan with this guy, which, now that I think of it, sounds a bit weird because Glenn's never mentioned Japan before, has he?"

"Don't know. Don't care," she says. "Just get out." And with that, BOSS slams her office door in my face. Presumably she is in the midst of entering sleep mode, and I'm left to find my way out; back down eleven floors and outside into the dark, frozen wasteland of Wall Street on a Wednesday night.

And yes, I did hear a tearing sound from the crotch of my pants. Dammit. The Silver Surfer's bald head is peeking out of my ass. I'm starting to wonder how much longer I can last here, as a walking wardrobe malfunction. Though, maybe this is the start of a new look, for this new all-honest, all-the-time Chester K. Eddy? I can wear torn, shit-stained sailor pants, a *SisQó Tour 2000* hoodie, and frilly pink socks, can't I? I think it's my natural, enviable aplomb, my *amour-propre* and *Go Forth and Conquer the World-ness* that simply allows me to pull off fashion statements like this. Like Prince. Or a classic Mr. T.

Shit. I'm pretty certain I left the Dick Butt rock somewhere back upstairs. So much for enviable aplomb.

My One Phone Call

"Hello?"

"How's it hanging, Ace?"

"Chester?"

I've got a single quarter left in my pocket after I scarfed two Whoppers at a downtown Burger King. I even stacked the two sandwiches one on top of the other and just ate 'em like that because, well why the fuck not at this point? *I trust you've been reading everything up until now, so there should no longer be any questioning of anything that's going on here.*

Anyway, because I've been running around the city like this was a bad movie about an infantile moron trying to piece his life together — *Shut up! This is very, very different from that!* — I've once again neglected to charge my phone. So why did I steal a charger from the hotel anyway? Beats me. A bad movie wouldn't need to explain away questions and plot holes such as that, and neither will I.

So, I've found myself half a block away from Chase Eddy's apartment at the last payphone in Lenox Hill, which just so happened to have a cigarette left inside from the last person to use this phone. *Which was probably circa 1998?* And apparently, I've dropped my last quarter in just so I can get sassed by my own brother.

"I'll be honest," Chase says, obviously jumping on the Honesty Movement bandwagon himself. *I knew it would catch on!* "I didn't think it would take this long for you to call me."

Is he really saying he assumed I'd crack long before now? I don't care, I'm taking that as a compliment, even if my impending response will no doubt say otherwise. "Screw you," I tell him. *Not my best; though I've obviously had worse responses. Yes, the winds of change are still a blowin'.* "Don't go and get up on your high horse now, Chase. I'm not calling because I need anything." *Shit. That was a total lie.*

"I don't believe you for a second, but go on."

Would Chase believe me if I told him I was merely trying to order a cheese pizza and dialed the wrong number? No, I want him to think I'm in a better place right now; that these last three days — *Christ, has it really only been three days? Two nights sounds pathetic, but three days doesn't seem too bad, does it? Am I reaching?* — have been nothing but positive changes. I stink of success right now, instead of Dorito dust, BOSS's cheap booze on my breath, shit on my leg, and whatever else I've got emanating from every nook and cranny and orifice. And a true hero of success, nay, a champion of success based on all-American honesty, would never be ordering a cheese pizza at eight o'clock on a Wednesday night, would he?

"I said go on," Chase says, snapping me back to reality.

"I, uh—I need a place to crash, bro."

"See? I told you you'd come crawling back, Chesty. And after only two days!"

"Hey, it's been THREE!"

"And you're a changed man now, right? Isn't that what you're going to say?"

"You wouldn't even recognize me."

"So, you're *not* still wearing your SisQó hoodie?"

From inside this phone booth, I look around like I'm some wanted criminal, afraid Ace Eddy has maybe got eyes everywhere in this city. "Of course not. I'm telling you though: you'd be *proud* of me! I've landed myself a new job, I got some sweet new pants, I motivated a convicted felon named Bullet to change his ways, and I've attended an SAA meeting." Of course, "attended" doesn't automatically mean I'm planning on going back for a second go-round.

"SAA? What does that stand for?"

"It's a personal growth thing. What have *you* accomplished in the last three days?"

"Not much more than usual. I did get some juice from the fridge. Yesterday, I think it was."

"Cool." Insert uncomfortable pause here. "Is there any juice left?"

"Nah. Sorry."

He's apologizing to me? One ticket for the Arm Pump Express, please. All aboard!

"That was a sarcastic *Sorry*, in case you were wondering."

Ka-Boom. And the train is off the rails again. "So, assuming you haven't already renovated my bedroom into a pinball arcade or a stripper's lounge, how about it?"

"Firstly, that was never *your* bedroom, Chester. It was just temporary, remember? And secondly: no can do, bro. I've already got someone else staying here."

"What? Are you running an Airbnb over there?"

"It's just Dad, actually. He's visiting for a week."

"Dad? As in, *our* dad?"

"No. It's the Dad's Oatmeal Cookies guy."

Okay, that was actually pretty good. Ace Eddy scores again. I take a good long drag off this cigarette. "Well, does Stuart Eddy know I've been unsanctimoniously kicked out by my own brother?"

"He hasn't even asked about you."

"How the fuck—? How could our father sleep in that bedroom, the one with The Afghan Whigs posters and my old Fraggle Rock bedsheets, and NOT ask about me?"

"Beats me."

"How about the couch?"

"The couch hasn't asked about you either. No one has, Chesty. Just keep telling people all the grossest shit about yourself, and keep cheating on your girlfriend. NO ONE cares, dude."

"Ouch. You know, in my defense, Melissa is *not* my girlfriend. And *she's* actually the one who's cheating on *her* boyfriend. With *me*."

"And you put up with that nonsense because—?"

Come on, Chester. Don't feed him some B.S. excuse to deflect your real reason for doing anything. Tell him the truth; he'll very likely sense your naked honesty and really appreciate it. He might even open up his home to you again. So: "It's because I love her."

"That is so, so sad."

This truth thing is far more complicated than I wanted to believe it would be. "So, do pity points allow me inside to crash on the couch for a night?"

"Listen, I told you to start figuring out how to function on your own. And I meant it. Because it'll do you some good. Now get on back to your personal growth meetings and keep on growing, big brother."

Okay. I realize you've gotta have balls of steel to play in the National Hockey League, but Ace Eddy must have a tight twosome of titanium testes 'cause this boy is not giving me an inch. "Can I talk to Dad at least?"

Click.

Did he really just hang up on me? After all I've ever—? *Scratch that.* After all the times I've paid for his—? *Nope. There must be something...okay.* After every time I've gone into his NHL video game and secretly adjusted every other teams' player stats, lowering them slightly so his fucking New York Islanders would have a better chance at winning, and he STILL hangs up on me? Actually, I guess it's likely he's never noticed the stat changes, so how could he be grateful for that? I don't know; I'm grasping here. Not that it matters; he still hung up and I don't even have enough change left to make another phone call.

Instead of letting anger win, I choose to take the high road: I Bang the Receiver* against the payphone Hard Enough and Long Enough* that tiny plastic bits and A Substantial Amount of Screws* start exploding within the phonebooth and all that's left is An Overextended, Dangling Cord.*[2]

I end up inside Chase's building anyway; there's a pretty sweet couch in the lobby, and Woody the apartment concierge is still cool with me (ie: my brother obviously hasn't spoken with him yet). I told Woody there was an intervention being held for Chase upstairs right now — *I was prepared to explain it was to encourage Chase to seek help for his pyromaniac and intermittent explosive disorders, but Woody never asked, so that's something I'll tuck away in the back pocket of my sailor pants for later. Shut up. I know there's no back*

---

[2] Man, I don't think I've ever used so many potential porno titles in one sentence before. Although "An Overextended, Dangling Cord" is admittedly a bit of a stretch.

pocket. It's a metaphor — and that I'd just be happy to crash on the couch until things up there were settled. He seemed to be legitimately concerned for me though, and even let me charge my phone at the desk and brought me a couple of packaged cheese danishes from the concierge's grotto for my hardship.

I didn't sleep great (turns out that couch was left there for a reason), mostly due to my uncertainty about what exactly I'll say to Glenn Workman in the morning, and where it is I stand with Melissa at this point.

So, I bugged Woody for some subway fare, and made sure to get out of there before Dad came down in the morning for his daily six o'clock 1980's power walk. He even does that ski pole thing sometimes, too.

Show no concern for me, Woody. Things are chugging along just fine over here.

Highlander Moment

TBH, I once masturbated while talking on the phone to my grandmother (on my dad's side though — *is that any better?*). Full disclosure: the phone call and the jerking off were completely unrelated, she just happened to dial me up while I was in the middle of stuff, and I'm too polite to let the phone go unanswered. You can't fault a guy for being too polite. The worst part of it all is that was the last time I ever spoke with my grandma; she died the next day (*also unrelated to my private business. Probably.*) I was too embarrassed to go to the funeral, which, in retrospect, might have served as some honest to goodness closure on the matter, but instead, I'm left with the memory of G-Ma Eddy's voice hacking and wheezing over the phone and chatting my ear off about the ungodly prices for cheese at her corner deli while I beat the salami to flashbacks of that night at the Madison, Wisconsin Christmas Tree Festival, with Shawnee Lazlo — *Consent!* — my first college girlfriend, and our seven minutes of heaven in the port-o-potty.

Side story: Shawnee Lazlo ended up dumping me for a dude who worked in the port-o-potty biz. Guess she had some sort of fetish. His job was emptying all the shit from the tank. Did you know they stick a big hose down inside the portable toilet and just suck all the excrement out of the waste tank? I'm pretty sure I assumed they just tipped the port-o-potty over and dumped all the piss and shit out into the ocean or a river somewhere. Either way, that's super gross.

So, I'm practicing my lines outside Theatre One Hundred. The snow is dumping down on me and my aching soul, but I ignore the cold, heavy flakes. I have to get in that zone. It's no different from the many auditions I've had up until now, it's just that *this* time I'm auditioning for the role of *Boyfriend Hunter*. Yes, that's still a working title; I'm hoping the ideal title will come to me through my line reads here.

Basically though, I'm going to convince Glenn Workman that I am the one who should be with Melissa. Not him. Persuasion and wheedling are specialties of mine, though please don't use the last few days as examples of that.

There's an old movie from the 80's called *Highlander* which was about a bunch of immortal swordsmen who ran around decapitating one another in the hopes they would be the last one standing. *"There can be only one,"* was their tagline. I think the winner got a new convection oven, or a trip to Orlando or something? I don't know. It had Sean Connery, which is an excuse people like to use to convince you a film isn't actually shitty, but Sean Connery also did *Zardoz* and *The League of Extraordinary Gentlemen*, so that argument does not hold any water at all.

Anyway, this is my Highlander moment. There can be only one boyfriend, and I am he. Also, I sure hope Glenn Workman has seen *Highlander* or else a lot of these lines I'm running through right now are not going to make a whole lot of sense later.

A gust of wind whips around Broadway and blows a sheet of snow into my face. I'm still spitting out chunks of ice and wiping flakes from my eyes when the theater door opens and I hear the sweetest sound known to man. Well, this man anyway.

"Whoa! Love the pants, Chestnuts."

"Melissa?" There she is, ponytail in all its freshly-washed glory. Defensively, I tell her, "They're sailor pants and there's a hole in the crotch and they're not mine." Then I ask, "What are *you* doing here?"

"You won't believe it, but I just got a lead in a play!" Instantly, I visualize her resume on the top of the submissions pile. In the very next instant, I think of her and Glenn Workman having just finished up a round of—*You know what? I can't do it. I just can't.*

The wind knifes around the corner again, chilling me to the bone. She asks, "Did you even know there was a theater up here?"

"Theatre One Hundred? Of course," I respond, all holier than thou. Like I'm the secret expert on all things New York Theater Scene. "Don't tell me you've never seen any of their productions! Hey, did you check out the façade?"

She almost looks behind her but stops herself. "Who the heck cares about a façade?"

"Some people seem to."

"Whatever. What are YOU doing here, Chestnuts?"

"Would you believe I've actually landed myself a gig here too?"

"*What—!?* Please tell me you're playing uber-horny, sex-crazed artist Matthew Willows!"

"Actually, I am playing the role of uber-horny *assistant* to the sex-crazed *director.*"

"You mean Mr. Workman?"

Mister.

Workman.

Right.

"Who else?" I catch her pouting a bit. It's minute, but my razor-sharp junior detective senses are on fleek this morning. I ask, "What's the matter?"

"I just got a bit excited there for a moment, when I thought you meant you got a part in this play. You know what that would have meant, don't you?"

That you'd have to immediately break up with your secret boyfriend Glenn Workman and stick with me full time? "I think I know. But why don't you just tell me? You know I hate guessing unless the potential for winning a mason jar full of jelly beans exists."

"No jelly beans, sorry. But it would have meant we were that much closer to finally fulfilling our dream."

"The one where we own the world's first orchard run exclusively by giants?"

"Uh, no. Our dream of acting together in the same production." She wipes a tear from her eye, though it could just be an errant snowflake.

Is she really this bothered by our near-miss of a fantasy? "Still," she admits solemnly. "At least we're working together again, right? Just like old times."

Man, I haven't seen Melissa this shaken up since I made up a story about Jonathan Van Ness shaving his head. *It's time to kick your barely-effective Honesty Movement into high gear, Chester! Don't downplay this tender moment! Don't pretend her stupid Serious Relationship business isn't really crushing your balls in a red-hot vice. Make this moment matter! Tell her—*

"I guess it's no big deal though," she says, beating me to the disastrous punchline.

FUCK! You missed your chance, Dick Butt!

"Also, you may have noticed I'm a bit despondent because I got laid off from my job this morning." *Uh oh.* "I walked right in like any normal Thursday, and BOSS just let me go."

"Just like that? Did she say anything?"

Mel's eyes lock onto my own. And in all seriousness, she simply says,

"Nothing out of the ordinary." *Okay Mel. You can stop looking at me any time now.* "Still, why would they just can me?" *Stop. Looking. At. Me.*

Finally, she shakes some fresh snowflakes from her hair. "Maybe it's a good sign though? Now that the play is happening. Those bank hours wouldn't work anyway."

"Everything happens for a reason, right?"

"Come on. That's what losers say." Then she gives me a jovial punch to the chest and that winning smile returns; all flashing teeth and just the right amount of gums. Her cheeks' tiny, fine hairs are like the follicles on an angel's bum. *I realize I'm assuming a lot about Angel bum hair here.* "I've got a good feeling about this play. Mr. Workman really has the kind of passion this city needs."

"*This* city? What about Japan? And the presupposed moving TO Japan?"

"There's change in the air, Chestnuts! Not just with me, but with The Boyfriend too."

She says *The Boyfriend* like she wants me to picture that rat tail tickling her nipples. *Too late. I did anyway.* "Well, Workman may not be the answer you're looking for. Or the one you need. The guy's not such a hotshot, Mel."

"Ah, he's not so bad."

"Did you know he attends Sex Addicts Anonymous meetings? Not all that regularly, but still. Though I suppose there's an argument there for saying, '*Hey, at least he's seeking help and maybe trying to better himself.*' But he's still the kind of weirdo who orders lettuce burgers, you know."

"What's wrong with a lettuce burger?"

"You may be visualizing that wrong. Not a burger with lettuce for a bun, but a burger with *no* patty and *just* lettuce *on* a bun."

"So?"

"You know what? The lettuce burger is not really the issue at hand here, Mel."

"Why'd you bring it up then, Dumbass?"

I love it when she calls me Dumbass. I absolutely love it.

"It's funny," she says without really giving me a decent chance to launch into something new, which is probably for the best anyway. "Mr. Workman told me his new assistant was a bit of a work in progress. A little *spacey.* He said he didn't even know where you were this morning. But he also told me he didn't have much choice. That he was pretty desperate. And you were right there. And I remember thinking, *Shit that sounds awfully familiar.*"

"I'm spacey? He didn't mean spacey like Kevin Spacey, did he?"

"I doubt it. But you never know."

"You do realize Glenn hired *me* to help him with the auditions and casting, but then he goes all maverick and gives *you* the part without letting me even do my job."

"I'm just going to assume it's because you don't really know how to *DO* a job. Based on your track record, that is."

I'd give Mel an amazing example right now just to prove her wrong, but nothing's cooking on the burner at the moment. I'll just smile instead.

"Would you have given me the part if you weren't busy choosing public drunkenness over showing up for work?"

Don't tell her about the trashed resume. Just keep smiling. "You're too good for this show, Mel."

"Chester, you have no idea what you're talking about. The play is wonderful."

"*Wonderful?*"

"Even beautiful in parts."

"*Beautiful?*"

"But you've read it. That scene when Madison and Miss Lee share a moment on the porch swing? *Ugh!* It's just breathtakingly heartbreaking."

"*Breathbreaking?*"

"You *have* read it, right?"

"To be honest, I've only flipped through it so far. I do recall a scene where one character is wearing a deer costume and protesting outside the all-you-can-eat barbecue buffet. What the fuck? Would you call that banality *beautiful?*"

"It's social commentary, Chestnuts. Like when you dissect the truths behind *Hot Tub Time Machine.*" *I love how she knows that.*

"First of all, HTTM is satire, not social commentary. And yes, I did just give it an acronym just now."

"First of all?"

"Yep."

"And this is the part where you have no second of all, isn't it?" *I love how she knows me.*

"Well, I was going to say—"

"Yes?" *I love how she totally calls my bullshit.*

"I was going to say, *When the Willows Speak They Sing in Unison* is a stupid title."

"Okay, well, those two points are not even related. But fine. You're welcome to your opinion."

"Don't you think it's a little long winded? A bit of a mouthful?"

I want her to say, "*So are you, Chestnuts. Nyuk, nyuk.*"

But instead, I'm met with: "It's full of theme, is what it is."

"Theme? Like because the characters' last name is Willows? Like that?"

"Here's how theme works: Matthew Willows is an artist. Madison Willows is a doctor. Native Americans used willows for pain relief and other medicinal purposes. And willow is also used to make drawing charcoal. Everyone knows that."

"I—I don't even know how you know *any* of that. You say this is common knowledge for people?"

"Also, the roots of a willow tree have extraordinary toughness, and a remarkable tenacity to keep growing. That is a direct metaphor for Madison and Matthew's hardships."

"Jee. Zuss. What did Workman have you smoking back there?"

"Chester, it's all right in front of you. You just have to look closely and really consider the details. Glenn's an incredible artist. A genius."

Me, I still just want to punch him in his stupid face. "Why don't you just marry the guy then?"

Mel sticks her cute little pink tongue out at me in attempted jest. But she doesn't know that I know what she thinks I don't know. "Considering this is a project you're working on, you certainly seem to detest it. Are you sure this is right for you?"

I'm just staring at her now. Her face looks a bit like a squirrel when her temper gets her chattering. A sexy squirrel.

"Listen. Just read it. Sit down tonight and read the whole thing. We can discuss it tomorrow." She makes a move like she's about to get going. Like there's somewhere better to be. Someone better to be *with*.

I say, "Well, we should at least celebrate, shouldn't we? How about with an Upper West Side Quickie?"

"Not now, sailor. I've got my hands full this morning." She punches me on the shoulder and I want to take it like a man, but my heel slides a bit on an icy patch and I slip, my ass landing in a snowbank.

Deflated, I say, "I'd settle for a Riverside Park Quickie. Most of the real pervy park creeps aren't usually too active at this time of the morning."

"We'll see each other here tomorrow. Read the script. You'll love it." Melissa bounds on over like that sexy squirrel's got her eyes on some real quality nuts, her sleek ponytail all a-flappin'. She helps me up with the effortless strength of an Amazon warrior, and gives me a tight hug. I pull her in even closer and put a hand on her bum. We both squeeze.

In this moment, I want to tell her everything: how I know about Glenn Workman and I don't even care, but I definitely don't ever want her to consider leaving the city again. Not just for someplace asinine like Japan, but even for somewhere as conveniently local as the Bronx. Okay, I do care about the Glenn thing too; that's gross and it's totally got to stop. Besides, *Highlander moment*, right? I want to apologize for my encounter with BOSS, and the subsequent loss of Mel's job. I want to pay her back for the charges at the Kitano Hotel, and my first couple of paychecks from the show will go towards that. A Chester K. Eddy promise is as good as gold. Or at least as good as the gold kids get when they go panning on one of those hokey mine tours. I want to show her that picture I took of the crazed wheelchaired beast in the bathroom. I want to stick her Black Stallion ponytail in my mouth right now. I really do. I want to apologize for these sailor pants — *of which she strangely seems to love anyway* — and the smell of my SisQó hoodie, and the very fact

I'm still wearing a SisQó hoodie in the year 2018, and my lack of oral hygiene over the last few days, and in general, for that matter.

But mostly, of course, I just want to tell Melissa I love her. That's really all that matters right now. I mean, fuck, I know I've loved Shawnee Lazlo, and Vicky Henderson, and this girlfriend, and that girlfriend, and that one super-classy prostitute who "accidentally" showed up at the hotel on my trip to Washington DC for Great-Grandpa's funeral. And I've even loved Dixie Carter and Bea Arthur, too.

But it's never felt like *this*.

Like a cheesy 80's hair band song, *It's Never Felt Like This. Was there ever an 80's song with that title? I'll have to Google that later. Mental note.*

I run through all of these thoughts in my head, but then the moment she lets me go, the only thing I can spit out is, "Hey, how come you never told me there was a *Wafels & Dinges* truck outside the Deutsche Bank?" I've still got my hand on her ass, too.

"I guess I never knew you loved waffles so much."

Ouch.

It's like she never knew me at all.

"Listen, Chestnuts. I've really gotta run."

Without even so much as a second-place kiss on my cheek, Melissa says goodbye and sashays on down West One Hundredth Street. She takes the snow with her too, and as the last of the flakes suddenly blows away, I'm left with this even colder feeling that I'm digging some sort of hole here which I'm never going to be able to climb out of.

I didn't even congratulate her on getting the part. Which is actually what seems most important to her. Even if I know the only reason she got the

part of Madison Willows is because Glenn's playing sexual favorites. I should
have told her he's married too.

The theater looms behind me. I plunk myself on the already-too-familiar
steps outside and take it all in. It's really not such a bad façade once you look
at it. Like Mel said: *When you look closely and really consider the details.*
Didn't Glenn say something like that too, a couple of days ago?

Shit. I'm in it deep, aren't I?

I give my lament another moment, but just as I rise to my feet again — *By
the way, this is a PHYSICAL rising to my feet, and most definitely not a
METAPHORIC one* — Glenn Workman comes bursting from the theater
doors. He stops his forward motion completely though as soon as he sees me.

"Chester! You're here! Finally!"

"Sorry, boss. I thought today was a national holiday."

He pauses momentarily to consider his calendar. "I'm not sure if I was
aware of—"

"I don't know the name of it, but I'm pretty certain it lands on the third
Thursday of the month? You celebrate by waking up hungover in a hotel
lobby, acting like a wuss around women, and reconsidering all your recent
life choices. I don't think it even *has* a name, come to think of it."

"Well, listen. There're some more callbacks I need you to make. I've got
notes marked on their resumes back in the—"

"No, you listen to me, Glenn." *This is it. It's happening! My Highlander
moment is nearly real. Finally, a rock-solid plan of mine is coming to
fruition. Yes, the Highlander moment is too a rock-solid plan. You'll see.*

"Pardon?"

There's a largish tree branch a couple of feet away from me, freshly broken off from the added weight of snow. I hold my finger up for a moment while I shuffle over to grab it. It's not a broadsword, and I'm fairly certain when it comes to quality decapitations this would likely not do the trick, but it does make me feel a bit manlier. Ouch. I think I tweaked my shoulder picking this branch up. Scratch that. Not feeling so manly.

Glenn's not really respecting the held-up finger however, and just keeps talking. "Listen, Chester. I don't have time for this right now. I was just about to—"

"No. Hold on. Let me speak, Glenn. Let me have my moment."

He shows me a bit of patience now, and exhales slowly. It's the same exacerbated exhale I've seen a million times from a million different people who've just realized the only way they're ever getting rid of me is by just letting me say a few words. His breath comes out all thin and wispy in the cold air. "Fine. Go ahead."

"Here it is: I love her, man. I love the sparkle that remains after she exits a room. The afterglow of her faded laughter. The space in the bed she leaves behind in the morning. It's everything about her. She means everything to me."

Glenn's just staring at me; a curious look upon his face.

I raise the branch, but only so far because, *shit, I really think I've legitimately hurt my shoulder. Fight through it, Chester! This is your moment!* "And if my feelings are trivial, if my words are meaningless to you, I'm prepared to let this tree branch do the talking for me."

Workman opens his arms theatrically, unorthodoxly making himself more vulnerable to my impending attack. "Oh, so you love her now, do you? But why is it you're baring your feelings to *me*, rather than telling Madison herself?"

Insert needle off the record sound here. "I'm sorry? Madison?"

Glenn puts his hands together and applauds as though we've just wrapped rehearsal. A street performance for no one but the Upper West Side pigeons and still-decaying rats. "Delightful, Chester."

"What are you—?"

"You've decided to audition for the role after all, have you?"

I look around, like there's a hidden camera around us somewhere. "Back it up, Glenn. I'm confused."

"Act Three. Page ninety-four. Where Matthew Willows confronts Melville, and realizes he still loves Madison."

"In the play, right?" I'm still holding the tree branch aloft, though more out of fear now instead of stark raving madness.

"Of course. So, are you telling me you're wanting to try out for the role of Matthew?"

"I, uh...I wasn't really—Wait. What I said just then; those were lines from the script?"

"Mostly. But I appreciated the improvisation of the tree branch rather than the rotisserie spit Matthew actually holds in the script."

How could I possibly have spewed lines from *When the Willows Speak They Sing in Unison* verbatim if I've never even read the damn script? Out loud, I think: "But that would be like monkeys on typewriters."

Glenn laughs. "So, you're calling me a monkey now?"

"No. I think in my example, I would be the monkey. But on second thought, I don't really want to be a monkey either. Jeez. I am really blowing my metaphors and bungling my similes lately. So, you didn't think I was actually mad at you right now?"

"I believed your anger, like a good actor would have me believe. But I mean, I realize you weren't seriously threatening me with a tree branch, Chester. How preposterous would that be?"

"Utterly preposterous. Super-duperly stupid. I don't even know the first thing about anger." I nearly launched into something about the Incredible Hulk, followed by some weird tangent about Bruce Banner's kinda-gay affinity for purple jeans. If only I did, that might have recouped some of my dignity.

He's still giggling a little, and slaps my shoulder now, like we're two old college chums fondly reminiscing our glory days and summer loves. Fucker nailed me right where it still hurts too.

"Listen," he says, gathering himself to leave. "I'll only be gone for an hour at most. But when I return we can read through some more of the script. See what else you've got."

I just stand here dumbfounded. There's really nothing at all I can think of saying in this particular moment. I'll admit, it's sort of transcendental to not be in the midst of burying my pride ever further. It's a new experience for me.

"Here, catch," Glenn says, tossing something my way.

But I'm totally not paying attention and a small ring of keys hits me right in the eye. *Fuck, that hurts! But I'm not going to show weakness here. My Highlander moment might still be salvaged, mightn't it?*

"Let yourself in the theater, Chester. I just put on a pot of coffee in the office too."

And with that, he simply walks away. A bit of a jaunty spring in his step. Glenn heads in the same direction Melissa went, not ten minutes before.

Well. That has got to be one of the worst Highlander moments ever attempted. Likely even worse than the movie itself, which is difficult to pull off. And don't give me any more of that Sean Connery bullshit.

I almost turn back to look at the façade once again, but I think I see a white van rolling up West One Hundredth Street; a white van with "Fuck the Police" spray painted on the side. The adrenaline of survival skills takes over, and on the first attempt, I instinctively find the right key for the theater door, and slip in faster than I can say *Edgar Allan Poe's Teardrop Prison Tat.*

The Pause of Relationship-Just-Rejected

TBH, I always try to peel my oranges so the discarded peel looks like a penis. Every time, always. The best part is that you can tell any offended party it's actually an elephant, even if you happen to be running around shaking the thing in front of your man stuff. Depends on the crowd, really.

The rich aroma of coffee leads me right back to the office, but along the way, I swear I can also smell the fading presence of Melissa. I can tell, because it's one of my favorite scents. Like flower petals tossed into the surf; like summer nights before the rain; like a freshly-washed and sanitized perineum. *It's too late to start judging me, so please.*

The last time I was here, Melissa's resume had suspiciously reappeared, and Glenn had asked me to add it to the pile of auditions for the Madison Willows part. Next thing I know, I've gotten her fired from her job, Lester McDoucheCrutches has informed me the secret Boyfriend is actually Glenn Workman himself, and now Melissa has officially landed the part in his shite play. *Metaphors and themes and social commentary and grown men in deer mascot costumes? Yes, it is so shite. Don't even question me on this.*

Things are looking pretty disheartening around here.

At least she's considering staying in the city though, rather than heading off to Japan. So, I've still got that, right?

Yes! There's always a chance at redemption! *Get that fucking chin up, Chester! No, higher! HIGHER!*

And my other pants — *The ones I willingly opted to replace with sailor pants. Remember those?* — have likely dried by now too, so I've also, thankfully, got that going for me. *We're gonna turn this thing around, we are!*

But then I open the office door to discover the coffee pot has exploded or something; absolutely every square inch of carpet is soaking, including the pants I'd left right there on the floor to dry.

Is there no hope for me? The only breaks I seem to be catching lately are of the Mr. Bean variety, if one considers anything in the families of food poisoning, broken bones, and extremities caught in inanimate objects to be considered breaks.

In the exact moment I'm considering ringing up Max Von Sydow to see if he can possibly exorcise this Charlie Brown demon from my person, I spot Melissa's familiar resume on Glenn's desk. In fact, it's the *only* resume on the desk. There's an open box for a brand-new coffee maker there too; I'll bet dumbass Workman didn't even read the owner's manual for this freaking thing before making a pot and conveniently slipping away on some pervy adventure of sexual miscreance, while coffee spewed from the machine like a demon-possessed Linda Blair—*Hold on. Am I making two Exorcist references in the same paragraph? I didn't even plan that, I swear.*

But what are the chances this is a set-up? Is Glenn trying to frame me for destroying his office in a jealous fit of rage? Is he trying to make me look bad in front of Melissa?

I take her resume into my hand. Mel's headshot is still defaced; she's still got that Sharpie'd beard drawn on it, as well as the square-framed glasses. But oh my god, is she ever still glorious.

Slumping down to the floor and not even caring a wit that my pants are now soaked brown with coffee stains, I give the resume a read through. I remember typing every word of this with her, including the stuff we made up, like her Notable Roles as Pregnant Woman #3, Sexy Troll, and The Reverse

Vagina. Not to mention her Special Skills of blood-chilling screams, exotic bird calls, and penny-farthing racing. It's a wonder we ever got paid for our time at the Deutsche Bank.

To be honest, I miss that.

It seems our time together has been strained of late. Sure, we've been pretty consistent with our bi-weekly romps in ever-changing, sometimes questionable, oftentimes body-contorting locales, but what I really miss is having Melissa around on a daily basis.

Cue the ringing phone. Somewhat muffled, however, due to sitting between the sandwich of wet carpet and my ass. But I know what's happening here! This is one of those classic story moments when our unlucky but lovable protagonist is realizing the importance of someone special in his life, and then: BAM! His phone rings and there she is. And okay, yes, I also realize I've already previously fallen for this, when Chelsea McMahon called me up after her audition yesterday, but I'm not stupid enough to fall for the same trick of fate twice, and besides, what are the chances? So, I take it in for a bit. I let my ringtone — *Which is totally not getting stale yet, by the way* — tease this moment with the extended time it deserves.

I'm a freak in heat
A dog without warning
My appetite is sex
'Cause me so horny

Then I fish the thing out of my back pocket, and launch right into my scribbled Zen rock affirmation from earlier: "Listen. I'm a dick, Mel. But the truth is, I love you."

"Chester?"

Not Mel. *Jeezus. Again? Really?*

"This is Chelsea McMahon."

I pull the phone away from my ear and check the number on the display. Nope. Definitely not Pornstar Jugz Sixty-Nine. I ask, "Were you the one who snuggles for a living?"

"What—? I had an audition for you yesterday."

"Oh, right. I'm sorry, but it's been a long couple of days. What can I do for you?"

"You just called me."

"I did?"

"You have a very poor memory; do you know that?"

"I'm very poor at a lot of things, so I don't really have a suitable model for comparison. Would you say my memory is *worse* than most guys you barely know?"

"It's worse than any person I've ever had at least three conversations with."

"To be fair, I don't know if what's happening right now technically counts as a conversation, Chelsea. But I'll concede." Did I just butt dial Chelsea McMahon? I've heard of butt-dialing, though it seems like one of those things that doesn't actually happen to people outside of Twitter feeds. I mean, no one is really that stupid. "Hold on a sec," I say. My phone tells me I redialed the last number from the previous conversation. Which was yesterday, when Chelsea called me.

"Looks like I butt-dialed," I tell her.

"I didn't think people actually did that," she jokingly comments.

"Oh, all the time," I say. "It's a national epidemic."

"So, is it good news or bad news?"

"Huh?"

"Did I get the part, or didn't I? I'm assuming that's why you're calling?"

How do I tell her I really did just butt-dial her without sounding like an idiot? There's no way, really. So instead, I'll just throw any answer her way. "Uh, no. Sorry."

Pause. I know this pause. This is The Pause of Audition-Just-Rejected. It differs a little from The Pause of Relationship-Just-Rejected, but the sting is nearly identical. It hurts. And I suppose Glenn is going to expect me to make this phone call to all the other auditioners. Because I'm a grown-up with a grown-up job. Suddenly the stink of responsibility has become quite stinky indeed. Thank god for voicemail, that's all I can say.

"I'm sorry," I repeat. But of course, I'm not really sorry, 'cause who the hell knows? Maybe she *will* get the part. I just want to redirect this conversation; get it out of the *Grown-Up Zone* and back into where my comfort lies: the *I'm Still Young So No Regrets Zone.*

The pause continues. It's like she just put her pause on pause.

"Chelsea?"

"I'm fine," she finally says. "Listen, what are you doing tonight?" *There's your No Regrets Zone. We're coming in fast. Now let's land this thing without too much turbulence.*

"What am I *doing*? I'm basically a Disneyland mascot. I just roam around directionless. Though I suppose even a Disney mascot must have *some* preordained path, now that I think of it. I mean, that's their job, right? But that's not what we're talking about here, is it? I'll shut up now. I mean, I'll answer your question: *Nope. I'm not doing anything tonight.* Okay. *Now* I'll shut up."

"Come out to Brooklyn. I'm meeting some girlfriends at a club."

Brooklyn? Why would I do that to myself? The last time I went to Brooklyn I woke up in Pittsburgh. "I don't like club scenes. But I do like the sound of the word girlfriends."

"It'll be fun. I know *I* could use some fun. And it sounds like *you* could use a night off."

I am literally the last living thing in Manhattan that needs a night off. But I can't shake the feeling there's a connection between the two of us, and not just the Ed McMahon thing. *Man, did I know Ed McMahon in a past life or something? There's no logical reason for my thinking about him so much.*

Instead of admitting any of that, I decide it's best — *Best for now, at least* — to say, "Sure." I mean, what else have I really got going on anyway? Besides one of these job things, and yet another awkward conversation with Glenn where he makes me feel inferior to him, which is totally absurd. I mean, it's absurd, right? I even ask Chelsea if it's absurd, but she says she doesn't really know Glenn all that well yet.

I dunno. I guess I assumed the answer would be obvious.

Anyway, she gives me the necessary time and coordinates for meeting up later tonight, and I agree to the rendezvous before common sense and future misgivings of the heart can wave me down and put a stop to any of it.

After taking one last look at Melissa's resume in my hand, I release my grip. The paper drifts back and forth in slow motion, landing upon the damp carpet, and I watch as the coffee seeps through it, until her headshot looks like an old photograph, weathered by the passing of both time and love.

I keep staring. And then the thought hits me: is *this* one of those moments? Is this when I'm meant to begin my getting over Melissa? Is this where I'm supposed to be giving up? Moving on? Letting The Boyfriend win?

Should I be honest with myself about the reality of who is meant to be with who? Or at least, who is happiest with whom?

Question: If my Honesty Movement has basically been about as successful as a Rob Schneider movie, do I cut my losses now or sit back and watch it continue to bomb?

Answer: I do enjoy a good shit show. Chester K. Eddy ain't ready to commit to change just yet.

One more look at this wet mess in the office confirms my decision. And so, rather than showing the eensiest bit of responsibility, I opt for putting my superego in a chokehold and immediately bolt from the premises. It's not until I'm on the subway when I realize I not only still have Glenn's theater key with me, but I'm also still wearing these blasted sailor pants, now complete with obnoxious brown stains on them.

To be honest, I don't even care anymore.

Proper Toiletries & The Continuing Quest for Ed McMahon

TBH, if were a little person or had some bizarre Elephant Man sort of deformity, I think I'd totally want to bring back freak shows. I don't see it as being made fun of — *Though it would probably happen, 'cause people are jerks* — and I don't see it as exploitation — *Though I guess by definition that's technically still exploitation.* I don't know. Can't me and my tent-full of Mexican wolfmen, balloon-headed babies, conjoined gymnasts, and Susan Boyles just be praised for being proud of our weird bodies? It's just the same as what those big-boned Southern black women are evangelizing about, isn't it? *"I'm proud of my pigeon-toes an' pinheadedness an' I'ma gonna preach it, Sugah!"* It's exactly the same, except I'd be making money off it.

Okay, that's *definitely* exploitation. Maybe some ideas do need a little filtering first before just going ahead with them.

Still. I'd pay good money to go to a really fucked-up freak show.

So, I'm in Brooklyn. It doesn't feel great, but I guess we're doing this now. This club I'm in is called *Halloo Nigh* — *Which is a definite sign I'm getting too old for nightclubs because that doesn't sound cool or make any fucking sense to me at all* — and I've been waiting for Chelsea at the bar for almost an hour. Granted, I did show up here an hour early, so I really have no right to complain, but this still gives me that feeling like she's not showing up. You'd think if I hate waiting for people so much, I'd start being the late one for everything, right? *You probably think a lot of things about me at this point, none of which have anything to do with making my life less vexing.*

I tried reading the Willows script that was in my bag. I gave it a real honest attempt, but it's just so stupid. And I'm not saying that simply to hate on

Glenn Workman. I flip ahead to Act Three, page ninety-four, where Matthew confronts Melville with a rotisserie spit from the Piggly Wiggly restaurant in his hand:

MATTHEW: I love her, Melville. I love the sparkle that remains after she exits a room. The afterglow of her faded laughter. The space in the bed she leaves behind in the morning. It's everything about her. She means everything to me.
[Raises the rotisserie spit] And if my feelings are trivial, if my words are meaningless to you, I'm prepared to let this rotisserie spit do the talking for me.

MELVILLE: Oh, so you love her now, do you? But why is it you're baring your feelings to *me*, rather than telling Madison herself?

Well, how about that?
There's a girl a ways down the bar who's chatting up some dude. She looks bookish, but not in the Jennifer Aniston-with-glasses sort of way, more like that girl in school who was obviously doing far too much homework to ever think about where to begin getting laid. This girl looks like she shouldn't even be out at a bar at all hours of the night; like she made a wrong turn when she was looking for a coffee shop to sit with a tea and plug away at her novel. She's got those sleep-deprived, ravioli eyelids too. But the thing that really bothers me is she's been chewing on the straw in her drink the whole time. I should just turn my attention elsewhere, but I can't. Her champing is rhythmic; the continuous, near-mastication of that plastic drinking straw makes me want to

yell at her to stop, but I can't turn away. I'm fixated on her oral fixation. And the dude doesn't seem bothered at all, which bothers me more.

I realize New York has an agenda to rid of the city of plastic straws, sort of like Batman cleansing Gotham of ridiculous super criminals. You know, like the Bad Samaritan, Kite Man, and Crazy Quilt. But let's stop discussing plastic straws and talk about The Riddler for a moment. I mean, the Legion of Doom would have gotten away with pretty much all of their Fort Knox gold brick-robbing schemes if the fucking Riddler would have just shut his trap. Lex Luthor and the Doom gang were always one step ahead, until The Riddler steps in and gives the Super Friends some ridiculous brain-teaser that takes Batman like three seconds to figure out and then the heroes stop them. Again. You could almost see the rest of the Legion of Doom off-screen rolling their eyes every time The Riddler stops to dish out another paper-thin conundrum. If I was Lex Luthor, I would have kicked The Riddler's ass off my team so fast. Even Toyman was more valuable, and he just had an army of wind-up tin soldiers. Like Superman ever shit his shorts over a tin soldier.

"Who shit their shorts?" *Ah! Inside voice! I'm bound to figure this out eventually.*

I turn around, and Chelsea McMahon's standing right there, two G&T's in hand. Instantly, I remember those silver-blue eyes, behind those crimson-framed glasses that shine like a Boeing from a 1980's American Airlines commercial. She's got her blonde curls tied back in a delicious mess, and under her coat a black dress, while under that dress an utterly obvious omission of a bra. And I mean Ob-Vee-Us.

Staring directly at her chest, I ask, "When you said you were bringing your girlfriends, is this what you meant?"

"The girlfriends aren't joining us."

"No?" Oh no. Have I just found myself in yet another unexpectedly humil-iating, but still-sort-of-amusing-when-I-look-back-at-it-later situation? How, in just one week, can one man be so oblivious?

"I thought we might get to know one another a bit better."

Her dress is clinging so tightly I can clearly make out surgical scars. I presume a lot of things, but I don't presume that's quite what she meant about getting to know each other better. It can't be this easy. "How about a warm up first?" I ask, somewhat nervously. Maybe subconsciously trying to give myself a break from another mistake? *Okay, that's a stretch.*

"A warm up?"

"Yeah. Have you ever gone in to do a line reading but the director has you loosen up on stage a bit first? Like you sing the alphabet, or a song everyone knows the lyrics to. *Wonderwall* or *Bohemian Rhapsody* or *Total Eclipse of the Heart*, for example."

Chelsea looks around the club nervously. Straw Girl is still chomping away. "You want me to sing *Bohemian Rhapsody* right here at the bar?"

"That was only an example. How about a Random Comment Faceoff? We take turns saying something totally random. Anything at all that comes to mind."

"You start."

"Okay—Shingles: sounds pretty funny. Not awesome at all." All right. I'll admit that's my go-to starter for basically every Random Comment Faceoff. No shame. Everyone needs a dependable opener. "Your turn."

"Hmm. How about, what's the deal with someone giving you a URL and they say '*backslash*' when they actually mean '*forward slash*?'"

"You're a natural! Yeah, I fucking *hate* that. Lazy bastards. Okay, my turn again. How come you don't see any Goth around anymore? Seriously, I don't think I've seen a Goth person in this city for ten years."

"Did you know a forward slash is also referred to as a solidus, virgule, or whack?"

"Hey, hold up. Are you going to talk about forward slashes all night? Also, those sound an awful lot like *Lord of the Rings* names."

She raises her arm dramatically, like she's onstage again. *"Solidus! Virgule! Whack! We must leave the Shire immediately!"* Whoa. Chelsea McMahon is actually funny. And I almost pinched her nipple right now, which is my standard *I approve of your witticism* response.

My go, again. "Somebody asked me for directions like a year ago, and I still catch myself worrying about whether or not they made it to where they were going."

She smiles at me like I'm really giving her something deep to ponder. "That is messed up." Okay, I might be in the midst of lamenting the near-destruction of my relationship hopes with Melissa, but maybe Chelsea McMahon can act as a suitable stopgap? "Did you know most people generate *more* pheromones if they never wash their perineum?"

"What? Really? You know what's funny, is that I was just thinking about the perineum earlier today. Amazing how a bit of skin between your genitals and anus can be such a hot button topic."

"I'll show you mine if you show me yours," she says. And then she squeezes my nipple.

Oh dang. This girl. "By the way, I *never* wash my perineum. So, my pheromones are probably thick like a good New England clam chowder."

"Yes! Your pheromones are shooting out of you like ball bearings."

I snort some gin out of my nose. I also realize Chelsea's chewing on her own little black straw now too, but it's not bothering me nearly as much as Straw Girl's habit. Chelsea bites on the end like she's nervous. In her shimmering eyes, little pools of wetness form upon the lids. It's not tears though, but more like there's something in the air that's bothering her. Maybe it's me? The Chester K. Eddy School of Nuisance says the only real way to tell if you're bothering someone is to ask them something you *know* will bother them. So, I go with, "How could you have made it this far in life and *never* have anyone ask you if you're related to Ed McMahon? It seems impossible."

"I guess it's because not everyone thinks about Ted McMahon as much as you. It's probably as simple as that."

Hm. Not too bothered. "It's Ed. Not Ted." The Chester K. Eddy Accelerated Annoyance Program insists you give it another go, just to be sure. "Is McMahon even your real last name? Did you just pick it so people would ask you about it?"

"Literally no one has ever asked me about it." Chelsea really does appear to be legitimately unfazed. "What about *your* last name?"

"Eddy?"

"Do you use it as a metaphor? Because your own life is running the opposite direction of the current, forming a little whirlpool and sucking in all the negative shit around you?"

Ouch. I squeeze my own nipple now, hard enough that Chelsea McMahon's accusation hurts a little less. "Is that really how you see me?"

"Just a thought."

I look at my hands on the bar, opening them to observe my palms. *Life line. Love line. Wisdom line. Horndog line.* Like I'm reading my own fortune and realizing I've got very little idea where it's all heading. Now it's me who's got the straw-chewing nervous tic happening.

She says to my glass, "I see you're empty."

"I am," I admit. "Empty of all hope, it seems."

"Your drink, I meant. Let me get you another one."

My beverage has been sucked down deep into my desolate, Charlie Brown whirlpool of shittiness. "Thanks," I say, but she's already off.

Straw Girl's still chewing away down the bar over there. Her guy's got his hand on her inner thigh, creeping higher and higher, but she seems completely oblivious.

When Chelsea returns, she slides a fresh drink right into my hand. "Don't get so bummed," she says. "Whatever it is that's getting you down, I can help you forget about it. A few more of these won't hurt, either." She clinks her glass sharply into mine.

"Thanks. It's been a rough week."

"You're in show biz. Of course it's been a rough week. That's what we do it for, isn't it?"

"I thought I was doing it for the groupies and my name in bright lights."

Nothing.

"That was a joke, by the way. Actually, I have no idea why I'm doing it." *Especially with Melissa and Glenn doing it, that is.*

"Dude. Yesterday you were being pretty negative, and it doesn't seem as though you've come very far."

"Maybe I haven't. But maybe that's an indication though?"

"Of what, exactly?"

"That I should get out of town. Leave New York. Maybe go back to

Madison, Wisconsin. Or maybe just a road trip would do me some good."

"A road trip? Do you even have a car?"

Shit. "That would probably help, huh? Have you ever noticed how, in movies when the characters decide to just get up and go on a road trip, and everything's all great and fun and they're bagging the hottest chicks in every state — and some provinces — but they never pack any dental hygiene products or other proper toiletries before they go. And they never ever seem concerned about it in the least. That really bothers me."

"Do you have proper toiletries with you right now?"

"I don't even *own* toiletries. I use a mascara brush to clean my teeth. And I've got a hand towel I swiped from a hotel six years ago. That's it." I can't tell if she's relating or if she's disgusted by my honesty. The two reactions can be very interchangeable sometimes. "Maybe I should go on a road trip with my brother? He could probably do with getting out of the house for a while. Might be good for both of us. Some good brotherly bonding, you know?"

"You'd actually choose to leave New York? And leave everything you're passionate about behind?"

Passionate? ME? "I tried once. Leaving the city. At one point, at my most jaded and disenchanted — well, before *right now*, that is — I decided a road trip was the only thing that could re-energize me, and maybe I could do with a little of that soul-searching bullshit you always hear about. I was going to hit the pavement and really see America and find myself, you know? But I planned terribly and packed poorly and I only made it as far as Hartford before giving up."

"Connecticut? Why would you head East from New York if you were traveling across the country?"

"I was back-tracking, so I could see America from one coast to the other. That's the dream!"

"Aren't we already on the coast here?"

"It doesn't matter."

"Can I ask, what is it you want to escape *from*?"

"I think it's the anonymity. Like, do you ever find yourself on the subway checking out all the other people? Stealing glances. Wondering why they're wearing what they're wearing."

"People in sailor pants and *SisQó Tour 2000* hoodies should not throw stony glances."

"Trust me. There's a lot worse fashion affronts than *this*."

"Unlikely. But okay, I'll play along."

"Regardless, I feel like no one's ever stealing glances *my* way. Like, I'm a fairly good-looking dude, aren't I? Why is no one checking *me* out?"

"You're kind of forcing my hand here Chester, but I'm just going to say again: sailor pants and SisQó hoodies."

"Funny. But there's got to be something I'm missing."

"I just think it's insecurities. And wishing you had what others have. And I think you're lonely."

In my head, I compile a quick list: My escalating tab at Philly's; the crabs these pants are surely giving me; Melissa, and the fact I can't tell her my true feelings. I visualize the caved-in sockets of the dead rat outside the theater. "You're right, Chelsea. I *am* kind of lonely."

"And leaving will make you *less* lonely?"

It's worth a try, I think. Melissa seems happy. So, who am I to mess with that? What kind of person would I be if I tried to dismantle her happiness, just because I'm miserable? Because I'm selfish. Because I love her. In all of time before me, men have loved and not been loved in return. I'm nothing new.

She says, "I wrote and performed a one-woman show — you might have noticed it on my resume — called *Anywhere But Now.*"

God, I think. Is there anything sadder than a self-written one-woman stage play they performed in the park in front of nobody but a bunch of Russians playing chess and dog-owners bagging up and pocketing their pet's shit? Is there anything sadder at all?

Maybe just my life.

"Do you remember that on my resume?"

Something tells me admitting that the only thing worth remembering on her resume was her glorious rack creeping up into her headshot might not be the answer she's looking for. So instead, *insert lie here*: "Yes. I totally remember. I wanted to see it too, but I had oral surgery that day."

"It ran for a week."

"I was laid up for a pretty extensive amount of time. Did you know they'll just keep giving you pain-killers and other anesthetics if you keep asking for them?"

"Well, anyway. *Anywhere But Now* was about a girl who was in love with a guy." *Yawn.* "And the guy liked her a lot but he couldn't love her back, not the way she wanted him to, because he was in love with someone else." *Isn't that typical relationship behavior patterns?* "But she wouldn't let it go, and it consumed her. She made everyone around her angry: her family didn't speak to her; her boss fired her unceremoniously; her roommate moved out—" *How many people were in this one-woman play?* "But what's worse was that she treated herself poorly. And she couldn't see that her loneliness was something she didn't need to carry with her."

"So, what did she do? How did it end?"

"That was where it ended."

"That's not an ending. Where's the closure? The new beginnings?"

"It's ambiguous. The viewers decide what happens, depending on their own feelings toward the character."

Hold on. Let me cue up that Neil Patrick Harris gun-in-the-back-of-the-mouth GIF on my phone.

"I'll be honest: I hate ambiguity in art."

"Well, most people don't."

"No, trust me. Most people do. They were probably just being polite. And, *Anywhere But Now*? What does that even mean? Doesn't any**WHERE** imply a *place*? But NOW is a *time*."

"It implies she doesn't like anything at all about the moment she's stuck in. No matter where she goes. So *Now* acts more like a place. It's *everywhere*."

"That doesn't make any fucking sense."

Chelsea angrily slides her own drink in front of me. "Here. You finish this."

"What? Are you leaving?"

"You know, I was only planning on seducing you to try and help my chances of landing the part in your play. But now I don't want it."

"The seducing or the acting gig?"

"Both."

"You're supposed to say *Neither*. Jeez, I thought you were the word worm?" *What is it with ladies getting me drunk and trying to take advantage of me?* "Listen, Chelsea. Sexual favors for professional benefits may have been cool at one point, but that is totally out of line in today's climate. *Me Too*, my ass. I feel so dirty." Do I tell her I lied about her not getting the part in the first place? How she actually still might have a chance? How it's not even up to me anyway? "But you can still seduce me if you want. We don't have to let the professional stuff get in the way."

She mumbles something about professionalism as she fumbles around in her purse before she pulls out a handful of yellow and blue pills and swallows them dry. Maybe because it would be too awkward to ask for her drink back at this point? "I think we'll just end it like this," she says with finality.

"I thought you liked ambiguous endings? What happened to *that* shit?"

"Goodbye, Mister Eddy. I hope you enjoy your miserable vortex of an existence. I'll be happy to not have to listen to any more of your ramblings about this Ed McMahon person."

"Ed McMahon is a national treasure! And you're sullying his name!"

Without another word, Chelsea McMahon exits the club, just as quickly as she appeared. At least I got a few free drinks out of it. Butt-dialing does have its benefits, apparently. I pour her drink into mine, not caring at all that the excess amount flows over onto the floor.

It doesn't make sense. I can't comprehend how someone would want a part in *When the Willows Speak They Sing in Unison* so badly they were willing to defile a half-assed director's assistant to get it. Am I missing something here? Is Glenn Workman not only a sexual virtuoso, but also a Broadway savant? I am definitely missing something. He's still got the kind of face that's worth punching though; you can't take that away from him.

I cannot believe I came all the way out to Brooklyn tonight for this. Man, actors are the worst. Present company included.

Where Everybody Knows Your Made-Up Name, You Big Fat Liar

TBH, I once went into what I thought was a FedEx shipping center, but it turned out to be a brothel instead. These companies can be very confusing sometimes! I mean, just tell me what your business is in very clearly-labeled signage, already. I don't appreciate — *though recent history might prove otherwise* — looking like an idiot. Trust me though, when I say they looked at me pretty strangely when I asked about their Puerto Rican rates. And third-party pre-payment. And my small package.

After Chelsea left, I actually spoke briefly with the girl who was still — *Still? Really? I mean, have some self-respect, girl* — at the bar chewing on her plastic straw. Though bookish and pure of heart she may have seemed, she was actually an incredibly terrible person. I mean, she was a fascist for one thing, but she also claimed *Hot Tub Time Machine 2* was far superior to the original. *What—?* Say what you will about fascists, but for the most part, they should still know how to recognize a good movie. So yes, sometimes first impressions really do matter. But I did manage to bum a smoke off the dude who was sitting with her, so sometimes things do happen for a reason.

Thanks entirely to Chelsea McMahon's malefic intentions, I stumble out of whatever this bar was called, and back out into the great, vast, stinking somewhere of Brooklyn. It's fairly dark, yet everything surrounding me seems brown. Just brown. The trees? Fine, I can buy that. The garbage in the gutters? Okay, maybe they're all paper bags from fast food takeout. But the sidewalk and the storefronts and the streetlight and the moon? That's too much, man. And way too weird.

I hate Brooklyn.

After some time spent wading my way through the borough's murky brownness — *I have no idea how far or long I've walked; my cell phone battery life was at three bars when I left and it's still at three. How's a guy to know?* — I spot some action up ahead: two people going at it right there on the sidewalk. Sex, I mean, not a fistfight.

Actually, upon walking closer — *Yes, I did so keep moving toward them. What? I'm supposed to just turn around?* — I realize it's not sex either. One lifeless shape is unmoving on the sidewalk, while a second body crouches above. A dead body! I wouldn't have ever thought that would get my blood pumping more than public stranger intercourse, but this is thrilling! My excitement level is supercharged.

You're redeeming yourself, Stinky Brown Brooklyn. Only marginally, perhaps. But it's something. I'll bet nobody's held you with this much esteem recently, aside from those annoying hipsters who keep trying to bring back tobacco pipes, but come on: even *you* wish they'd shut up already, don'tcha?

Smoking the last cigarette I found in my bag, I boldly ask the conscious fella, "What seems to be the problem here?" Yep, just like I'm a beat cop trying to keep trouble off my streets.

"This guy just hit the ground," he tells me. He points to some bar behind us. "I was sitting in there and saw him collapse. Right on his face."

I look at the body; eyes rolled into the back of his ugly head, pointed up at the brown stars above us. His nose and mouth are bloodied. "So how come he's on his back?"

"What—?"

"If he landed on his face, how come he's on his back?"

"Because I turned him over. Do you know CPR?"

"Should you be manhandling a body like that? I mean, you have no idea how injured he might be."

"Who in the—? Who are *you* anyway?" This guy looks at me. Searching for answers maybe, while I'm just looking back and realizing how handsome he is. I can appreciate a good pulchritudinous countenance when I see it. The dude's got the classic chiseled mug, freshly trimmed salt and pepper hair, piercing blue eyes — *Turns out not everything in Brooklyn is brown* — and a five o'clock shadow he probably started growing at six o'clock.

"Who am I?" Another drag on my cigarette, and I flawlessly blow smoke out the side of mouth. "Just a passing leaf on the wind, friend. Just a leaf on the wind. Hey, what's CPR stand for anyway? I mean, I know what it *is*, but I don't really have any idea what it actually stands for. Do you? Can't be Canadian Pacific Railroad, can it?"

"Listen, can you help or not? Have you got a phone? You could call 911."

Just as I'm about to reply with 'Actually, no, sorry. But I'm expecting a phone call' — *Which is true, because what if Melissa chose this time to call me back? I know she would, too, because that's how these Karmic retribution situations seem to work* — someone else bursts from the bar spitting out something about an incoming ambulance. I'm not really paying attention though, since I'm still distracted by Rico Suave's superhuman hairline. That shit would make Zac Efron weep. If Zac Efron wasn't weeping somewhere already.

"Well," I say, before adding a triumphant: "I guess that's that." It doesn't take long before we hear approaching sirens in the distance.

I hold out a *Put-'er-There* fist for him to bump — *Hoping he won't finish it off with one of those annoying exploding fist numbers. I fucking hate that*

— but he just coolly ignores it, and places a manly palm on my shoulder instead. "Don't worry about panicking back there," he tells me calmly, flashing his weatherman teeth. His grip is firm, yet gentle. "It happens to the best of us in moments like this." God, his hand is so warm. Like a heating pad.

The ambulance is already rounding the corner and pulling up alongside the curb, unloading whatever equipment is needed to deal with whatever the hell is going on over there. I don't know and I honestly don't care, really. Which likely makes me look like a complete dick, but Superdude here doesn't admonish me any. We both take this moment to sit down on the sidewalk and allow for the flashing red lights of the emergency response vehicle to wash out some of the brown of our surroundings.

He says, "I would have called 911 myself, but I dashed out of the bar so fast I just left my stuff at the table. But that's how it goes sometimes. We've all got our moments of heroism, don't we? That adrenaline that just comes out of nowhere, right?"

I dig deep inside attempting to find anything at all that could be positively misconstrued as a flash of heroism. My special Wite-Out love note for Melissa? My moment of bonding with a possible fugitive named Bullet? Certainly not yesterday's trip to the Deutsche Bank. I'd like to erase those events from my personal records.

I got nada.

Maybe offering to help Glenn Workman with his play might be the closest thing, but with the current suspicion that Glenn is actually Mel's secret boyfriend — *As well as my overactive imagination's blatant misuse of sexual fantasies involving massage oil, rat tails, and poorly written stage plays —* my distaste for him is currently trumping anything positive.

So, all I tell the dude next to me is, "Don't I know it."

God, it's like this guy's been genetically engineered to show the world what a man is supposed to look like. This is the kind of guy Mel should be in love with. Not Glenn Workman.

He says, "We're on top of the world one minute, and then—" And then he tags a Bronx cheer onto the end of his sentence, adding a big thumbs down for good measure.

I consider his life lesson for a moment, before naturally sidetracking the conversation. I think conversation sidetracking must be my superpower. I'll have to get working on a codename as soon as I find the time. "That's a dumb saying: *On top of the world*. Because technically, we're ALL on top of the world, aren't we?"

"You mean, because anywhere on the surface of the planet is the top?"

"You nailed it." *Finger gun!*

"Well, then sure. We are all on top of the world."

"Sure are. Well, except for the mole people."

"Uh—? I don't think—"

"You know what, fuck the mole people. They get too much attention."

"I've literally never heard anyone talking about mole people before. Do mole people even exist?"

"I've never seen one."

"So, who cares? Why let them bother you then?"

Damn, this dude has got life figured out, doesn't he? Sitting next to him on the sidewalk and eyeing him up and down, I can't help but guess he's some sort of messiah — or an *It's a Wonderful Life* Henry Travers ghost, but much better looking — sent to Great Brown Brooklyn tonight in order to show me something miraculous. Something awesome that will open my eyes. Like the honesties I think I'm gushing are not really the truth. Like maybe I'm not being honest with *myself.*

Whoa. That was pretty good. I can't believe I just came up with that. This sexy messiah works fast.

"Come on," he says, rising to his feet. "Let me buy you a drink. You look like you could use one."

But let's just put the honesty on hold for a moment; there's more free booze to be had!

Do I tell him I'm basically a walking advertisement for inappropriate drinking schedules right now? Not if I can disguise my inebriation this well, I don't. So, we head inside the bar, just as the body that was on the sidewalk is being gurneyed into the rear of the ambulance.

***

The sign of a good man is when he asks you what you want to drink before he asks you for your name. I imagine this is exactly the opposite if you're a woman though, but I'm not a woman, so it's pretty much the best thing in the world right now.

Prince No-Name returns to the table and slides my bourbon across the smooth, lacquered surface, and right into my open, waiting hand. "Thanks, man. So, what's your name, anyway? I'm honestly not comfortable calling you any of the names I've got floating around in my head." *Names like: Cowboy, The Candyman, Don Draper, Doctor Hot Butt, Burrito Grande, His Royal Waffle, Babes McBaberson. I could go on.*

"Brook Bonhomme. How about yourself?"

Cue bourbon spit take. "Your name is actually Brook? My friend and I know a guy named Brook too. Not too many dudes with that name, are there?" He doesn't confirm or deny this statement, choosing instead to slam back some incredibly dark beer. I imagine Sidney Poitier and Marlon Brando slammed their incredibly dark beers back in much the same manly fashion. I can only imagine what it might look like if Charlie Brown attempted the same move. At my most blunt, I ask, "What's your email address?"

Brook wipes his mouth with the tiny square napkin that came with the drink. Meanwhile, I didn't know anyone was ever supposed to use those napkins. He says, "That's a little forward, don't you think?"

"Maybe. But I like to use it as a conversation starter. I mean, everyone's got an email address, right? BAM. There's something we've got in common straight away. Aside from our remarkable good looks, that is."

Then he actually gives in and tells me his email address. And it's very, very boring. Like *Name + Birth Year* boring. Guh. So disappointingly forgettable.

I pester on. "But have you ever had another email you used for the sole purpose of fucking around with folks?"

There.

Right there. That's it. I catch him squirming just a tiny bit. A tell so miniscule, only someone like Chester K. Eddy with his staggering junior detective skills accumulated from watching too much Carmen Sandiego as a kid could pick up on.

"You know, I used to have a very different — much less professional — one."

"It didn't happen to have a Sixty-Nine in there somewhere, did it?" *Pester on, Chester. Pester on.*

"How did you know?"

"All the good ones do, Brooky."

Oh.

My.

God.

Shitting.

Gods.

This is definitely the guy. It's pornstarjugz69@aol.com himself, sitting right across the table from me! I should be soiling myself right now, but as far as I can tell, these remarkable bell bottoms are miraculously still poop free.

"All the good ones do," I repeat. But then again, if this *is* actually the guy, he sure as shit doesn't match any of Melissa's graphic descriptions. Brook is handsome — *like Black Stallion Tail handsome* — and totally without any of the deficiencies Mel had included in her reports. I go ahead and ask, "I thought you were supposed to have a peg leg or a neck goiter or a weird Jason Momoa forehead or something?"

He stiffens up a little. Not as much as if he actually *had* a peg leg, but enough to indicate he's considering changing his mind about me. "Do I know you?"

"Do you remember scheduling a meeting with someone at the Deutsche Bank?"

"Two months back?"

"Correctomundo."

"That was *you* I spoke with?"

"Nailed it again, Doctor Hot Butt." *Damn. That one slipped out.*

He gives his head a shake as if to say *Never mind* to my comment. Then he concisely and jovially explains how he never made it into the office for our scheduled meeting — *The one I would have missed anyway due to getting fired for—Okay, we really don't need to get into that again* — but then he felt bad for canceling and rescheduled, eventually meeting briefly with someone else there.

"Melissa?" I ask.

"That's her," he clarifies. And then he asks, "So you are—?"

Hmm. "My name's Jeff. With a J. But it's not short for Jeffrey. Just Jeff. My parents liked the name Jeffrey, but then Jeffrey Dahmer was all over the news so they chose to rethink things a little."

"Jeff and Jeffrey? That's not much of a difference, when you think about it."

"What can I tell you? They were really married to Jeffrey. It was probably the toughest decision they ever made."

"So, in an effort to *not* name their child after a notorious serial killer, they still sort of named you after a notorious serial killer?"

"Uh. Well, when you put it like that. But Dahmer wasn't *that* notorious. He worked at a chocolate factory, you know?"

"Hey, I'm just joshin' ya." He takes a fair-sized gulp of beer before asking, "So, do you still work at the bank?"

"Not really, nope. But we parted on excellent and very professional terms, if you were wondering."

"I wasn't. But when you specifically point that out, it does make me a little suspicious. So, what do you do for work these days, Jeff?"

Think fast, Chester. "Animation. Stop-motion Animation, actually." *Nice. A totally believable profession. I almost bought that myself.* "That's the stuff where we use paper dolls and clay models and move them in tiny increments and snap a picture. Takes like two years to shoot ten minutes of film."

"That doesn't sound right."

"It is though. Dude, who's the expert here, you or me?"

"Fair point." Then he finally holds out a hand. "It's nice to meet you, Jeff. To tell you the truth, Brook was not the first name my parents had for me either."

"I was going to say. It's not really the most masculine name. Kind of girly."

He ignores that last comment completely. "As a kid, my father always threatened to go to City Hall and change our names if we ever misbehaved. Dad finally had enough one day, and changed my name to Brook."

"Wow. Your dad had amazing balls."

"He still does."

"I'm not going to ask you how you know that. But still, I suppose you could have done worse than Brook."

"Legally, he changed it to Brooklyn."

"Ugh. Okay, that's definitely worse. What the hell did you do to finally put your dad over the edge like that? Did you flush the toilet while he was in the shower? Draw a penis on his forehead when he was passed out drunk?"

Brook takes a good, long sip of beer now. He stares out at the fogged-up bar window, trying to grasp a distant, fading memory. It's the same sort of stare I have when I'm trying to come up with a good lie.

Not that I lie anymore. Honesty Movement, remember?

Shit. My name is Jeff — or Galahad, depending on who you ask — and I work as a stop-motion animator? Could be creeping a bit too far from the truth. Whatever.

"What did I do? I don't even remember now," he finally says.

"That's okay. Whatever it was likely got pushed down into your subconscious with all the beatings, right? You'll probably figure it out in therapy later."

"That's a positive outlook."

His phone buzzes happily on the table. I pray my own won't be going off anytime soon. Don't need to be putting a damper on this special, new friend bonding moment with some classic but objectionable 2 Live Crew. But still, how nice would it be if Melissa called me right now?

Brook looks at the number and respectfully raises a finger to excuse himself. He answers with a, "Hi, love." Like he's some British soap star.

Pause.

"No. I'm just talking to a guy." *Just a guy? Did these last thirty minutes mean nothing to you?*

Pause.

"Jeff." *That's better.*

Pause.

"What? Ha ha! No, definitely not THIS guy." *He's not laughing at my expense now, is he?* Brook looks me over quickly, evaluating my wardrobe choices. "A little eccentric, maybe. But he's cool." *Hell yes, I am. Even in these throwaway theater costume pants and frilly pink socks, I remain the biggest eye of the Hurricane of Cool. Wait, is it possible for a hurricane to have more than one eye? And is being a hurricane a positive metaphor? Maybe destruction is not the right way to go?*

As my own thoughts once again distract me from reality, Brook finishes up his phone call; congratulating her for something or other, and extolling her achievement at being the luckiest gal on the planet for getting to see him shirtless every night, and then finally saying goodbye. "Love you," he says. As effortlessly and inexorably as I'd like to one day say it.

"Sorry," he apologizes, turning back to me. "My lady love's just checking in. Calling to tell me she misses me."

"That's sweet. *My* lady love's cheating on me with my boss."

"Well, that totally sucks."

"Tell me about it. But don't worry about me none. I'm planning on drinking my sorrows away."

"That sucks too, Jeff."

"Listen, I'm going to be honest with you, Brooky. I think I'm going to barf."

"Just not into all the lovey-dovey stuff, are you?"

"No. I'm really going to *barrrr*—" I taste the bile coming up from my stomach, and I hold a bit in my mouth long enough to wobble-run out the front door. Brook's hands firmly grasp my shoulders the whole way out to the sidewalk.

And out it comes. Right into a dirty snowbank. More brown for Brooklyn.

He helps me to the curb — *So chivalrous!* — and we slide down a ways from the stink of my festering puke. Now that I've gotten that out of my system, I realize it's actually not so gross out here. Throw up notwithstanding.

"What's gotten to you? Was it the bourbon?" he asks.

"One-part bourbon mixed with five-parts bad nightclub G&T's mixed with thirty years of *this*."

"So, you're in a bit of a rut?"

"I just—One minute I've got this confidence and unbridled enthusiasm, and the next I'm wondering how the hell I've gotten myself into pretty much every situation I ever get in. It's almost like I don't think about things before I do them."

"Nobody is so horribly uninstinctual, are they?"

With my face buried between my knees, I say, "I'll just let my track record speak for itself, thank you very much."

"Well, perhaps you're nothing more than a creature of instinct? Millions of years of evolution have to eventually lead to the creation of beings so advanced they wouldn't even need to waste energy with such nonsense as thinking."

"So now I'm a highly advanced super being? I'll admit, that's one I've never heard before."

"Well, I'll be honest. You can't be too highly advanced, or you wouldn't stink so much. When was the last time you showered, Jeff?"

"I'm on a thirty-six-hour shower schedule."

"So, thirty-six hours ago?"

"I'm not very good at the maths."

"Well you smell like a pirate."

Shaking a leg flirtatiously, I say, "I'm a sailor, actually. And I think I've gotten vomit on my pants. Sorry. I should say, *MORE* vomit."

"Let me ask you this, sailor: when it comes to life goals, do you want to be the one hoisting the sails, or the one scrubbing the deck?"

"Is your scenario assuming that hoisting the sails is the most-esteemed sailor job? Because I'd lean more toward navigation. Or shore leave. Yeah, shore leave seems to be where it's at."

"Jeff, all I'm trying to say is that no matter what you do, always strive to be the best at it. Don't settle for being the lowest man on the totem pole."

Just what I need: more helpful advice. I can't take any more helpful advice, especially when it's not even all that helpful. Totem poles? Where are we anyway, the Pacific Northwest? This is fucking New York City. Ain't been no totem poles around here since the colonies burned 'em down. I bury my head further between my legs, not caring at all about the puke smell. *And by the way, Brooky, the lowest man on the totem pole has to be the strongest one so he can hold all those other dudes up. Especially that lazy fucking eagle, who could just fly and make things easier on bottom guy, but oh no! He's got to just sit there at the top being a dick.*

"You know," he says with a rugged rumble in his throat. "I just live around the corner from here. How about you come on over and we'll get you cleaned up. A fresh start! I can give you some new pants too, if you want. You look about my size."

The sign of a good serial killer is when he invites you over to his place and you don't even stop to think about the possibility that he's going to chop you up and stuff you into his stockroom full of sausage casings. So, is Brook a bad serial killer or not a serial killer at all? Either way, I shouldn't have to worry, should I? How dangerous could a bad serial killer be? You never hear about them. And hey, if I can score some new pants out of the deal, it's really a win-win.

"What's the worst that could happen?" I say, like anyone who's never seen the worst of anything.

Rock and A Hard Place (Chester K. Eddy: Boyfriend Hunter)

TBH, I'll sometimes clean my body with wet wipes instead of having a shower. Mostly just so I can sleep in a bit longer, but usually I just do it because I'm lazy. Sometimes — *Okay, every time. Have you ever seen the price of wet wipes?* — I'll use toilet paper. But hey, I'll wet it first. I'm no troglodyte. So, it's not uncommon for someone to point out the dried scrap of paper stuck to my neck, chin, forehead, or ass crack. The trick is making sure that someone is a *different* someone every time, just to keep the judgmental glaring to a minimum.

So, I realize I've probably talked a lot about serial killers. I can't help it, really. It's one of my Top-Three Fallback Subjects for Jumpstarting Boring Conversations. And *What are the rest*, you didn't ask? Without further ado (because who needs more ado in their life anyway?):

#3: Hot Tub Time Machine's intricate plot, as well as its social and moral commentary (And how the sequel is not much more than a bad fart joke — *Yes, there are so good fart jokes*)
#2: Ear anatomy (Man, I really boned up for that role of Doctor Lauchlan Twindler, disgraced Manhattan ear, nose, and throat specialist, didn't I?)
#1: Serial killers (But mostly just the glitzy American ones; you talk about the Russian and weird European ones too much and people assume the worst shit about you)

But here I've found myself at pornstarjugz69@aol.com's apartment, which, honestly, is a fair bit bigger than it probably needs to be for some dude who just bought me a drink and had his meaty palms on my quivering shoulders as I barfed it up onto a sidewalk. I mean, no mentally unhinged person could afford a place this size in New York. It's tidy, but I take into account the few boxes piled up in the corner. Just moving in? Just moving out? Seen the movie *Se7en* one too many times?

Also, I cannot believe I didn't ask him what he even does for a living. Total rookie mistake on my part.

Question: Would it sound worse if Brook told me he worked at a chocolate factory, or that he is currently between jobs?

Answer: I feel like it's far too late to matter much either way.

As we breezed through his apartment, my keen senses noted the details of a telescope at the window — *Hello, instacreeper* — a dart board behind the door with no darts stuck in it — *Curiouser and curiouser* — more than one samurai sword mounted on the walls — *Let's be real here, more than zero is a safety and security risk* — and dozens of boxes of tissue paper scattered around — *'Cause serial killers are chronic masturbators. Everyone knows that.*

So yeah. Maybe I do talk about serial killers enough to make John Q. Public a little uncomfortable, but I think it's only prepared me to watch out for the tiny details that could lead to potential *Me-Being-Murdered* situations.

This I say as I walk right into the killer's den. Totally drunk too, I should add.

Also, I'm currently showering in his bathroom, the door slightly ajar. *Did I mention that part? I probably should have mentioned that part.* His shower curtain has a muted design of animal skeletons all over it too. I thought they were innocent seashells at first. But no. Rodents. Birds. You know, various creatures who have very little in the way of defense mechanisms. There are also a few bottles of feminine body cleaning products in the shower (a lavender mesh sponge and a loofah exfoliating pad, exotic fruit-scented body wash with moisture beads) so who knows how unstable this person really is.

And maybe I'm wrong in thinking there's dried blood around the drain, but I'm completely willing to blow things out of proportion at this point. My prerogative.

What the fuck have I gotten myself into?

I turn the water off and opt for an air-dry, since I don't know where these towels have been and what they've touched. And this is when, as I stand here naked in another man's bathroom, I spot something else in the waste bin.

Yep. Human hair.

The ultimate sign.

Reaching into the garbage, I pull it out. It's lengthy, maybe eight inches, and tied together with a hair elastic. Looks like a pony tail was snipped off and tossed away. It's a bit more peppery than salty, but definitely the same color as the stuff on Brook's head. Did Brook have a ponytail? What's with all the dudes lately and their long hair?

Weird.

I toss it back in the waste bin, and take the clothes Brook left for me on the vanity. Beneath the neatly folded shirt and pants I discover a pair of scissors, hair clippers, and little hairs everywhere. I guess he cut this thing off just before going out tonight?

Curious.

These clothes are cool: chinos, a *Dismemberment Plan* t-shirt, and even a pair of Calvin Klein boxer briefs, which seem to be brand-new (*Does he just have unopened packages of undies in this place? Is that a serial killer thing too?*) And he's right: we are the same size. The clothes fit me perfectly. Better than my own clothes ever did.

Convenient.

I check myself out in the mirror, palm my hair into place, and decide I'm looking pretty decent. This may be the first time in a long time that I've put any effort at all into looking good, even though it was someone else who made the effort, really. Dressed to kill. Or dressed to *be killed*, as it were.

I peek through the open crack in the door, but there's no movement out there.

Ugh. How am I going to just walk back out there, thank him for his hospitality, and then excuse myself without getting Highlander'd by a samurai sword? There's really no polite way to part company with a presumed serial killer, is there?

"Excuse me, I know you were just about to turn my skull into a crude masturbation device, but I just remembered today was Buy-One-Get-One at the Cinnabon. Did you need me to pick up some more Kleenex while I'm out?"

But then, with a trembling hand on the doorknob, I notice something unusual. On a shelf beside the towel rack, almost tucked out of sight, is a rock. Flat, heart-shaped, and painted black.

My Zen rock.

Oh.

My.

God.

Shitting—You know what? I think my God has got to be about done with all the God-shitting by now. Let's give the poor guy a rest.

I take the rock in hand, and I'm surprised to find it doesn't say "I'm a Dick Butt." The whole thing has been colored black, and there's a new note written in fancy silver marker — *Yes, even fancier than Wite-Out* — that reads:

"BREAK A LEG"

Okay, I'll admit I can be fairly slow on the uptake at times, but it's all coming together now: the Zen rock; the pomegranate body wash in the shower; the chopped ponytail in the garbage. And the Deutsche Bank connection. Brook said he met with Melissa. He *knew* her.

But it seems he knows her a little better than I thought. Like, *"Penis, meet Vagina"* better.

Glenn Workman isn't The Boyfriend after all. It's Brooklyn Bonhomme.

Even Lester from the office told me what I needed to know: Melissa's boyfriend had a ponytail, he's about the same size as me, he likes chinos, and he's handsome.

Maybe Brook *isn't* a murderer, but he's certainly just killed my confidence and chopped it up and jerked off on it and stuffed it into a suitcase.

I definitely don't think I can give my Highlander moment another go right now. There can be only one, and you know what? I'm withdrawing myself from the competition. I've lost out to a dude named Brooklyn. So, go on and decapitate me with that samurai sword. Chester K. Eddy: Boyfriend Hunter is better off simply Charlie Browning his way out of here: admitting defeat, and walking away, head down about as low as I can get it.

Pocketing the rock — *File that under S for Small Victories* — I simply walk right back into the living room, hands up. Brook is just standing there, right in the middle of the room. Like he's been doing nothing but waiting for me to come out.

"Jeff! You clean up well, my friend. What else can I do for you?"

"You can answer one question for me, Brooklyn."

"Shoot."

"Are you The Boyfriend?"

Pause. But is this a processing sort of pause or a calculating, gotta-stay-one-step-ahead-of-you pause? "I'm *A* boyfriend. I don't know if I'm important enough to be *THE* boyfriend. Though it might depend on what you're really asking here. You seem agitated."

"Melissa? The girl you met at the Deutsche Bank? Are you *her* boyfriend?"

He gives me a cocked head, and a look that seems to wonder why on earth I'd ever be making a deal about this. "I'll tell you something. When I eventually made it in for that meeting, we really hit it off. We've been seeing one another ever since."

So, she's been lying to me about him the entire time? I finger the Break-a-Leg/Zen rock in my pocket, and I really want to use it to break *his* legs right now. He paints over MY rock and takes credit for it, using it to wish her luck on her audition? Not cool. "So, *you're* the asshole? And the asshole who I *thought* was The Boyfriend was really just the weird, pervy, lettuce-burger asshole I originally thought he was all along? But it was *you*, asshole, who's been secretly dating Melissa, who — *now that I think of it* — has kind of been being an asshole *herself* lately. And those assholes at work who were all lying to me, too? And my asshole brother who kicked me out? And of course—"

"Listen, listen. Let me stop you right there. I want to give you some advice my dad once gave me—"

He goes to put his hands on my shoulders again, but this time I swat him away. "Oh, no. Not more fatherly advice. What is it about me that seems to warrant fatherly advice? Am I lacking guidance?"

"You do seem a tad directionless."

"Also, it's occurring to me that the only dad who hasn't given me any advice lately is my *own* dad. In fact, he came all the way to New York and the asshole *still* didn't want to talk to me."

"So, I was going to say, my dad once told me that when you feel like everyone in the room is an asshole, the asshole is probably *you*."

Me? I'm the asshole? Not to nitpick, but doesn't it sound like it's BROOK who's the asshole here, if it was HIS dad giving him the advice in the first place?

"Just try not be the asshole, Jeff."

"My name's Chester, actually."

"Chester? You lied about your name? You see? That right there is a real asshole thing to be doing. What else have you been dishonest about?"

"Hey, I started an Honesty Movement! It doesn't get more genuine than that."

"So, you really *do* work as stop-motion animator?"

Uh. "I very easily *could!* It's not outside the realm of possibilities! The truth is, I haven't worked anywhere since I got fired from the bank, and then *you* came in the next day and took my girl."

"*Your* girl?"

"I'm sure she's talked about me. What's she told you?"

"I don't remember her ever mentioning anything about anyone named Chester."

"My name hasn't come up in conversation? Not even once?"

"Not once. Unless you've given her a fake name too."

Ha, frickin' ha. "That's just insulting, Brook. I'm insulted."

"I think it'd be best if you got going, Chester."

"Fine. Great. I get a drink and clean clothes, and you get to run off to Japan with Melissa. That sounds like a really fair deal."

"Japan's not happening anymore."

"No?"

"No."

"Huh." *I sense an opening here.*

"I'm...in between jobs at the moment." That actually does sound worse than *worker at the chocolate factory.*

"You know what? I think I'll just see myself out."

As I make for the door, which doesn't have nearly as many deadbolts on it as I would have originally assumed, Brook calls out to me. "Forget about Melissa, already. She would never sully herself with the likes of you, Chester."

And because I barfed it all out already, I don't have the guts to tell him I'd been sullying Melissa long before he came along. And I've *continued* to sully! Instead — *and much more to the point* — I trip over a box before leaving and tumble out into the hallway, my face eventually coming to a stop against the cold elevator door.

Yep. That's an image that's really going to haunt his dreams for a while.

Rising to my feet, I coolly push the elevator call button and dust myself off. Straighten the nice shirt he gave me. And the pants. Adjust my balls a bit to the left. Actually, over to the right feels a bit better. Palm my still-wet hair down.

I push the button again. Christ, his door's still open and he's still just standing there in the middle of his apartment.

What is taking this elevator so fucking long?

"That button isn't working properly," he calls out. "You'll have to take the stairs down."

Now I notice the button never lit up.

"You know, I'll just take the stairs down," I say, before heading the wrong way down the hall.

Well, that could not have ended much worse.

When the Willows Speak They Sing in Unison

TBH, I used to be so naive that when we had Sex Ed in school, I raised my hand and I asked: "So when boys have their periods—" Fortunately, I don't recall what my question was going to be; I was way too bombarded with laughter and ridicule and spitballs. It didn't help that in the very next class, when we watched the infamously dreaded childbirth video, I passed out and fell out of my desk and onto the cold, laminate floor. I claimed I'd actually fallen asleep, but who am I kidding? No one believed me in the least. I thought they were supposed to give us a one-class warning, you know, so we could all plan a good excuse in advance for not showing up, but the teacher just sprung it on us. One minute we're etching our favorite band names into our desks, and the next we're blurring our vision and wilting in our seats because of a screaming, goopy, veiny extraterrestrial.

The other kids at my high school started handing me sexual educational pamphlets in the hallways; my locker was full to the top with brochures like *Teen Pregnancy*, *Am I Gay?* and *Puberty for Boys & Girls & Everything In-Between*. I still don't get that last one. Probably should have read it. One kid who was proficient at making balloon animals stuffed my locker with poodles and giraffes made out of condoms. I think his parents owned a convenience store or something, and he pilfered them all. Awful kids, all of them.

Still, free condoms. That's like finding the dragon's gold when you're a horny teen.

Speaking of balloon animals, did I ever mention that Mel's dad is a clown? Not a clown in the Chester K. Eddy "let's stick my tongue to this frozen flagpole and see what happens" sense, but in the "he wore makeup and attended children's birthday parties" sense. And I realize this could still be misconstrued, and one might understandably be led to believe he's not that far off from the land of John Wayne Gacy, but trust me, he's not that. He's quite simply a professional clown. He went to clown school, even. Have you ever honestly thought about that? I mean, there are actual, legitimate institutions devoted to the training of clowns. That is literally the dumbest thing ever.

Still, even though I've never met the guy, Melissa's described her dad as being pretty cool. For a clown, that is.

Her mother, on the other hand, is apparently an obnoxiously humorless, never laughing, always stressed pony trainer. Like, real ponies. Not that super weird cosplay stuff. I dare you to look it up.

I can only imagine how her parents met. The obvious scenario would see the two of them being hired to attend the same snotty seven-year-old's birthday party, where they fell in love while pitching in to clean vomit out of the bouncy castle, but I like to believe in the magic of serendipity. And serendipity doesn't happen in such an obvious manner. My serendipity involves a *Die Hard*-type hostage situation, though at an indoor equestrian show, where the off-duty birthday clown has to John McClane his way through some air vents (you can imagine what air vents at a horse venue in the dead middle of summer might smell like) in order to take out a murdering — and very generically European — terrorist who's come to steal millions of dollars in super-rare, Medieval horseshoes.

Yep, that was the fourth time I've brought up *Die Hard* now. Thanks for paying attention. Also, I need to be writing screenplays, like yesterday.

Mel told me all about her family dynamics during one of our drunken nights at the Chelsea Piers. I don't know how she ever managed to turn out so well-adjusted. Still, I've never asked Melissa how her parents actually met, because I know I could only ever be woefully disappointed.

Speaking of dreams crashing down around me like I've just been standing at the business end of a woolly mammoth after overdoing it at a prehistoric chili cook-off, the fact that Jack The Boyfriend is actually Brook of pornstarjugz69@aol.com fame is finally sinking into my formerly-shit-canned but now-quite-lucid headspace.

All I can say though, is thank God Glenn Workman gave me a key to the theater, because I literally have no idea where else I'd have spent the night. Certainly not on Brook's bed, in sheets reeking of pomegranate body wash and Melissa farts, and filled with molted strands of both of their ponytails. I'm not sure what time I got here — *Christ, I'm a little uncertain HOW I got here* — but I wake up on Stage Left; with a sandbag pillow and a dusty theater curtain for a blanket. My hoodie is still damp from the snowfall.

It's been a hell of a week for Chester K. Eddy, hasn't it? Let's refresh. We kicked it off in Washington Square Park with a bit of Mark Twain-inspired honesty, followed by getting tossed from my brother's apartment, the embarrassment at The Kitano Hotel, that weird SAA meeting, my visit to Sugar Hill, my return to the Deutsche Bank, and last night's jaunt into Brooklyn. I've hooked up with Maya Custner and Ariel — *or Jasmine, or Mulan, or whatever her name was* — and I've been sexually harassed by both Chelsea McMahon and the Brainless Office Shit Supervisor. I've verbally assaulted around two dozen people, with maybe five or so who didn't deserve it. Then there's been the whole Jack The Boyfriend revelation, as well as this job I stumbled my way into. Aside from the astounding amounts of alcohol consumed along the way and the embarrassingly low number of showers taken, none of this has been anywhere close to being a normal week for me.

Yikes. These are the kind of adult stories your parents warned you about when you were in high school, aren't they? The kind of "If you're not careful your life's gonna turn out like that guy's" stories. *Yes, kids. I am that guy.*

I sit up, and shake the cobwebs from my head. Sighing, I'm surprised by just how much air I'm letting out. Like I've had more negativity built up in me than I knew about.

Still, what am I planning on doing next?

Like any good immediate answer, the theater lights come up, and both Glenn and Melissa enter, Stage Right.

"Chester?" they sing in unison.

My emotions are all out of whack; I've been feeling one way towards one person, another way towards someone else, and then back and forth and back again. Glenn's a weirdo but he gave me a job and he bought me chicken parm, but now he's secretly in love with Melissa and then he isn't so he should be cool again? And Mel is my best friend, but The Boyfriend is hers, who happens to be Glenn Workman, but then it turns out it's some guy named Brooklyn instead, and he's whisking her away to Japan but now he's not?

I should apologize to both of them, really. Maybe? It's growth, right? Isn't this a story about growth? Or is it a story about honesty? I wish it was a story about a hot tub time machine because that shit would be so much easier to keep up with.

I was making an effort to be honest from now on, but then people just started lying to me more. How's that for fair?

Still. I can't say any of that. Instead, all I can come up with is, "Hey guys."

Nice. Playing it real honest and cool, Chester.

"How long have you been in here?" Glenn asks, though without the sprinkling of suspicion he used to ask me questions with. He should be asking me where the hell I disappeared to yesterday, but he doesn't. He's drinking a coffee too, so I know he does like coffee, just not the crap I bring him. Jerk.

"Are you okay, Chestnuts?"

"What's not to be okay about?" I say to Melissa, hoping she'll launch right into her admission about The Boyfriend. At least then I won't have to bring it up myself.

"You're sleeping in the theater for one thing. What's happened?" Melissa looks me over carefully. I wonder if she recognizes the new duds, and exactly what closet they may have come from. She's still bundled up from the cold out there; gloves, scarf, and a big furry hat.

"I'm fine," I say. "I am perfectly fine." I think we can safely say now, that officially puts an end to the Honesty Movement right there.

Glenn claps his hands like a good director will do to get everyone back on track. He explains succinctly how yesterday, after I disappeared on him, he held the auditions for the Matthew role. And there was one dude he really liked who he scheduled to come in this morning to read with Melissa. He doesn't even make me feel bad about not being here to help. You know, to actually do my fucking job. Is he super understanding, or has he already given up on me?

"So, where is he?" I ask, looking around for this mystery actor. Melissa's come up onstage with me, with two copies of the Willows script in her gloved hands.

"In jail, actually."

"Jail?"

"He called me just now. Used his one phone call too."

"That's a pretty romantic gesture. Though if he's anything like me, he's probably set all his other bridges aflame by now and had no better option. What did he do?"

"I didn't ask." He waves his hands and nod-bobs his head, obviously unsure of how anyone might do anything in this big, messy world.

"You *didn't ask*? The guy is in the slammer, Glenn! That is the *one* thing you ask. What *did* you ask him about? Outlandish sex fetishes? His high school tetherball team?"

"Nothing quite so personal. I merely told him I'd find someone else."

Way to keep things professional, Glenn. How does such a presupposed creative person play things so safe? *Two words for you Chester: Lettuce. Burger.*

Melissa's handing me a copy of *When the Willows Speak They Sing in Unison.* It's no bigger than a typical stage play, but it looks like fucking *War and Peace* to me. I sense it's about as bleak, too. "So, did you read it last night, Chestnuts?"

"I was—*busy*? I think that's where I'll leave the extent of last night's details." I look at Glenn now, who's already taking a seat in the empty house. He's got a DMX console set up to work the stage lights. "Wait, you're not saying you want me to take the part? Are you?"

He twists a few dials on the console, slides a few sliders up and down. Reminds me of my high school Home-Ec teacher getting her sewing machine ready. "Heavens no. I only need you to stand-in this morning, so Melissa can run through her lines."

I still cannot believe Melissa landed a part in this train wreck. I suppose it's more of an oncoming train, since there hasn't been a crash yet. And no signs of bodies yet either.

Glenn wags a hand at the two of us and says, "Now, what do you say we start with Scene Thirty-Two? Where Matthew Willows realizes how much he actually loves Madison—"

Oh yes, this will be perfect!

"—just as she's decided they should separate."

Oh.

Melissa asks, "This is her big monologue, right? Where she convinces herself they will never work."

Um...

"And lists all the reasons he's completely wrong for her?"

Oh, come on!

"That's the one," Glenn confirms, still adjusting his knobs.

My pride interjects. "Are we sure that's really where we want to start? I mean, isn't there a scene where Matthew gets to shine? Where we realize maybe he's a pretty decent dude after all?"

"There really isn't a scene like that."

"Don't you think there *should* be? I mean, I totally read it of course — last night when I wasn't doing anything weird at all. Yep, totally normal stuff going on— and thought that was a pretty key scene missing."

"Besides," Glenn says, once again shitting all over my feelings. "This isn't really about *you* right now, Chester. This run-through is for Melissa. Now go ahead and start with Scene Thirty-Two, please. Matthew is running toward the dock on the lake, where he finds Madison searching for her lost frog."

A lost frog now? It's far too late to ask what this play is all about, isn't it?

Melissa finds her spot on stage, and closes her eyes for a moment, focusing on her transformation into Madison Willows. She clears her throat politely, just as I imagine the Duchess of Cambridge would before going to town on the ol' prince. She says, "*Oh, Matthew! You surprised me. Your presence is typically betrayed by your footsteps creaking upon this old dock. Or how the wind through the reeds never fails to signal your arrival.*"

"Uh—" I still haven't yet found the page we're supposed to be reading from. "Yep. It's me all righty. Good old Matty Fabulous."

Mel rolls her eyes, grabs the script from my hands, and gives me hers, already open to the correct page. It's covered in handwritten notes in a variety of colors, no doubt forged from stolen Deutsche Bank office supplies. She flips to the exact spot she needs to be, and continues her lines, not worrying about whatever dribble I'm half-spouting. "*And yet, the frog remains missing. Lost to me. A metaphor for what I need to say to you now.*"

In real life, if I had any clue at all about what a woman was about to say, I'd totally say it. So, I skip ahead in the script a line or three and cut to the chase. "*It's that a prince can be lost, just as easily as he was once thought found.*"

Mel whispers, though still projecting enough for Glenn to hear. "That's *my* line, Chestnuts."

"Cut!" Glenn calls out suddenly, holding up an awkward finger. I'm assuming he's about to concede, and confess picking me to stand-in this morning was a terrible, terrible idea. Maybe the most terrible idea he's ever had, if he never had ideas about cheating on his wife, that is. But instead, he quickly explains how the DMX console doesn't seem to be working properly, and then promptly excuses himself to run up to the booth to adjust things to where he wants them.

Leaving Melissa and I alone on the stage. She breaks the ice with a, "Come on, Chestnuts. You didn't really read it last night, did you?"

In my best Yoda voice, I say, "Quick to assume, you are."

"I knew it. I knew you wouldn't take this seriously. Just like everything else."

"*Everything?* Come on, I gave you a fairly serious orgasm a couple of weeks ago."

"No, you didn't."

"The time before that then?"

"Nuh uh."

"Before that?" She just stares at me; she doesn't even take this conversation serious enough to answer me. Now who's being the immature one? "Well, it's not my fault I've got this Charlie Brown curse hanging over me all the time."

"Come on. Your whole Charlie Brown thing is getting a bit old, don't you think?"

"I don't think so, no. Why would I keep bringing it up?"

"Charlie Brown was a failure, but only because of his *own* insecurities. He never used anything as an excuse though."

"You sure you're not thinking of Charlie Brown the steakhouse guy?"

Some of the lights above us come alive now. Melissa takes her scarf and hat off, tossing them to the stage floor. She gives that amazing hair a good toss too. The stink wave of pomegranate hits me, instantly reminding me of every time I've ever had my face buried in her scalp, but also taking me right back to last night, standing naked in Brook's shower-for-two.

"But do you really want to be talking about character falsities and mistaken identities right now, Mel?"

"I just think if you want to be comparing yourself to someone, there should be some amount of accuracy there."

"How about The Boyfriend? How do I measure up to him?"

Melissa stops for a fraction of a second. I know her body's every move, so it's easy for me to detect the absence of such. "You don't compare to Jack." She gives my duds another look over; a double take at the Dismemberment Plan t-shirt I'm currently sporting. "Although I think he owns that exact same shirt."

"It's a funny story, Mel—"

This, of course, is when Glenn comes running back to his seat. "Okay, let's pick up at the top of Scene Thirty-Two again. And Chester, please try to stick to the script this time."

It's not my fault the script sucks, Glenn. "Isn't there room for any creative modifications? Some of this still reads a bit rough to me."

"Rough? Like which parts?"

"Well," I flip to an arbitrary page. "Like this line here: *I'll run as fast as the clock?*"

"What about it?"

"That doesn't make any sense. The clock only ever runs as fast as YOU, doesn't it?"

"Perhaps it's an acknowledgement of—"

I don't have time for this shit, Glenn. I'm trying to debrief my lady-friend at the moment, and no, I'm not going to go for the obvious debriefing joke there. Not in the mood. "Let's just get back to it, okay?"

Melissa takes her place once again and waits for Glenn's signal.

And, go! She turns to face me once more, and there's a look there. *"Oh, Matthew! You surprised me."* Or rather, there *isn't* a look there. That way her eyes would light up, with just the smallest glimmer of hope for another Deutsche Bank workday half-spent in that weird, perpetually-empty office in the back corner. *"Your presence is typically betrayed by your footsteps creaking upon this old dock. Or how the wind through the reeds never fails to signal your arrival."* It's like that office was only there to lure the two of us inside, and we fell for it every time.

But that look isn't there. Maybe she's just really focused in on her character right now.

I can't believe I've lost my place in this script again. But I'm not going to show weakness here. I'm not going to use this as an excuse. *Come on, Chester! You're better than Charlie Brown anyway. Be one of those other Peanuts kids. The one hunched over at the piano, maybe? He seemed like a bit more of the lady killer type. Women love that silent, head-down-and-focused-on-the-job type, don't they?*

Now the look in Melissa's eyes is the, *What the fuck are you doing to me right now?* sort of look. Like it's *my* fault this dude I'm standing in for is in jail right now. You can blame me for a lot of shit that's gone down in Manhattan over the past few days, but as far as I know, this isn't one of them.

And then the lights suddenly blink off, and I have no idea what look is now in Melissa's eyes.

From the darkened house, Glenn Workman shrieks, "Crap!" and he goes running back up to the control booth.

With this fuzzy, half-blackout between us, we can both tell each of us is sizing the other up. From my pocket, I withdraw the Zen Rock of Leg Breaking-ness (formerly of Dick Butt-ness), holding it out for her.

Immediately recognizing it, she asks, "Where did you get—?"

"I got it from The Kitano Hotel. But where did *you* get it?"

Melissa's caught in another one of those frozen moments. She usually knows exactly what sort of dickhead move I'm gonna pull before I pull it, but this is a new one.

She says, "This new guy at work. Lester. He gave it to me. But—"

"Lester?" He must have rooted through my stuff when I'd forgotten my bag on the cubicle. That prick!

"He's kind of a creep, to be honest. But I told him I had this audition and he gave it to me for good luck. It was sort of sweet."

"Lester McDoucheCrutches took credit for MY act of kindness? What the hell?"

"I think he likes me."

"Of course he likes you! Every dude in this city with half a hard-on is in love with you, Mel. The Boyfriend, Lester. Glenn Workman basically hired you on the spot. I'll bet that waffle truck guy outside the bank gives you free meals, doesn't he?"

"Only a few times."

"You're like the second coming of *Something About Mary*! So help me if Brett Favre shows up right now. That rock was from *me!* I stole it and defaced it so I could give it to *you!*"

"But Lester told me—"

"You don't understand. I wrote *I'm a Dick Butt* on it, but then he covered it up."

"Why would you write *I'm a Dick Butt?*"

"I didn't finish what I was really trying to say."

"It just doesn't make any sense is all."

"It doesn't matter Mel. The fact is — *the truth, the actual honest TRUTH* — is that I love you. You make me feel like I've never had my heart broken before. Like all the bad stuff and lack of basement bedrooms before you never even mattered."

Cue the lights. Thanks, Glenn. Brilliant work.

Mel is staring at me, not quite *jaw agape staring*, but she's nearly there. Her eyes search me up and down like I went to throw a handful of shit at her but missed. *Come on, that's a pretty decent metaphor, all things considered right now.*

"That is such a dick butt move, Chestnuts."

"My point is, I know about Brook. The Boyfriend, Jack, or pornstarjugz69. Whatever his name is at the moment. I don't know how one guy manages to get so many nicknames, but I know all about him. And you know what? I'll give you a piece of advice that some guy in the park muttered to me last week: *The truth is fucking awesome 'cause you don't have to remember shit.*"

"Is that a Mark Twain quote?"

"Parts of it are, I think. I was sort of drunk at the time. Also, he didn't say it directly to me either. I was eavesdropping."

"Well, you're a fine one to be giving advice on honesty, aren't you?"

"Why wouldn't you just tell me about him, Mel? It's not like it was a secret worth keeping from me."

"I—I guess it's because I felt sort of guilty. I mean, one day you're my favorite thing in the world, and the next day you get canned and that's when Brook shows up. And I realize what we have is just a *friends-with-benefits* sort of deal, but even when Brook would pop in to work and we made out in the janitor's closet, I'd still feel sort of guilty."

"OUR janitor's closet? You made out in our janitor's closet?"

"Yes, our janitor's closet. And the janitor's too, I suppose."

"I don't recall ever seeing a janitor in there, now that you mention it."

We both take note of Glenn returning to his seat yet again, and stop momentarily to refocus. Well, Melissa's refocusing; I'm still reeling from my one true moment of honesty. *I did it! I told Melissa I love her. Maybe now she'll start seeing—*

"Hold on. That's Brook's t-shirt, isn't it? Why the hell are you wearing Brook's clothes?"

"I, uh—I was at his place last night. Does that sound any less incriminating than it should? It sounds fairly irredeemable when I say it out loud, actually."

"I can't believe you would stalk my boyfriend, Chester! That's unforgivable! What, did you end up murdering him and taking his clothes?"

"Hey! *I'm* not the serial killer. HE is!"

"I've told you, he's a nice, sweet guy."

"If you haven't noticed, the dude owns multiple samurai swords. Multiple!"

"He loves Japan. Remember when I told you about Japan?"

"Barely."

"Maybe you'd have a better memory if you stopped and listened to people for once, instead of making up these crazed stories in your head. You're certifiable, Chestnuts."

"I doubt I could afford to be certified."

"Guys, guys!" It's Glenn, who we've conveniently forgotten was still here. He's standing on his seat, arms and palms splayed outward in a look of perturbation.

Melissa — *in all of her super-professional glory* — apologizes first. "Sorry, Glenn. I'm sorry."

"Don't be sorry. This is some raw emotion here. You two have amazing chemistry, you know that?"

"*I* know that," I say without a lick of hesitation or doubt. Melissa, however, is just standing there, hands on her glorious hips. I wish I was holding those hips right now, too. "But what's indisputable to some, is not always so obvious to others." Melissa crosses her arms, and I can't tell if it's because she's pissed at me or whether she's starting to see my point. I do have a knack for making pretty convincing arguments, I'd say. "I mean, tell me I'm wrong, but you can bear your nasty, nauseating soul to someone you love, and all they want instead is to move to Japan with some obnoxiously handsome dude who has a ponytail, who buys drinks for strangers, and who knows CPR."

"Well, I have no idea what that means. But whatever it is, you two are great together."

"Thanks Glenn," I say, taking credit for something.

"Great on *stage*, I mean." *Fuck off, Glenn.* "I even jotted some of that dialogue down in real-time. See?" He holds up a pen and notepad as undeniable evidence.

"You say you love me," Mel says, turning back to me. "And I know you mean it, but you have to know I don't feel the same way. I mean, I love you too, but not like that. This is all it ever was, Chestnuts." She wipes an all-too obvious tear from her cheek, absorbing it instantly with the woolen gloves she still has on.

"So, what you're saying is that you're sticking it out with a guy named Brooklyn? *BROOKLYN?* And that's that?"

"I'm saying I love him, Chester. I've never told you otherwise."

"Well, technically, you only ever told me you *liked* him. Now it's love? That sounds pretty fucking otherwise to me."

She pulls her gloves off, and I'm assuming it's because her hands are sweaty or the material is soaked with the sort of tears that only Chester K. Eddy can make a woman produce, but she holds her hand up in the stage's fine-tuned lighting and I see it.

A big, fucking, glittering rock.

Shining like the Black Stallion's magnificent tail.

Like the Highlander's broadsword catching the sun's glare as it swings my way. There can be only one. And it's not me.

My decapitated head is still rolling across the stage as she continues the blitzkrieg of truth.

"I gave him an ultimatum. I realized I didn't want to go to Japan. I wanted to stay in New York and pursue my dreams. Also, I asked him to chop that ponytail off too."

"Well, I have to say, he does look good with the short hair. Good call there. But in Brook's defense, isn't he allowed to chase his own dreams too?"

"Love is compromise. And maybe you'll find the strength to compromise *this*, Chestnuts. This you-and-me thing."

"That is such a great line..." Glenn mumbles, still standing on the seat cushion and scratching another bit of dialogue down onto his notepad.

"Listen, why don't the two of you jump to a different scene? One where you *both* can shine. I can tell you're in the zone right now; you're really firing on all cylinders up there!"

I don't even turn to Glenn Workman; I only want to see Melissa right now. But I still say to him, "I can't be your Matthew Willows, Glenn. And I can't be your Second Place, Mel. I'm not sure *where* I'm going to be, but I think I'm better off elsewhere."

"Go to your Someplace," she says, reminding me of her own little bench on Grand Street. "Find your own place to go when you're lonely, Chestnuts. To dance or sing. Or just scream if you need to."

"I think I'll drink instead. But thanks for the advice, Melissa." Finally, I turn to Glenn. "And thanks for everything you offered me, Glenn. Really. I don't know how far I would've made it without either of you two. I hope you both find your frogs, or whatever the fuck this story's about."

Another light burns out as I walk off-stage.

And resisting the urge to pick my nose and eat a booger when I exit out onto West One Hundredth Street, I shoot the dried snot out into a crusty, greying snowbank instead.

Fallopian's Colossal Tube

TBH, when I hear someone I've actually met before has died, I use that to get out of work for as long as I possibly can. If it's somebody I actually worked *with*? Even better. Cut to the counseling support story:

ME: "Alberto died? The guy who does the Three AM bathroom cleaning shift? Oh man. I'm just not functioning properly right now. It's affecting my productivity and my usual positive and sunny disposition."

TRAUMA COUNSELLOR: "His name was Rohalio. It was a car accident. You scheduled this meeting to talk about your feelings of grief over the loss of Rohalio."

ME: "So, how much time off does one typically ask for in situations like this?"

TRAUMA COUNSELLOR: "It depends on the person, really."

ME: "What if this person was someone who was looking for as much time off as he can get?"

And there you have it; Chester K. Eddy got himself a sweet three weeks off work. I literally got paid to hit on girls and eat Chinese takeout and egg creams in Bryant Park for three weeks. Not a bad gig at all. Thanks, Rohalio. I still think of you every time I see piss on a bathroom floor, which is quite often. I'd say that's a pretty decent compliment.

So, after my blow-up with Melissa, I've found myself back at Washington Square Park. *This is it!* My lonely Someplace, just as she suggested. Because of the coming winter season, the water in the fountain should be turned off, but it still seems to be trickling slowly and sadly from the nozzles. Like the whole thing is just letting go of whatever it's got left.

Still, I sit down and dip my fingers into the murky quarter-inch of disgusting water, making shapes of various levels of inappropriate sexual innuendo within the algae-smeared surface.

To summarize: I've lost Melissa and I am now in a position where I'm required to swallow my pride in order to have any future at all on Broadway. And, Honesty Movement be damned, I very likely could have avoided all of this by simply being true with Mel in the first place. If only I'd admitted my feelings months ago. I'm honest with myself, in my own head, but I know I've got to preach it. Can I get an amen?

"Amen, brother!"

Shit. I've done it again. *Inside voice, Chester. Inside voice.*

"Sorry," I say, turning toward the person next to me.

Who just so happens to be a dinosaur.

Yes.

A real-live, talking dinosaur. Triceratops, specifically. But what it's doing here today in Washington Square Park and not laying eggs in a tar pit circa eighty million years ago is beyond me.

Then it says, "It's because I'm actually NOT here, Chester K. Eddy." This massive thing is lying beside the fountain like a lazy dog, the tip of its thick tail twirling around in the shallow fountain. However, no one in the park is paying any attention at all to the presence of this living triceratops.

Except for me. I give my head a shake. "So, you know my name and you can read my mind?"

"I'm IN your mind, dude-bro."

"And you use colloquial slang, apparently."

"Apparently. But that's all up to you, really."

So, my assumption here has to be I've passed out drunk and am now dreaming up conversations with a triceratops. Sounds like something that might happen to me, actually. So, who's surprised at this point? One time in college, after dropping a wee bit too much acid with Dorothy Doppelganger — *Coolest name ever, by the way* — up in the catwalk during the school's opening night performance of *Oklahoma!* we were convinced we'd seen the ghost of Chris Farley in an Oscar Mayer hot dog costume up there, rubbing his big wiener on the stage lighting. We freaked — *Naturally, because, well, we were on acid* — and I tried to tackle him, which — *More specific details aside* — only brought about a quick end to the show.

Still, I remain convinced people must have talked more about what actually *did* happen that evening than they would have discussed had the alternative happened; if they had to sit through yet another overwrought and over-acted production of *Oklahoma!* and if Dorothy and I had just dropped acid off-campus, out behind the veterinary hospital like a couple of respectable folks would do.

"But I'm not a triceratops," he says, reminding me I'm still here. "I'm a tricera*cocks*. You know, from your dinosaur porn fantasies."

"My wha—? You mean Jurassic Pork?"

"You have more than one dinosaur porn fantasy?"

"Wouldn't you know that?"

"Touché."

I recall my recent conversations about this very subject with both Melissa and Ariel.

Question: How does one well-adjusted individual bring up the idea of dinosaur porn multiple times in the span of a couple of days?

Answer: Did I just say well-adjusted? I'm giving myself way too much credit, aren't I?

"So, has dino porn been done before? Melissa said the idea wasn't very original."

"I'm just a figment of your imagination, Chester K. Eddy. I'm not all-knowing."

Looking him over though, I'm confused by the lack of penis-shaped horns. The way I see it, I figure any legit triceracocks worth his weight in colossal piles of dinosaur shit would have penis horns.

"I *am* a legit triceracocks," he says, reading my mind again.

"Seems like a missed opportunity though. Evolution really screwed the pooch on that one."

"It's not evolution, it's your imagination. Blame yourself and your own limitations, Chester K. Eddy."

And me being me, I'm simply not willing to let this one die on the operating table. "But — and correct me if I'm wrong — 'triceratops' literally means 'three-horned-*face*' doesn't it?"

"If you think you're right then I can only agree with you."

I have to say, having this guy around might be exceptionally good for my ego. "But then 'trice*racocks*' would mean—"

"See for yourself, bro." He stands up now, and lifts a hind leg so I can take a look underneath. This creature has three long, veiny spikes coming out the sides of his massive penis.

"Jesus! Forget those creepy human hands on the Swedish Chef: THAT is the most frightening thing I've ever seen."

"Dinosaur porn is not for the weak-kneed," he comments, placing a heavy foot back down on the ground. The entire fountain jumps a little; those Jurassic Park water ripples happening right before my eyes.

"I'm getting that. But, so, why are you visiting *me*? If you can read my mind, you'd know the last thing I need right now is a talking, freaky sex dinosaur."

"I don't read minds. I told you already: I *live* in your mind."

"In my—?"

"You're unconscious right now, and dreaming all of this, Chester K. Eddy."

Unconscious? How did that happen?

"You came to Washington Square Park and ended up watching those drunk guys impersonating Mark Twain—"

"That was a *week* ago."

"No, that was roughly four-and-a-half *minutes* ago. You slipped on the fountain trying to do a handstand, and you hit your head on the concrete here. Everything you've experienced since then has been nothing but a dream."

"Why was I trying to do a handstand?"

"Beats me, dude-bro. You did manage to do a killer Worm, however."

I always do a killer Worm. I rub my forehead, checking for any sign of a wound, but everything appears to be copacetic. "Man, I do *not* remember that at all," I say. Looking around with a bit more focus, I watch the bundled crowds of people gathered around the fountain. I end up spotting those same two Mark Twain impersonators, still trying to impress the same two girls who are, for some reason, still wildly fixated on them. "So then, my Honesty Movement never actually happened?"

"Well, you did come up with the idea. Right after you heard Shorter Twain say, '*If you tell the truth, you don't have to remember anything.*'"

That was the line. I knew it was something like that. "And then?"

"And then you decided to kick off your Honesty Movement by doing The Worm and attempting a handstand for some reason. I don't know why exactly. Have you ever noticed you often make very erratic decisions?"

I punch him right in his big, wet eye, and my hand regrets it immediately. *Ouch! Who knew dinosaurs had such hard eyeballs?*

"You see what I mean?"

"You are one smart triceracocks, uh...um—wait, what should I call you? Do you have a name?"

"You haven't given me a name yet."

"I was supposed to?"

"This is *your* dream sequence, dude-bro."

"Let's do some word association. You say a word — any word at all will do — and I'll say the first thing that comes to mind. And *that* will be your name."

"Okay: *Fallopian.*"

"Vomitorium," I shout out.

"Vomitorium it is then."

"I'll be honest, I was going to say vomitorium no matter what." But if dinocock here is really just in my head, then maybe he knew that already? I hate stories that tread into psychic, mind-reading territory like this. Hurts my *own* head. "You know what, I actually like the name Fallopian better."

"Well, okay then. Call me Fallopian." Wait. This was his plan all along, wasn't it? See? This is why I hate psychic stuff.

For the hell of it, I get up and try doing a handstand.

I fail miserably, falling backwards and hitting my head on the cold concrete again.

"So, if the Honesty Movement never actually happened, then that means everything else — getting kicked out of my brother's apartment, Glenn Workman's play, that Sex Addicts Anonymous meeting, naked in Brook's shower — all of it *never* happened?"

"I would think not."

"And Melissa being engaged to pornstarjugz69@aol.com?"

"Dude, that is so stupidly preposterous. I mean, I know coincidental shit happens all the time, but seriously. How could that possibly *ever* be a thing? The odds alone would be—"

"All right! Shut up, already. It is stupid, isn't it?" *Almost as stupid as me having a conversation with an affable dinosaur named Fallopian who has horns on his penis.*

"I heard that," he says. "But listen, you've likely got a shitload of questions, huh? Look at it like this: forget everything that happened that you *thought* happened. It's like you've got a brand-new lease on life!"

"Yeah. I've just time-traveled into the past and now I get to remake the future! You know, just like in my favorite movie."

"I've never seen a movie. I'm a dinosaur."

"Generally, you're not missing out on much. But *Hot Tub Time Machine* is a work of art. It's genius how the film really makes you *think* about what it means to actually travel through time."

"That sounds incredibly introspective and philosophical."

"Trust me. It is."

"And I really love how when anyone at all calls a movie a *film*, they think they're sounding more highfalutin."

To be honest, I only pick up on Fallopian's sarcasm after I'm mid-way through my next thought. "Craig Robinson was robbed for the Oscar that year. Flat out robbed! Friggin' milk-drinkin' Christoph *That's-a-Bingo'* Waltz."

"Couldn't agree more," Fallopian says.

"Really?"

"Only 'cause that's what *you* think."

"Oh yeah. Right."

"So, if you *could* travel through time, where would you go, Chester K. Eddy?"

"I always imagined if I had the ability to time travel, I'd use it to go back to conversations I really sucked at, just so I could be wittier. More memorable. Maybe steal the killer joke that guy always had, primed to make me look stupid."

"That seems like a terrible waste of near-unlimited power, Chester K. Eddy." He's crouched down further now, and is scratching his underside on the ground.

"It's the little things that count in the end, Fallopian."

"I guess so." He grinds a bit harder now.

"What are you doing? Are you rubbing that giant schlong of yours on the concrete?"

"I can't help it, dude. Those horns down there can get pretty sweaty and itchy."

"I can imagine. Still, that's sorta gross."

"You'd do the same."

"Probably constantly."

"Knew it."

There are no words now, and barely a sound; only the scraping of his three-horned dinosaur-hood on pavement. Makes me a bit queasy, to be honest.

There's a gentle rustling of leaves in the park; the sound seems to muffle that of the crowd gathered around the water fountain, rather than the other way around. The mid-day sun feels a little tilted, if that's even a possible detail to notice.

"What's going to happen when I wake up then?"

Fallopian rises, standing up on all four legs now. He turns his face to mine, at an inquisitive angle.

"I mean, if none of what I thought happened ever *actually* happened. I wake up and just...what?"

"Well that's really up to you, isn't it?"

"That's not very *Spirit Animal* of you. I thought you were here to guide me?"

"You want guidance? Here: take advantage of this opportunity. Live your life just as you were, but how about this time you avoid the same mistakes? Make better decisions." He resumes his crouching position, and gets back to rubbing himself against the base of the fountain. "Wouldn't you love to avoid that last argument with Melissa? How about the other night at the Deutsche Bank? You could sure do without *that* whole embarrassing debacle. This is an opportunity you might not ever have again."

Shorter, Mustached Twain and Taller, Mustacheless Twain are still going on over there. Man, those girls are eating out of their hands, too. I remember being a starving acting student — *Which was actually incredibly similar to my life nowadays, just with many more Still-Yet-To-Be-Pulverized-Into-Fine-Powder dreams* — and busking my way through college. I was no better than these two guys. Just like them, I also had passing teens and drunks reminding me I sucked; I also had garbage and cigarette butts tossed into my hat. But I recited monologues for multiple character plays (ie: four terrible performances instead of one forgettable role); I was a shitty living statue; I actually tried ventriloquism with my feet; and I also discovered you apparently need a permit to have a flea circus in a public dog park. Who knew?

But these dudes are killing it, and they don't appear to be wanting to kill themselves either. They're actually happy. Maybe they're *already* avoiding their own mistakes?

Or maybe, just maybe, they're fixing their mistakes right now? Right this very minute. Could they be enacting change in their lives, as I sit and stare at them? Is what they're doing now for the betterment of their lives?

With my gaze still stuck on the twin Twains, I say: "I don't know, Fallopian. Maybe instead of *avoiding* mistakes I should just man up. Make all the *same* mistakes, just so I can fix everything that's happened. That seems a bit more noble, doesn't it?"

No answer.

"Doesn't it, Fallopian?" I turn to him but he's gone. Now, where does a triceratops just off and disappear to anyway? As I look back behind me, water from the fountain suddenly sprays me in the face, like a pipe burst or something.

Wiping my face, I realize the Mark Twains are now gone also. I notice I'm wearing Brook's chinos and t-shirt still, so it couldn't have been the past that was just happening now, could it? Well, obviously in the sense of the word, it *was* the past, but it wasn't a *Week Ago Past*, only a *Few Seconds Back Past*. Of course, there very likely wasn't just a big talking dinosaur here either, so what I experienced was some variation on one of my drunken stupors. I wish I'd noted in my fantasy just now what it was I'd been wearing. That might have helped. Maybe I *always* owned a Dismemberment Plan t-shirt? So then maybe this *was* a week ago? I'm starting to rethink everything now.

Maybe Melissa and I are actually the same person, like a Fight Club sort of thing? *Can I be Brad Pitt?*

I hear a voice above me saying something. Listening closer, I hear: "Chester?"

And this is when I realize I hadn't just been caught in some hyper-convoluted time warp encompassing the past, the future, reality, consciousness, and dream states. No penis dinosaurs either. Damn.

"Chester?"

And the water fountain didn't spray me, either. It's just Maya Custner who poured a drink on my head. She's standing here looking me up and down.

I run my hand through my hair and lick a finger out of curiosity. Mountain Dew, I think. That's not bad.

"Oh. Hey," I say, super coolly like I wasn't just spaced out and lost in an imagined conversation. "How have *you* been, Cuntster?"

Truth Redux

TBH, I don't want to do this part anymore.

So, Maya Custner and I have found ourselves at some tiny Chinese restaurant in the Bowery. The seats are sticky and the windows are yellowed and there's some hair on the floor, but just enough that it's obvious *Ming's Empire* makes a killer sweet and sour crispy pork. I think I've already eaten my weight in food, which shouldn't be a surprise considering how much attention I've paid to my dietary sustenance over the last few days.

This place still has Halloween decorations up too, which are nothing more than fingers cut off from white rubber gloves, sporadically taped to the walls, each one with two dots for eyes and one for a mouth. It's pretty fucking sad. Though I don't know if I'm more bothered by the fact it's late November and still Halloween in here, or that these ghosts are so terrible.

It was about an hour ago when Maya, sitting across the Formica table with chopsticks all ready to go, asked what I'd been up to over the last week. *Five days, actually.* It was five days ago when she'd left my apartment leaving nothing behind but a Sharpie'd note on my bag and the lingering smell of too much booze on my pillow.

I'm surprised she even asked to grab a bite with me, all things considered. But I always say New Yorkers are a much more charitable bunch than people give them credit for, even if the most charitable of the bunch are likely from the West Coast or Canada originally. I think that's one of the things I'm always saying. Everything is a bit of a blur right now, to be fair. I don't really know why she dumped a Mountain Dew on my head at the park, but it didn't take us long to decide to come here and discuss it all.

And I told her everything. Right up to the Mountain Dew part, where I realized I hadn't been dreaming up everything that had happened. I really *did* do all of those things.

"He lied to me!" I say at the end of my storytelling session, slamming my hand on the tabletop for the umpteenth time and knocking the same bottle of soy sauce over once more. "That fucking, talking penis dinosaur lied to me. Never trust talking dinosaurs who show you their penises."

Stuffing one more bite of crab rangoon into her mouth, she says, "I try to avoid getting into those kinds of situations in the first place. But that's still good advice."

"Invaluable advice," I confirm.

"But tell me, Chester. Do you actually think drunk Mark Twain impersonators are really the best source for life-changing inspiration? It sounds to me like you're on the precipice of setting the world record for bad decisions made." With a chopstick, she pushes her glasses up the bridge of her nose a tiny bit, enough for my heart to skip a beat.

"I'm starting to rethink some of my life choices, to be honest."

"On the subject of rethinking, I'll add that the nose-picking might be a good place to start."

"Noted." One of the rubber finger ghosts falls off the wall and lands between us, right into the almost-empty bowl of cold, hardened chicken chow mein. "Though I'm actually considering dropping the idea of being super honest now. I think I'm going to focus more on being just *sort of honest*. You know, then I'll be more like everyone else."

"Sounds noble," Maya says with a titch of sarcasm. But then follows that up with, "I think that's actually a very good idea, Chester." Like she doesn't want to hurt the broken, little ol' me too much. I am nothing more than a wounded bird learning to fly again.

I ask, "But what about Melissa? Was I right in just walking out of there?"

"How should I know if that was right or not?"

"Well, I'm assuming you know women better than I do."

"I am woman. Hear me scratch my head in astonishment over your utter confusion in the matter. And in *most* matters, if you really want the truth."

"So, tell me. 'Cause I have NO idea."

Maya places her chopsticks down on the table, and she sits back pensively. "Hm. Okay. Well, bearing in mind the fact that I don't even know her—"

"She's amazing."

"Of course she is. But it sounds to me like what the two of you had—"

"Yes?"

"Well, it seems like, in the immortal words of Marc Almond: '*It was a kind of so-so love.*'"

"I have no idea who that is. Baseball player?"

"Yes. Because baseball players are so incredibly well-known for their quotable statements on the power of relationships. He was from *Soft Cell*, you Philistine."

"Philistine? I've never even *been* to the Philistines." She gives that look. The one I've been getting a lot lately, so I recognize it immediately. "Sure. But, yeah. Maybe you're right. It *was* a kind of so-so love. I guess." But that look actually looks a lot better on Maya Custner than it ever did on Melissa or Chelsea or Glenn or Brook or my brother or even Darren the bartender.

"Hey, you asked my opinion, and there it is."

I think about it more than I need to. "Maybe I've just lost my mind though?"

Maybe I'm going insane, and Melissa picked up on it, but maybe she was too afraid to call me on it. Like, because I actually AM that crazy. Does insanity sound like something applicable here?"

"Chester, you can't plead insanity in a relationship."

"I can't, can I?"

"Nope. It has to be *somebody's* fault. The good stuff is great and all, but it's the mistakes that really put a stamp on relationships. And I don't truly know which one of you made the most mistakes, or the most hurtful ones, so I'll just leave that for *you* to decide."

Wow. "You should work with Glenn Workman. He gets a hard-on for dialogue like that."

"You think I should contact him?"

"Truth be told, he gets a hard-on for most things. This was the guy who took me to that SAA meeting I told you about, remember?"

"Maybe not then. God, show me a man in this business who isn't a raging perv."

She is asking the wrong dude that question, isn't she? You've read enough of this by now to know. I can't help it, but sometimes — *Oftentimes; that's more than ONE sometimes, right?* — I make lewd, lascivious, borderline-inappropriate comments in passing to women. Honestly, I can't help it. I'll be heading toward the washrooms at the same time as a woman, and I'll stop at the ladies' room door and say something like, *"After you."* Or, *"Should we grab adjacent stalls, or share?"* I don't know why I do it. Or I'll be on an elevator or on the subway, blatantly checking out a girl and when she makes eye contact I'll accuse her of treating me like a sexual object. Again, I know it's wrong, but I just can't help it. There's something about how my brain is wired.

But I'm sure as hell not telling her that. I'm not opening myself up *that* wide for Maya Custner tonight.

She's leaning back into the squeaky, plastic booth about as far as humanly possible. I honestly can't tell if she wants to say something but is holding it back; the ol' brain wiring in me makes my assumptions a little cloudy. "Hey," I say bravely. "Thanks for listening to me, and for being honest with me. It's nice to just talk to someone. Also, I'm going to assume you're getting the check since I have zero funds at the moment."

"Not so fast," she says, brows furrowed. "You don't get to talk about *your* life for an hour and then we simply pack it up and ride off on our sad little horses."

"I don't? What *do* you want me to talk about next?"

"You haven't asked ME anything yet. Do you realize that? I had a week too, you know."

I thought this was my story? But man, I didn't even *think* about asking her anything about *her* story. What is wrong with me? "So? What's new, Ballyhoo?"

"Do you remember one of last things you told me?"

"Was it, '*I can't come if you've still got your socks on?*'"

"Before that. One of the last *bits of advice* you gave me."

"Always take your socks off before intercourse?"

"I wasn't the sex or socks stuff at all. After your audition for Luuk Meijer, when you and I spoke in the alley behind the theater? You told me I should cut my ties with him; go do my *own* thing. You told me I had the skill to do it on my own. And you said it really nicely to me, too. You were genuine, and I appreciated that so much."

"So much that you came to my place for horizontal refreshments, is that right? And then you vandalized my bag and disappeared."

"Sure. But skip ahead to *after* that part. When I decided to do just what you suggested. I quit the project with Luuk Meijer and I've decided to start figuring out how to direct my own play."

"Really?"

"Yep. And I'll probably fail and get a poor reputation around town, but at least I'll have tried."

"And you want *me* to take credit for all that, right? You're thanking me, aren't you?"

"That wasn't the point, actually. No."

"Well, I appreciate how you not only listened to my advice, but actually acted upon it. Especially since I very rarely give anyone advice ever. Especially good advice."

Question: Do I tell her a bad reputation in this town is basically career suicide?

Answer: Not if I can help her avoid said reputation in the first place. Growth! Achievement unlocked!

Instead I ask, "So why *do* you keep your socks on during sex, anyway?"

"It was a quickie, Chester. I wasn't exactly planning on sticking around."

"And yet. Here you are."

"Here we are." She takes the last of the crab rangoon from the plate and chews it up victoriously. "I've quit drinking too."

"I definitely can't take credit for that part. Unless it was from setting an example of how *not* to balance alcohol with a healthy lifestyle."

"It's only been three days. But my head already feels clearer. So, as you can see, I'm all about change too."

"I'll drink to that!"

"Nice try."

"Maybe we should have a drink to celebrate your new venture?"

"Stop it, Chester."

I do stop. I stop to think about exactly what is happening here. I feel like I'm flirting with Maya Custner, which, in itself, is not so hard to imagine. Because she's cute? Because I'm a dirtbag? Take your pick. But I'm still pretty upset from the whole Melissa thing. Plus, I'm still a bit pissed about the message Maya left on my bag in black Sharpie; the note which stated I was terrible at pretty much everything. Not exactly the type of statement that would spark a bit of horndog philandering, the likes of which desperate and damaged women haven't seen since early 2000's Wilmer Valderrama or John Mayer came creeping around the club scenes.

But.

Maya Custner is not so desperate. Nor does she seem particularly damaged. Though I may just be comparing her mental health to my own right now, and I was doing handstands for an imaginary dinosaur less than two hours ago.

"Change is tricky," I tell her. "I mean, in the realm of visionaries attempting something new. One moment you're Elon Musk while the next you're trying to wipe your ass with your opposite hand. Have you ever tried wiping your ass with your other hand? It's fucking impossible."

"Scratch my earlier comment about your thoughtful moment of encouragement. THAT was the most inspiring speech I've ever heard. And I studied Black History in college."

"Of course you did."

Maya keeps her eyes on mine a little longer than what feels natural, before shaking her head and pulling out her purse. *Is 'purse' the right word still? It gives me an antiquated feeling; like it's one of those things women have been fighting to change lately. I don't know. But it's a good sign that I'm even thinking about that, isn't it? I've got growths on top of my growths over here!* "You know, I still think you'd be a good fit for my play," she says, folding a few bills and gently laying them upon the table top.

"I'll think about it. Send me the script." For my audition, I'd only been sent a script sample. I don't even think the project had a name at the time, but it sure wouldn't have been anything I'd have paid any attention to whatsoever.

"You'll sit and read it in its entirety?"

"Your presumptions are cute, you know that? Totally erroneous, but cute."

She digs in her Personal Stuff Bag — *On second thought, Purse sounds less offensive than Personal Stuff Bag* — and extracts a semi-thick script. "It's a good thing I always carry one of these around, isn't it?"

For basically the first time ever, my phone vibrates instead of ringing, like it's supposed to do. What do you know? If my settings are actually starting to take, is that a metaphor for something? I look at the number: Glenn Workman. Probably wondering what dumpster my drunk ass has stumbled into. I hold a finger up for Maya, indicating I'll only be a minute, but she just leaves her contact info behind on the script in her familiar Sharpie scrawl, before withdrawing herself from the restaurant.

Glenn doesn't ask where I disappeared to. He jumps right into talking about his shit play once more, and noting again how Melissa and I have such amazing chemistry.

"Yeah," I tell him. "We sure do."

I catch Maya Custner stealing a glance back in the yellowed window of Ming's Empire. I'm already feeling a lot less dyspeptic.

Glenn has also realized, he tells me, that I am a terrible assistant. He says it quite happily, too. But he likes me — *Not as much as he liked his previous assistant, thankfully* — and he insists I just take the lead part in *When the Willows Speak They Sing in Unison*. The whole thing still just feels like some sort of pity fuck, and I politely decline.

The script Maya left on the table is called *Cerulean Sunflower*. It's highly likely that, even as little as an hour ago, a title of such nature would have made me throw up in my mouth a bit. Now it sounds kind of hopeful.

A little bit honest, too.

Truth Redux Again, But Better Than Last Time

November's early snowfall led to a quiet Christmas, and from there we watched New Year's fireworks from the rooftop of some midtown office tower we weren't ever supposed to be inside of. I don't even like fireworks, but that view was something else. I remember thinking how New York was amazing from no matter where you stood. But some parts just can't help being more amazing than others. Good company and being sober can go a long way too.

December also saw me spend a night in the hospital after having contracted some twenty-six-letter virus. The doctor told me she sees a lot of children with the same infection, claiming it's usually from too much mucus consumption. I told her I didn't know anything about that.

I barely saw the faded amber/pinkish daylight of January, busy in the theater every waking moment. We found this small, recently renovated theater in the Meatpacking District that gave us a deal due to some earlier carbon monoxide-related deaths in the building. Honestly, you can't be afraid of everything you hear. The truth, we found out later, was the details were mostly just covering up a non-carbon monoxide-related death anyway. Me, I like to think it was a serial killer, but I've been trying to do a better job at keeping a lot of the figments of my imagination to myself.

When the Willows Speak They Sing in Unison opened to decent reviews in mid-February. It was Theatre One Hundred's first-ever hit. Melissa was impeccable and luminous as the erudite Madison Willows.

Cerulean Sunflower opened one week later, and went mostly unnoticed. It might have been partly due to my promoting the show with the made-up title I preferred: *The Booger Kazoo*. Who knows though? It's early days and

Maya Custner's work may catch on yet, even with me in the lead role. Upon my own suggestion, the owner of the music shop got his own song in the play. I wrote it myself, too. It's not very good, but at least it makes more sense thematically.

The snow just seemed to stop as soon as I let Melissa go. Maya and I have been together ever since. Still, I'm a bit nervous for next winter's snowfall, because I know it will only remind me of Mel.

I hate stories that give annoying wrap ups with everyone being happy when they don't deserve to be. I'm not doing that. A little mystery and ambiguity never hurt anyone. Unless you happened to be one of the eleven poor unfortunate souls who attended Chelsea McMahon's one-woman show. So, I'm not going to tell you if Melissa and Brook are still engaged, or if Glenn Workman and his wife are working things out, or whether or not Bullet ever pursued a career in children's literature, or whatever happened to the sailor pants with the hole in the crotch. I did figure out how to change my phone's ringtone though. Pretty proud of myself for that bit.

Ace and I have reconciled too. We had a long talk about a lot of things. I told him about how I visited him a lot when he was in the hospital after his career-ending injury. He was basically half-cyborg, being hooked up to as many beeping contraptions as he was. One time, I sat beside him and burst into tears. I was whimpering and slobbering and I opened up my heart about everything; all the shit that had been tossed in my face from childhood to adulthood. Broken hearts, jealousy, and plans gone horribly awry. But I only admitted all of it because I thought no one was listening. Ace remembered it clearly though, recalling how he was awake during my breakdown but didn't want me to stop. A *catharsis*, I think he called it. He thought I was better off just letting it all out.

Maybe I was?

He explained that, in a way, I've always been that super-honest guy. The difference was, I was currently doing it publicly and in a far more revolting way. I couldn't really disagree. But I decided that moving out from under his shadow was probably best for both of us. I've been shacked up at Maya's place in Park Slope, with her consent of course. Turns out there are parts of Brooklyn that aren't as brown as I once thought.

So, I don't know. Maybe that's it? I realize a good majority of the crap I've been through has been my own fault, but I think we all need to make a disgusting mess sometimes, just to see it. Like digging a wiry hair out of your face and sticking it to your bathroom mirror as a kind of hunting trophy. We've all done it.

END

From the Author

I've learned something recently about my books. Though each is quite unique in genre, tone, and story arcs, there's actually a common thread through them all. And it's kind of a negative one: not-easily likeable protagonists. They're not full-on UN-likeable, they just take a little more time. Maybe this is the fault of my own writing, or maybe, subconsciously, I'm drawn to characters like this. Let's go with the latter. But through many reader comments, I've found my story protagonists can be a bit...prickly. Isabelle Donhelle (Molt) can frustrate the reader with her inability to make sensible decisions. Tommy (The Inevitable Fall of Tommy Mueller) can come across as a bit of a bully, and oftentimes puts his feelings ahead of his friends. Epic Small (This Never Happened) is certainly more of a spectator in life than a participant.

And then we have Chester K. Eddy. With his awkward fascination with serial killers, propensity for public F-bombs, severe lack of very basic morals, and even his admissions to having masturbated while talking on the phone with – *well, let's not bring that up right here*. Chester is rude, crude, and unfiltered, and he is definitely not the hero we need.

Or is he?

All I know is writing Chester was FUN. Sure, maybe readers won't be calling him the next Mr. Darcy, but hopefully they will take pleasure in simply reading the comedic exploits of an irrational, erratic, and sexually incompetent thirty-something anti-hero.

Chester K. Eddy means well, though. Attempting to be super honest is not a bad thing. But sometimes, incredibly-open honesty is only going to get one into more trouble than it's worth. And I hope you enjoy the troublemaking.